"Joelle Charbon... ... ...experience to *Murder* ... ...enjoy her heroine Paige Marshall's take on high school show choirs. Music and drama lovers who can't get enough of Rachel, Finn, Kurt, and the gang will have enormous fun with this delightfully witty take on 'Murder, She Sang.' Encore, encore!"

—Miranda James, *New York Times* bestselling author

"Charbonneau hits all the right notes with her show choir coach sleuth."

—Denise Swanson, *New York Times* bestselling author

"An intriguing mystery . . . I'm looking forward to future entries in this series."

—Donna Andrews, *New York Times* bestselling author

"Imagine if Stephanie Plum joined the cast of *Glee*, then someone proved to be more felonious than harmonious."

—Deke Sharon, vocal producer of NBC's *The Sing-Off*

"Like a little harmony and humor with your homicide? You've found your match in Joelle Charbonneau's *Murder for Choir*; it's a heckuva fun read." —*The Maine Suspect*

"*Murder for Choir* has plenty for both mavens of the performance world and those who never set foot in a theater. It's a very promising start to a new series." —*Fresh Fiction*

Berkley Prime Crime titles by Joelle Charbonneau

A Chorus Lineup

♩ ♫♩ ♫♩

JOELLE CHARBONNEAU

BERKLEY PRIME CRIME, NEW YORK

THE BERKLEY PUBLISHING GROUP
Published by the Penguin Group
Penguin Group (USA) LLC
375 Hudson Street, New York, New York 10014

USA • Canada • UK • Ireland • Australia • New Zealand • India • South Africa • China

penguin.com

A Penguin Random House Company

A CHORUS LINEUP

A Berkley Prime Crime Book / published by arrangement with the author

Berkley Prime Crime Books are published by The Berkley Publishing Group.
BERKLEY® PRIME CRIME and the PRIME CRIME logo are trademarks of Penguin Group (USA) LLC.

For information, address: The Berkley Publishing Group,
a division of Penguin Group (USA) LLC,
375 Hudson Street, New York, New York 10014.

ISBN: 978-0-425-25249-9

PUBLISHING HISTORY
Berkley Prime Crime mass-market edition / January 2014

PRINTED IN THE UNITED STATES OF AMERICA

10 9 8 7 6 5 4 3 2 1

Cover illustration by Paul Hess.
Cover design by Rita Frangie.
Interior text design by Laura K. Corless.

Chapter 1

A singer knows she's arrived when a limo picks her up and whisks her off to a luxurious hotel, where she's greeted by hundreds of roses and cards wishing her well before her starring performance the next night. The fact that I currently rode in a yellow bus with duct-taped vinyl seats, surrounded by a bunch of high school kids hopped up on sugar on the way to a Holiday Inn, spoke volumes about the career choices I had made. Sadly, no matter how much I wanted to be an opera star, at this moment I was not.

"Ms. Marshall, could you help me, please?"

I sighed at the sound of the voice of Music in Motion's captain, Chessie Bock—who, despite her strong singing and dancing abilities (or perhaps because of them), was a pain in my proverbial backside. Up until a few months ago, Chessie had gone out of her way to speak to me only when absolutely necessary. During those exchanges, she was pushy and unpleasant. But dodging gunfire had made a serious adjustment on Chessie's personality. Since then, she'd felt it necessary to consult me on everything that involved the Prospect Glen High School's competitive show choir as well as on all facets of her life. Lucky me.

"What's wrong, Chessie?" I asked as across the aisle my boss and the official leader of this adventure, Larry DeWeese, chuckled.

Thus far on the trip from the Chicago suburbs to Nashville, Tennessee, Chessie had needed help with geometry (not my best subject) and chemistry (really not my best subject), and tips on how to apply eye shadow so your eyes looked their best onstage. Minus the bus hitting a large pothole as I was demonstrating the correct technique for using eyeliner, the final request was actually helpful. Music in Motion was currently en route to the National Show Choir Championships, where they would compete with the other top twelve teams in the country. Each team had to win several contests throughout the season in order to be awarded the coveted invitation to compete at this final event. With that kind of competition, we needed every advantage we could get.

Chessie took my question as an invitation to walk up the center aisle of the bus and slide into the seat next to me. She then looked over her shoulder to make sure that no one was listening. Oh joy. After being trapped for eight hours on a bus with eighteen high school students, I wanted peace and quiet. Not more drama.

Still, I asked, "Is everything okay?"

Chessie bit her lip and shook her head. With another glance behind us, she whispered, "Megan has a sore throat."

After listening to them talking nonstop for eight hours, I'd be surprised if all the students on this bus didn't have sore throats. "I'm sure it's nothing. But if it is, we'll deal with it."

I had a bag of zinc lozenges, zinc vocal spray, and a host of other remedies to make sure my singers were in top shape by the end of this week. While I still wasn't sure I knew how to teach teenagers, I was more than equipped to handle their vocal dilemmas.

Unfortunately, Chessie wasn't willing to let the issue slide so easily. "She had a sore throat yesterday, too. I heard Megan tell Breanna that she was scared to tell you or her parents. She didn't want anyone to say that she couldn't come compete. But I thought I should tell you in case you want to give the understudies a heads-up. I know they've been practicing, especially since Megan's sister had to go on for her during the winter concert, but they might need some extra rehearsal time."

I studied Chessie's pretty face, trying to see whether there was another agenda lurking behind those big brown eyes. Chessie was never one to let an opportunity to snag someone else's solo pass her by, and Megan had one that Chessie had angled for. Chessie's eyes were wide with concern as she nervously twirled a lock of long dark hair with her fingers and waited for my reaction. There was none of the calculation that typically went along with Chessie's power plays. Unless Chessie had taken a really good acting class in her spare time, her concern for Megan was completely sincere. Chessie didn't just want to shine this weekend. She wanted to win.

"I'll talk to everyone later about what they need to do this week to stay healthy for the competition." I gave

Chessie what I hoped was a reassuring smile. "If Megan or anyone else looks like they're worried, I'll pull them aside and talk to them in private."

Chessie stood and smiled back. "Great. I told Eric you wouldn't think I was being catty. And don't worry about him. His cold is gone, and he promises that he's going to go to bed early and get lots of sleep before the preliminary competition on Thursday."

And I was going to go downhill skiing in hell. I remembered taking a couple of overnight field trips when I was in high school. We quickly figured out that whatever chaperones were roaming the halls did so only until our rooms were quiet. A half hour without shrieks or giggles meant the chaperone could go to sleep and the rest of us could venture out into whatever town we were visiting. Any night that we got more than four hours of sleep was considered a wasted opportunity to experience life. Needless to say, I wasn't terribly optimistic about having rested performers a few days from now. The good news was every other show choir was going to be equally fatigued. Teenage misconception about the necessity of sleep was the great equalizer.

Even better, I wasn't the person the school put in charge of this adventure. That job was squarely on the shoulders of the head of the choir program, Larry DeWeese. If the principal knew that Larry had locked himself in the music room storage closet—twice—he might not have been so keen to trust Larry with keeping a close eye on our students. On the upside, I had learned how to jimmy open a lock. So, if one of my kids got a case of stage fright and barricaded herself in the bathroom, I'd be able to get her out. Being back in high school had certainly broadened my life experience.

"Devlyn's right, Paige," Larry said, sliding into the seat Chessie had just abandoned. "You've worked miracles with those kids. Especially Chessie. The school board and Principal Logan agree. They're going to renew your contract for coaching Music in Motion and offer you an additional one to direct next year's musical. Isn't that great?"

Great? Um. That wasn't the word I'd use. When I'd started this gig, teaching show choir was the last thing I'd wanted to do. I only took the job because I needed the paycheck until I got my big break. Now that I had gotten a chance to sing for one of the most publicized versions of *The Messiah* in recent history and landed new management, my phone was starting to ring with offers.

I'd managed to squeeze in a couple of gigs in between show choir competitions, but Alan, my new manager, told me he was certain bigger things were on the horizon. If events worked out the way we both hoped, Prospect Glen was going to need a new show choir coach. Something Larry should have already figured out from the hints I'd been dropping. Unfortunately, Larry was either totally oblivious or being incredibly passive aggressive. At some point, I was going to have to be more direct. But the happy grin on Larry's face and the squeals of laugher behind me told me now wasn't the time. Not unless I wanted to feel like the Grinch that drop-kicked Christmas.

Larry smiled. "I just thought I should let you know about the offer so you're ready to answer when they ask."

"I promise I'll have a suitable reply ready by the time

the school year ends." *Hell no* was probably a little too pointed. I'd have to work on that.

"You might need one a little sooner." Larry's smile grew even wider. "Principal Logan and four of the board members will be in Nashville for the final round of competition. They're going to offer you a new contract when we win."

Yikes.

"Of course, we have a lot to do before that happens." Larry pulled out his phone. "I don't think we'll get to Nashville in time to load into our staging room today." Larry sighed. "Jim isn't going to be happy about leaving the band's instruments in the bus overnight."

Jim Williams was the head of the Prospect Glen instrumental music program. He also was in charge of the Music in Motion band, who were traveling in the bus behind us. In the great choral director/orchestra leader tradition, he and Larry didn't always see eye to eye.

"You can use my room to store the instruments." I had already agreed to store the costumes since we didn't want to risk anything getting spilled on them before showtime. "That way we know nothing will happen to them before they're loaded into the facility."

While I didn't love the idea of sharing my space with a bunch of dusty instrument cases, it was better than the damage control I'd have to do if Larry and Jim got into a shouting match. Last time, Jim had refused to show up to rehearsal and Larry had stuttered for two days.

Larry gave me a relieved grin. "That'd be great. I'd volunteer my space, but Devlyn's rooming with me. Jim's rooming with Mr. Mitchell." One of the band boosters who came on the trip to supervise. "Actually, it's probably a good thing we aren't loading in today. I got an e-mail from Christine McCann telling participants the stage-left loading dock door is broken. That's the one closest to our room. They should have the problem fixed by tomorrow morning when we officially check in."

I hoped so. Otherwise, I would be climbing over saxophones, drums, and trumpets all week. Was my life glamorous or what?

While Larry rearranged tomorrow's schedule to accommodate our new load in and read e-mails to make sure nothing else had changed, I leaned my head against the window and closed my eyes. I was already exhausted, and the first round of competition wouldn't start until Thursday. However, it was recommended that we arrive several days early to practice in the space, participate in a master class series, and rest up before the first big hurdle—the preliminary round, where half of the choirs in each division would be eliminated. Normally, this wouldn't concern me. My group was strong. The five first-place trophies we'd received over the past two and half months proved that my Music in Motion kids knew how to strut their stuff. But those competitions were open to any choir who wanted to pay the entry fee. This event was by invitation only. After looking at the YouTube videos posted online from some of the regional events, I knew we were going to need to be at the top of our game to make the cut and compete in Friday's final round.

"So what do you think?" Larry asked.

I blinked. "About what?"

Larry sighed. "About helping with Wednesday's

master class? This e-mail says they tried to get ahold of you but your phone has been going straight to voice mail. You must be having reception issues."

Or I could have shut off my phone so I wouldn't receive any more texts from my aunt Millie or her live-in boy-friend, Aldo. There was enough drama on this bus as it was.

"The good news is the chair of the competition decided to send me an e-mail before looking for another option. It seems that Donna Hilty had a family emergency, which makes her unavailable for Wednesday's class. The com-mittee would like you to stand in."

Donna Hilty was the coach of Nashville High School's show choir and an accomplished country-western singer. Her résumé included concerts at the Grand Ole Opry, several CDs, and singing the jingle for a national chain of barbecue joints.

"Why me?" I asked.

"Because you're famous."

I rolled my eyes.

Larry laughed. "Everyone here knows that you're the singer who helped catch David Richard's killer. You're also the most exciting new talent on the musical stage, accord-ing to the *Chicago Tribune*."

"I'm flattered," I said, remembering how the same critic also said my high notes sounded thin and slightly strained. "But I think the committee should ask one of the other instructors. Show choir students aren't terribly impressed by operatic singers."

I should know.

"They'll be impressed by you. I think you'll enjoy doing it." When I crossed my arms over my chest, he let out a sigh and admitted, "It's something Greg Lucas used to volunteer for, and look how it helped him and his choir."

Since Greg Lucas was no longer among the living, I thought Larry's pep talk left a lot to be desired. Still, I got the point. Greg Lucas had never been the poster child for educator of the year, but he had understood what it took both on and off the stage for his team to win. Which is probably why his choir took top honors at this competition three years running before his murder. Without Greg Lucas at the helm, the North Shore High School show choir had failed to place higher than third at any of the competitions they'd attended and hadn't received an invitation to this event. Greg Lucas had been a less than stellar human being, but he excelled at schmoozing. I sucked at it, which no doubt had something to do with why I was trapped on this bus instead of jet-setting around the world, performing for adoring throngs. While wanting to get hired because of your talent was admirable, it was also stupid.

"What time is the master class again?" I asked.

Larry beamed and tapped the screen of his phone. "Ten o'clock to noon. You'll be coaching the students with a guy named Scott Paris. He's the instructor for the team from Atlanta. They gave me his phone number in case you want to coordinate strategy. You're going to have a lot of fun, I promise."

Right. Two teachers from competing schools working with a room full of emotional, tired students guaranteed to doubt every word we say because our kids are going up against them. What could possibly go wrong?

Over the next hour the kids ignored Larry's requests

to quiet down and the bus driver's insistence that everyone stay in their seats. I ignored it all while going over the words to one of my favorite arias. Which was the only reason I didn't look as if I'd shoved my finger into a light socket when the bus pulled into the hotel parking lot.

After haggling with the front desk clerk to make sure that all of our rooms were on the same floor and that I had extra keys for my room so that Devlyn, Larry, and Jim could all have one in case they needed access to instruments or costumes, Larry and I handed out room keys. We then asked everyone to carry their costumes to my room, and turned the kids loose. By the time I'd made sure my students were all in their designated rooms with instructions to meet back in the lobby for dinner in an hour, I was ready to collapse on my bed.

Of course, for that to happen, I'd first have to be able to find my bed. Garment bags filled with costumes and black, scuffed instrument cases were piled on both beds and the rug, giving me nowhere to walk let alone sleep. As a teacher, I was certain I was supposed to treat this as a learning opportunity and knock on doors, get the students back here, and insist they hang up their costumes and stack the instruments in a responsible and considerate manner. Clearly, I was more concerned about peace of mind than education because I rolled up my sleeves, propped my door open so claustrophobia wouldn't set in, and got to work.

One by one, I stacked the instrument cases in the hall outside my room. When I could finally see the floor again, I approached the problem like a game of Tetris. Wishing I had the nifty music to entertain me while I played, I stacked, restacked, and arranged until the reconfigured instrument cases allowed me to reach both the bed closest to the door and the television. The window was completely blocked, but I'd just have to learn how to survive without a view of the blinking neon cowboy from the restaurant next door. My loss.

Now that the instruments had been dealt with, I turned my attention to the garment bags strewn across the bed I desperately wanted to curl up on. I had just grabbed the first bag when a warm, rich voice asked, "Can I give you a hand?"

I turned and spotted Devlyn lounging against the frame of my open door. At more than six feet tall, with deep blue eyes, a slightly crooked nose, and unruly brown hair that his mother almost certainly would tell him needed a trim, Prospect Glen's drama teacher Devlyn O'Shea was every high school girl's dream of a leading man. Add in the body-hugging pink T-shirt and the fitted gray-wash jeans and I doubt there was a woman alive who would turn down his offer of a helping hand. I certainly wasn't about to. Of course, I had an ulterior motive.

"I left the door open when I was restacking the instruments, but you can close it now," I said with a slow smile. "I wouldn't want the students to think I was keeping it open because I didn't trust them."

"You're a smart lady, Ms. Marshall." Devlyn shut the door and then walked across the room and kissed me.

And wow, could Devlyn kiss. My knees went weak. Or maybe they were already weak from the exercise I'd gotten relocating instruments. Regardless, I wrapped my arms tight around him and lost myself in the moment. Devlyn was sexy. Smart. Wonderful. And mine.

Okay, maybe he technically wasn't all mine. I mean,

we hadn't . . . wow. His hand ran down my back. I shivered and pressed closer, wondering how it was possible that we hadn't yet moved our relationship into something more physical. The sparks were there. I gasped as his lips touched my neck. Okay, the sparks were more than there. But . . .

Knock. Knock. Knock.

"Ms. Marshall?"

At the sound of Chessie's voice, Devlyn moved away from me and to the pile of garment bags. Sighing, I walked to the door and opened it to find Chessie standing on the other side with a garment bag draped over her arm.

"I forgot to bring you my costumes." Without an invitation, she strolled into my room and gave Devlyn a smile. "Hi, Mr. O'Shea. It's too bad you weren't on the choir bus. We were running lines for the musical, and I was having trouble understanding the motivation for one of the scenes. Do you think you'll have time to work with me on it this week? We only have two weeks until the show opens, and I want to make sure I'm doing everything exactly right."

While Devlyn assured her that he'd schedule a few minutes to run lines and ushered her out, I hung Chessie's garment bag in my closet. Once the door was closed I looked at Devlyn, waiting for him to pick up where we left off. Instead, he grabbed another bag of costumes and began to clear off my bed. Drat. There was nothing like high school kids and the reminder of Devlyn's secret identity to kill the mood. Though the kiss he'd just given me and the ones we'd been sharing on and off for months proved he was attracted to me, the rest of the Prospect Glen community of students, teachers, and parents believed the rumors that Devlyn O'Shea was gay. Further complicating matters was the fact that Devlyn not only encouraged the rumors; he was the one who'd started them. While that prevented passes from high school girls like the one that derailed his mentor's teaching career, it made the pursuit of a real relationship challenging. I had tried to talk about the problem on a number of occasions, but Devlyn only assured me that things would get better. That I was currently handling hangers and large plastic bags instead of Devlyn's well-toned shoulders told me we hadn't reached the better stage yet. And if I didn't say something, it was possible we never would.

"The bags aren't going to all fit in your closet," Devlyn said. "I'll take the last four down to my room." With a quick kiss on my cheek, he headed for the door and then added, "Oh, and make sure you turn on your phone. Larry's been sending texts. When you didn't respond he was worried you'd slipped and fallen in the shower. I'll see you downstairs for dinner in ten minutes." And with that he was gone.

Flopping on the finally cleared bed, I pulled my cell out of my pocket and reluctantly hit "on." The chimes telling me I had texts, e-mails, and voice mail made me sigh. Ignoring the texts, since I knew most if not all were from Larry, I hit "play" on my voice mails. The first was from Aunt Millie, asking me to call when I got to the hotel. She was finishing packing and wanted to make sure I really didn't want the girls to wear false eyelashes. Applied correctly, the eyelashes could really bring out the girls' eyes. They could. They could also come loose and make it look as if a tarantula had climbed onto my student's face. Some judges were turned off by spiders. Go figure.

Both Millie and Aldo were driving into town tomorrow,

bringing with them Millie's array of products and the expertise she'd earned while becoming one of Mary Kay's top sales representatives. I just hoped they didn't bring their current argument with them.

I closed my eyes as the second and third messages played: Christine McCann, the organizer of this year's competition, asking me to step into teaching tomorrow's master class, followed by Larry wondering why his cell service worked just fine and mine didn't. Sigh.

"Paige, where the hell are you?"

I sat up as the angry voice of my manager, Alan Held, filled the room.

"Call me as soon as you get this." Click.

Yikes.

I got up and paced as the phone rang. Two rings. Three.

"Paige, where have you been? I specifically said that I needed to be able to get ahold of you at any moment."

"I told you I was going to be in Nashville this week. My show choir is performing at the National Show Choir Championships."

"Well, they're going to have to do it without you. I need you in Chicago first thing on Friday morning to sing for Sir Andrew Davis."

My heart stuttered, and it became hard to breathe. "Andrew Davis wants to hear me sing?" Sir Andrew Davis was a world-renowned conductor and the current musical director of the Lyric Opera.

"He heard a recording of *The Messiah* and was impressed. He'd like to hear you in person and potentially use you in a recording he's conducting that features Andre Napoletano. Andre personally requested your consideration."

My head spun.

"There's also a chance you could be offered a role in next year's Lyric season. One of their performers had to cancel her contract, and Andrew thought you'd make a very interesting choice."

Roles at the Lyric were often cast years in advance by world-renowned artists. This was an once-in-a-lifetime career-making opportunity.

But . . .

"I'm in Nashville," I said, trying hard to catch my breath. "The kids are counting on me to help them get through this competition." They'd worked so hard. They might not have wanted to do what I asked of them, but they had.

"Well, they're just going to have to get through it on their own. Andrew has pushed back his flight to London in order to see you. If you don't make this audition, it won't take long before the entire opera community learns that you were a no-show. If that happens, you can kiss ever having a real career good-bye."

Chapter 2

"You okay?" Devlyn asked as I stared at my slice of now-cold pizza.

"Sure." I shrugged and forced a laugh. "I guess I'm not in the mood for pepperoni."

"There's a McDonald's down the road," he teased. "I can ask the bus driver to make a stop."

While I loved the fast-food chain's salty French fries, my stomach curled at the thought. "I wouldn't want to set a bad example for the team. Besides, the last thing we need is for someone to have a major acne breakout from the grease. Can you imagine the drama that would cause?" Probably just as much as if I talked about my phone call with Alan here where the kids or Larry might overhear.

Devlyn's eyes turned serious as he studied my face. Apparently, my acting skills weren't up to par tonight. However, before he could ask questions, Larry stood up and called for everyone's attention. The bus would be leaving to go back to the hotel in ten minutes. Breakfast would be at eight tomorrow. We would leave for the performance venue at nine. "I expect all of you to be up and ready to go on time."

Teenage eyes rolled and then glazed over. Larry and his continued speech on curfew, comportment, and responsibility had been officially tuned out in favor of food and whispered conversation.

When he was done, I stood up and said, "One more thing."

Each member of my team went silent as they waited for what I had to say. Just months ago, it would have taken a lot of yelling or threatening to get their attention and even more effort to keep it. The kids still drove me crazy when they came to rehearsal late, forgot to tell me their costumes were in need of repair, or got careless with their dance steps. But over the past few months, they'd earned my respect with their work and dedication. Their silence now told me that I'd earned theirs in return. We were a team. At least, we were until this competition was over.

Ignoring the ache in my gut, I said, "I couldn't be prouder of the work you've done to get to this point. Keep that work in mind when you're tempted to stay up all night. It would be a real shame to get this far only to screw up before the final competition. And, understudies . . ."

Four sets of eyes glimmered with interest.

"If I think any team member is too tired to perform, you'll be called on to take their place. So make sure you're rested and ready. We came here to take first place, and that's what I intend to do."

The team cheered and exchanged high fives, but in the

middle of the celebratory moment, I could see Chessie's eyes narrow as she looked at her fellow teammates.

"Chessie's going to make sure they all go to bed early," Devlyn whispered. "And unless I am totally mistaken, she's currently talking Eric, Megan, and John into being the bedtime enforcers in their rooms. I couldn't have manipulated them better myself. And you used to think you weren't meant to do this job."

Devlyn was right about Chessie getting the kids to adhere to their curfew. When I opened my hotel room door just after eleven, the hallway was silent. Which meant no one saw me head to the business center to book a flight to Chicago. I assuaged my guilt by only looking up flights that would allow me to be with my team during their preliminary round competition and return in time to help them prepare for the final round—if they made it that far. Still, I couldn't shake the feeling that by getting on a plane, I'd be letting everyone down. Which was crazy. The last thing I'd ever wanted to do was teach. This job was temporary. Everyone knew that when I started. Larry. Devlyn. The kids. They had been there to watch me sing in December. They'd read the reviews and cheered when I secured a more influential manager in addition to several Midwest concert appearances. If I told them about the audition, I was sure they'd insist that I go.

Yeouch!

I stared at the screen. The cost of the cheapest round-trip ticket was more than what I earned in a month of coaching the choir and teaching voice lessons. This trip could be for nothing. How many auditions had I gone to in the past where I'd heard nothing more than "don't call us; we'll call you"? As much as rejection was part of this business, it still stung every time. But that risk was part of the job. As was the financial investment of getting to the audition.

Plane ticket and aisle seat confirmed, I pushed back my chair and went in search of a Diet Pepsi, a Snickers, and two bags of deep-fried, artificially flavored cheese-and-sour-cream potato chips. Then I headed back to my room to drown my uncertainty in sugar and carbs.

I tore into the Snickers bar and took a big bite as I slid the key card into my room door. The sound of giggles from the room across the hall told me that some of the Music in Motion team were still awake. I could only hope that by the time midnight rolled around, they'd be in bed asleep. With any luck I would, too. Between the pre-competition events, the high level of teen anxiety, and the audition that could potentially change my entire future—well, it was going to be a very long week.

———

"I'm glad you decided to have the kids leave their costumes and instruments at the hotel," I said, walking back to the bus. Despite the promise that it would be operational by today and our attempts just now to open it, the stage-left loading dock door wouldn't budge.

"I'm grateful you're willing to live with your room being a storage area for another day." Larry smiled. "There's no point in our team having to lug all of their stuff farther than necessary. Especially since our dress rehearsal isn't until Thursday morning. The band was especially grateful since it meant they could spend the day lounging around the hotel pool instead of coming here."

Larry yelled to the bus driver to go around front. Then

he trekked around four Dumpsters to the stage-right side to try that door. Whoever said theater was glamorous had never had a stage door near the trash.

Eureka! This door opened and we stepped into a dimly lit backstage that was bustling with people shouting orders, carrying risers, and unwinding microphone cables.

Larry and I followed the signs through the wing space, down a side hallway, to a room with a large sign with the word *Registration* written in hot pink glitter. The boys in my choir were going to love that.

"Name." The bleach blond woman behind a long, folding table strewn with boxes filled with folders and papers looked up from the enormous purple bag she was pawing through.

Larry smiled and waved at a dark-haired woman on the other side of the room. She smiled back. "Larry DeWeese and Paige Marshall with Prospect Glen High School."

The blond woman set her bag on the chair next to her, glanced at me, and then flipped through the folders and pulled out a yellow one marked with our school name. "In here you'll find the most up-to-date rehearsal and competition schedule, your backstage passes that allow you to have access to the staging rooms while the competition is in session, and a map of the facilities. You'll also find a list of activities for your students to participate in." The woman dug through the large cardboard boxes behind her and snagged two large plastic bags filled with pink and purple T-shirts. "Let me know immediately if the sizes don't match the ones you sent us. We've had some issues with someone ordering the wrong sizes."

The blonde glanced across the room at the dark-haired woman and gave her a nasty smile. To the dark-haired woman's credit, she didn't react. She just went back to collating papers.

Frowning, the blonde handed me a separate folder. "In there you'll find the room assignment and other information for the master class you'll be teaching. We're counting on our instructors to keep the class limited to the assigned time frame. We're running on a tight schedule, and the coordinators need everyone to do their part to make this week run smoothly or the competition will suffer."

Translation: Let the kids out of class on time or I'll see the coordinators' annoyance reflected on the judging sheets.

"No problem," I assured the woman as Larry handed me my name tag and backstage pass. "Do you know if Scott Paris has checked in yet? I'd like to meet him before we teach together."

"His team loaded in yesterday." Her expression made it clear that this was the way things were supposed to be done. "They're in staging room 118. Who's next?"

Stepping to the side to put on my badge, I watched a woman with teased hair step up to the table and be greeted like an old friend. While the two exchanged photos of their kids, Larry and I went in search of our staging area.

Staging room 101 was located at the end of the hall, next to two large double doors that separated this area from the front lobby of the theater complex. It was also the room farthest from the stage. Most teachers would be annoyed by the placement. I was overjoyed. Being on the edge of the chaos was way better for my team's focus than being in the middle. The real problem with the space was the room's small size.

A quick peek into the other rooms made it clear ours was by far the smallest staging space in the joint. It also told me that feathers and gold sequins were all the rage this year. Despite the fact that our group had better taste in costumes, the staging room's size was going to cause problems. Between the four makeup mirrors sitting against the back wall and the costume rack near the door, there was barely enough square footage for all the choir and band kids to fit in this room. While a great deal of the time surrounding competition was spent in the audience watching the other teams or pacing the halls and hoping no one got so nervous they threw up, there were times when Larry and I would need to address our entire group. As it stood now, this room was barely going to cut it.

As Larry ranted about our room, I considered our options. We could ask for more space as Larry suggested, but I doubted it would get us anywhere. This competition was filled with teams who were invited year after year. They were going to get the big rooms and the preferential treatment. Making waves would only count against my team in the long run.

"The room will be fine," I said with more enthusiasm than I felt. "But we should wait to move the instruments and costumes in until just before the competition on Thursday."

"Are you sure?" Larry asked. "Those instruments take up a lot of space."

The black-and-blue toe I'd gotten getting up in the middle of the night attested to that fact.

"This way, there's no chance anything will get spilled on the costumes before we perform," I reasoned.

Larry smiled. "That's an excellent point. Let's go get the kids and show them where they'll be camping out between classes and our practice time."

As Larry pushed open the double doors, my cell phone buzzed. My manager, Alan, had texted:

> Audition set for Friday at 9:30 A.M. Meet you at 9:00 in the Lyric lobby. Don't let me down.

"Everything okay?" Larry asked.

"Everything's great." Or it would be if I could figure out how to turn off the guilt I felt every time I thought about leaving the team in the middle of the competition.

Larry gave me a look that said he didn't believe a word I'd said.

Hoping to change the subject, I shoved the phone in my pocket and said, "I'm surprised I haven't heard from Aunt Millie or Aldo today. If they left when they planned to, they should be over halfway here." Especially if my aunt was driving. Millie might be light on her feet while prancing around in four-inch heels, but when she was behind the wheel, Millie's foot was pure lead.

"It's great that your aunt was willing to come help with the team's makeup." Larry dodged a couple of girls in sparkly, tie-dyed tops and promptly tripped over a potted plant. Grace had nothing on my boss.

I gave him a hand up as several more kids raced by. With the twenty teams arriving, twelve in our mixed-company division and eight in the all-girls category, the lobby was a zoo.

"Millie's always happy to show off her products," I said. As Mary Kay's top saleswoman for the Midwest region for almost a decade, Millie wasn't about to let an opportunity to showcase the new spring line go to waste. And unless I was mistaken, she'd not only have her pink Mary Kay Cadillac but a trunk full of saleable product in tow.

I only hoped she and Aldo would leave their personal issues aside. While the two were obviously head over heels for each other, they had very different ideas of what they should do about it. Aldo wanted Millie to wear his ring. Determined never to get married, Millie wanted Aldo to move out and never call her again. Aldo refused to budge. Millie didn't have the heart to throw him out, and as Millie's houseguest, I was caught in the middle.

Ignoring Chessie's constant concerns about Breanna's stash of HERSHEY'S KISSES (they might cause her to break out or the chocolate could coat her throat and make it hard to sing) and Jason's sore arm (caused by arm wrestling over who got to take the first shower this morning), I led my team to the room, explained that we would not load in costumes until Thursday, and then gave them the schedule. Master classes would be held both today and tomorrow in the mornings. They would have a choice of two different classes to attend. After lunch, teams would each have fifteen minutes to rehearse onstage. Full dress rehearsals for all-girls teams would begin tomorrow after dinner. Mixed-company dress rehearsal would begin at eight A.M. Thursday. When the groans at the time subsided, I told them our preliminary competition was scheduled for two P.M.

"That will be the first time the judges see you on this

stage," I said, "but that doesn't mean they won't be watching you in the halls or making note of your behavior. The difference between getting cut in the first round and making it to the finals could be a fraction of a point. I don't want to give them reason to judge anything other than what they see on the stage. Got it?"

The way Chessie glared at everyone as they headed for the door made it clear she planned on making sure they followed my instructions as they participated in this morning's vocal jazz and tap dance master classes. When the students were gone, Larry, Devlyn, and I headed for the auditorium to take a look at the space.

Wow.

There were more than eighteen hundred plush blue velvet seats. Ornate trim framed the thirty-foot-tall proscenium stage. Since the bands would not be allowed to use the pit, it was not lowered. The rules for this competition stated that the instrumentalist must be in full view of the audience and judges. How their musicality enhanced or detracted from the performance would be added to my team's total score. In the past, our band's abilities had helped put us over the top. I was counting on their skill to help us again.

"So now what?" I asked.

Larry glanced at the schedule. "I think we should look in on the master classes and make sure everyone's behaving. I saw Christine McCann in the halls. One word from her to the judges and our team will end up with more deductions than we've seen all season." Larry turned to Devlyn. "It probably wouldn't hurt if you introduced yourself to her. Greg used to flirt with Christine and look how well his team did."

I shifted, trying not to look uncomfortable with the suggestion. After all, Devlyn was supposed to be gay. Larry didn't know we were dating.

Devlyn laughed. "Why don't I try and do that now? It'll also give me the chance to scope out a better load-in door in case the one on our side of the stage door doesn't get fixed before Thursday. Paige, do you want to meet up in the lobby in an hour? We can talk about the spacing changes we need to make."

"Sure." I smiled. Talking about how we wanted to alter the team's spacing now that we'd seen the theater made for a great excuse to spend some quality time alone together. "I'll see you then."

Since the last thing I wanted was to see Devlyn flirting with another woman, even for a good cause, I headed toward the stage. By the time I climbed up the escape steps and walked to the middle of the wooden floor, Larry and Devlyn were gone.

Even with every chair in the audience empty, there was something magic about standing onstage. Remembering the glare of the lights, the swell of the orchestra, and the feeling that I was a part of something greater than myself was the reason I could brush myself off after every rejection and risk being told "no" once again. Performing was about more than the paycheck and the applause. It was part of who I was. Who I needed to be. It was the reason I had to be at that audition on Friday. The team would be fine without me.

Telling myself to stop feeling guilty, I exited stage left and went in search of staging room 118 to find my co-instructor for tomorrow's master class. Drat. Except for racks of satin and rhinestone-studded costumes and neatly stacked black instrument cases, the staging room for Scott Paris's team was empty. So much for that idea. I called the number that the planning committee had e-mailed to me. Voice mail.

Now what?

Since Devlyn and I weren't planning on meeting for another forty-five minutes, I decided to follow the sparkly pink signs to the stairs that led to the greenroom—the site of the master class I would be teaching. It was also the location of today's vocal jazz class. Like most greenrooms, the large, fluorescent-lit space's paint color didn't match its name. Instead, the chipped paint was closer to mustard yellow. Teens sat on the scuffed gray linoleum floor, listening to a quartet of male singers. One of the tenors reached for a high note and missed. A few kids on the floor snickered. I was thankful none of them belonged to Music in Motion.

When the kid missed the next high note, I decided it was time to leave. Turning, I smacked right into a guy coming down the hall. Thank goodness the wall was there to catch us or we would have both gone crashing to the ground. As it was, the loud thud drew the attention of several students, as did the sight of me pressed up against the guy's partially exposed and somewhat hairy chest.

Scrambling upright, I kept my voice low so as not to cause further disruption as I said, "Sorry. I didn't see you."

The man I'd nearly toppled flashed his pearly, professionally polished whites. Or maybe they just appeared bright next to his deeply tanned skin. It was hard to tell. His voice was amused as he said, "I'm the one who should apologize, Paige."

I blinked. "Do I know you?"

The man shook his head. "But let's see if we can't remedy that. I'm Scott Paris. Perhaps if you have a moment, we can talk somewhere less . . ." The quartet hit their final, out-of-tune chord, and Scott sighed. "Boisterous."

"Going upstairs sounds good to me," I said as we walked back upstairs.

"I hope you don't mind my saying," Scott said as we reached the blissfully quiet hallway, "but your pictures don't do you justice. You're far more attractive in person."

"I'm flattered you took the time to look up my website."

"I'm embarrassed to say I haven't." Scott shrugged. "Greg Lucas was a friend. I followed the story of his murder and your part in bringing his killer to justice. The art of performance choir lost a bright and shining star the day Greg died." Scott bowed his head for a moment, and then looked up with a smile. "Luckily, we also gained an angel in you. Can you say kismet?"

Can you say smarmy?

"I'm sorry you lost a friend," I said.

Scott sighed and leaned against the wall next to the poster for an upcoming production of *The Music Man*. "Greg understood how to get the best out of his students. That's why his program competed year after year at this competition."

The fact that he was known for romancing the female judges probably didn't hurt, either.

"I tried to encourage the board to invite North Shore High School's performance choir this year, but they just didn't score high enough in the regional contests to warrant an invitation." He winked. "And even if Greg were still alive, I don't know if his team would have given yours a run for its money. I've seen tapes. I'm impressed."

"Thanks," I said. "I hope that means you don't mind my teaching with you. I was hoping we could talk about the class and make sure we're on the same page."

"That sounds great." Scott's smile lost a little of its sparkle. "I hope you won't be offended if some of the students are disappointed that Donna won't be teaching. She and Greg taught this class last year. It was standing room only. Some of the judges even came and listened in. When it was over, Greg and Donna arranged for a few of the kids to perform for a talent scout. Donna and I were working on something even bigger this year, but—"

We both jumped as a high-pitched scream rang through the hall. The scream faded and then started up again. This time even louder. "Oh my God!"

I dug into my pocket for my cell as we raced toward the screams. The same woman who'd given Larry and me our schedules staggered out of one of the staging rooms and yelled, "Call the police!"

"LuAnn, what's wrong?" Scott took the woman's arm.

"Just look." Her lip trembled as she lifted a hand and pointed into the room she'd just exited. In recent months, I'd come in contact with several dead bodies. The last thing I wanted to see was another. Still, I took a deep breath and stepped into the room, prepared for blood. Instead, I found—clothes?

Satins. Tulle. Lamé. Bright costume colors. Perfect for catching the light and the attention of the audience. Or they would have been if they hadn't been shredded. The costumes looked as if they'd had a fight with a couple of disgruntled cats and lost. Big-time.

"Who would do such a thing?" Scott stooped down and picked up a bronze lamé top that was now in tatters.

"I'll tell you who."

Scott and I turned toward LuAnn, who was now standing in the doorway. Behind her, I could see other people who must have heard her screams and come running.

"It was her," she said as she raised a hand and pointed it directly at me.

Chapter 3

I looked behind me in case someone had materialized since I'd turned my back. Nope. No such luck.

"Me?" I squeaked.

"You were in this room earlier." The woman's eyes looked as if they were going to pop out of her head as she stomped her red cowboy boot–clad feet. "I saw you."

Was she kidding? She actually thought I played arts and crafts with another team's costumes?

Trying to keep calm, I explained, "I wanted to meet Scott and talk about our master class."

"Then why, Ms. Marshall, did I see you going into other staging rooms earlier today?"

A tall blonde appeared behind LuAnn.

"Christine." The way LuAnn said the name told me everything I needed to know. This was Christine McCann—the head of the National Show Choir Championships. "Thank goodness you're here. Never have I seen such a blatant attempt to sabotage another team."

"I didn't sabotage anything," I shot back.

So much for my attempt to remain calm.

"No one's accusing you of anything." Christine took a step into the room, carefully skirting the fabrics on the floor.

"But, Christine." LuAnn frowned. "I saw her—"

Christine held up her hand, cutting off whatever new accusation LuAnn planned to hurl. "This competition is filled with high-strung teenagers with a competitive streak. I think it's far more likely one of them caused this kind of damage. This wouldn't be the first time a rivalry between teams bubbled over." Christine sighed and turned her attention to the man to my left. "Scott, I promise we'll get to the bottom of this. Please let me know if there is anything I can do to help you get replacement costumes."

Angry and excited whispers from the hall told me the story of the costumes was spreading. Turning to me, Christine added, "And just to make sure there is no whisper of impropriety on your behalf, Ms. Marshall, could you please explain why you were near this room when LuAnn made this discovery and what you were doing in the other staging rooms earlier today?"

The way she glanced over her shoulder at the people hovering in the doorway told me that whatever I said was going to determine whether I would be branded a saboteur by the masses. If that happened, I wouldn't be the one to pay the price—my team would.

Was that fair? No. But if there was one thing I had learned from my performing career, it was that fair rarely applied to show business.

Projecting my voice so everyone listening could hear, I explained how Scott and I bumped into each other at the master class and came upstairs to talk about our turn at teaching tomorrow. "And the director of my choir program and I were looking in the other staging rooms to see if we were the only ones who had chosen not to load in due to the broken loading dock door." Okay, that wasn't really the truth, but sometimes honesty was definitely not the best policy.

Christine nodded. "I appreciate your candor and your willingness to answer the question. If I were in your position, I might not be so understanding. Please accept my apology for asking. Also, I apologize for the loading dock malfunction. I'm hopeful the mechanic will arrive and everything will be back to normal tomorrow. Now, LuAnn, if you could please track down one of the teachers from each of the teams, I would like them to check their staging rooms for signs of tampering. Scott, let me know if you or your team need anything at all. Kelly?"

The dark-haired woman I'd seen earlier in the check-in area stepped around several people and walked into the room. "I'm here."

"Good. Please meet with each coach and document any and all damage. Also, contact the media who were supposed to come today and ask them if they can reschedule. We want them to focus on the teams and their talent, not a juvenile prank."

With that she turned and headed toward the door. Kelly followed behind her. Shooting a disgruntled look at me, LuAnn hitched the enormous purple purse she was carrying onto her shoulder and walked out of the room, leaving Scott and me alone with the mess.

"Nine," Devlyn said as we stood in the corner of the lobby, trying to ignore the looks we were getting from the teens and adults in the large, chandelier-lit space. "Nine other teams reported some kind of damage to the belongings. The good news is that none of it was as bad as Scott's team. A few ripped dresses, some missing cummerbunds, and a couple of missing instrument mouthpieces. Christine has already made arrangements to replace the mouthpieces and has asked one of the local costume designers to help with the rest."

I took a sip out of the water bottle Devlyn handed me. "Were all the teams from the mixed division?"

"That's what it sounds like. Ten out of the twelve teams have been sabotaged in some way. Only Music in Motion and Donna Hilty's team from here in Nashville escaped the vandal unscathed. Because of her family emergency, she decided not to have the kids load in their costumes and instruments until she was here to supervise. Guess we both got lucky."

I glanced past Devlyn to where the sour-faced LuAnn stood whispering to a group of women while pointing at me. Luck wasn't what I would call this particular turn of fate.

Trying to ignore them and the unease growing inside me, I said, "I helped Scott go through all the costumes. A lot of the tears were on the seams, and the costumes that were shredded the worst weren't going to be used anyway. Scott brought them in case of emergency. So it could have been worse."

"Well, that's good. I hope Christine will find the

person behind this and things will go back to normal. Or at least as normal as a show choir competition can be." Devlyn grinned.

"She was there," LuAnn's shrill voice rang out.

My smile faded as everyone in the lobby went quiet.

LuAnn didn't seem to notice as she waved her arms in the air. "I'm telling you. We've never had this kind of trouble before, and she's had all sorts of run-ins with the law. Those kinds of things probably gave her ideas. Mark my words: This will just get worse until she and her team are sent packing."

I looked back at Devlyn and sighed. Yeah, something told me things weren't going to get back to normal anytime soon.

———

We met the students back in our staging room after the morning master classes let out. News about the sabotage had already spread, and emotions were running high. Several of the girls looked decidedly freaked. A bunch of the guys took the opportunity to strut and flex their muscles and promise to guard our costumes when we loaded them in. The macho routine might have worked had it not been for the bright matching tie-dyed shirts they were wearing. The phrase "I'm too sharp to B-flat" printed on streaks of pink, yellow, and violet wasn't exactly bodyguard attire.

But while most students showed concern over the plight of the other teams and worry about what might befall us when we loaded in, there was one person who wasn't disturbed by the recent happenings. Chessie. Despite the downturned mouth and the wringing hands, there was excitement and satisfaction in her eyes. The girl had a

powerhouse voice and great dance technique, but her acting needed serious work. And while everyone else looked
shocked by this turn of events, Chessie didn't seem at all
surprised.

This couldn't be good.

"The bus is waiting outside," Larry announced. "We're
going back to the hotel to pick up the band before heading
to lunch. The band will come back here for rehearsal."

"One second," I said as kids started to bolt for the door.
When they stopped and turned, I said, "If anyone hears
or learns anything about what happened today, I expect
you to talk to Mr. DeWeese, Mr. O'Shea, or me immediately. Mrs. McCann is determined to get to the bottom
of these incidents. The sooner that happens, the sooner
we can focus on why we came here. Got it?"

Chessie looked down at the floor as the rest of the team
nodded. Yep. Something was going on here. And from
the way Chessie's boyfriend, Eric Metz, was looking at
her, I'd say he agreed.

"Hey, Larry said he can handle lunch with the kids by
himself," Devlyn said, putting a hand on my arm. "That
means you and I can eat on our own and you can tell me
what's bothering you."

"Aside from being accused of playing Jack the Seam-
Ripper?" I asked. "I'd say that's more than enough."

"Maybe for other people. But I know you're not like
everyone else. Come on."

As soon as the bus headed to the hotel with Larry and
the team on board, Devlyn and I walked down the sidewalk on the hunt for food. The early April sun was bright,
making me sweat in my tan pants and long-sleeved
cream-colored shirt. But I didn't care. Just being away

from the trouble at the performing arts center made me breathe easier, and being here with Devlyn . . . Well, that didn't hurt, either. I reached out for his hand, but came up empty as he pulled away.

"Sorry," he said, giving me an apologetic smile. "There could be other teachers or students around. The last thing we need is to add any more confusion to this week, right?"

"Sure," I agreed, even though the knot in my stomach made it clear I didn't.

Devlyn didn't seem to notice my discomfort as he kept an eye out for the perfect restaurant while talking about the conversation he'd instigated with Christine McCann. "I can see why she and Greg Lucas got along so well. She certainly likes attention from men."

"Did you tell her you were gay?"

"I would have thought my outfit today would have made that obvious."

The powder-blue dress shirt was layered over a T-shirt of bright pink. The shiny gray pants and bright pink high-tops completed the outfit. Still, despite the color palette, there was something about the way he looked at the women we passed that belied the gay persona he worked to exude.

"Aside from the flirting, I think the conversation was productive. Don't be surprised if you get a lot of attention from the attending media."

"Why?"

"Christine's been using the story of the novice show choir coach who has been inspiring her students to greatness ever since finding a championship-level director dead and helping bring his killer to justice." Devlyn pointed to a small Italian restaurant and ushered me inside. "She said the story's drawn larger than usual media interest, which is probably why she jumped to your defense this morning."

"That might also have something to do with the fact that I didn't have anything to do with the sabotage."

Devlyn gave my hand a pat as a waitress led us to a small, butcher paper–covered table in the back. Once we were seated, Devlyn assured me that no one who knew me would ever think I'd have anything to do with the destruction. "Screwing people to get ahead is tried and true, but totally not your style."

"What is my style?" I asked, feeling the warmth of Devlyn's smile melt the icy knot in my stomach.

"You work hard. You fight for what you believe in, and as much as you want to succeed you'd never take the easy way out. Cutting up other people's costumes is the cheap way to achieve a goal. You wouldn't consider that kind of win a victory."

"That doesn't sound like a compliment."

"It wasn't meant to be." His hand found mind under the table and gave it a squeeze. "You try to do what's right even when it lands you in danger. It's a trait that scares me to death. Which is why I wanted to talk to you alone. That woman's accusations aren't making you consider doing something crazy, are they?"

"Like what?"

Devlyn raised an eyebrow. "Like trying to track down the person responsible for this morning's incidents."

I blinked. "Why would I do that?"

Devlyn laughed. "Because you can't seem to help your-self. But I guess I don't have to worry about that this time, which is good. I don't know if I could handle it if you ended up in danger again." All traces of laughter faded as Devlyn's eyes met mine. The intensity of emotion in them made my breath catch and my heart beat faster. "Between musical rehearsals and competitions and grading papers, we haven't had a lot of time to spend on us."

"Life's been pretty busy," I agreed as the waitress brought us a basket of warm bread and took our drink orders. Iced tea for Devlyn. Water with lime for me. If I was going to audition for the Lyric Opera, I needed to keep my throat hydrated.

Just thinking about the plane ticket confirmation sitting in my inbox made the guilt I'd almost squelched bubble anew. But maybe Devlyn was right. Maybe I did take the hard path too often. I bet if I told him about the audition, he'd inform me that the kids would hardly notice that I was gone and that I would be insane not to take this opportunity. Devlyn wanted the best for me. And wasn't that following my dreams?

By the time the waitress returned with our drinks and took our order, I had decided to tell Devlyn everything. Only he started talking first.

"School's kept me busy, but that's not the main reason we haven't spent as much time together as I've wanted." Devlyn frowned. "I figured it was best to wait until the end of the school year before we really explored a relationship. That way if we decide it isn't working, we don't have to worry about anyone else finding out. No reason to complicate things at work if we don't have to."

The bread I'd just swallowed felt like lead as it traveled to my stomach. "You're worried about people at work finding out?"

Devlyn shook his head. "Not really. Although, I'd rather not have to deal with that until we absolutely have to, and I thought summer would give us more time to just focus on us. Especially after everything that's happened over the last couple months. Some alone time away from the kids and the craziness will give us time to talk about the things we really want out of life." Devlyn's fingers tightened on mine. "Once the musical is over, I'd like us both to start putting some more effort into this relationship. The way things are going, I think we have a real chance at building a future, both at the school and in our personal lives—together. What do you think?"

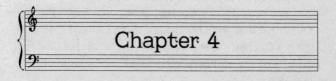

Chapter 4

What did I think?

The waitress arrived with our plates, which was good because I was having trouble formulating a coherent thought. Hearing Devlyn talk about building a future with me made my breath catch and my heart skip several beats. He was talented and sexy, and the two of us shared so many of the same interests. But the way he put school in the middle of that future put a damper on any excitement I might feel. I wanted a performance career. Teaching, as much as I'd come to enjoy it, was just something I was doing until that happened.

I still wasn't any closer to a response after Devlyn assured the waitress that our food looked wonderful and we didn't need anything else. What I needed was some-thing our server couldn't provide. I seriously doubted Parmesan cheese was going to help me understand the turn this conversation had taken.

"So?" Devlyn asked, picking up his meatball sandwich.

I picked up my fork and stabbed a ravioli.

"You're really not worried about your job?" I asked. Okay, that was probably the last thing I should have said, but it was a place to start. Besides, the whole handholding thing just ten minutes ago called that statement into question.

As if to prove his point, Devlyn put his hand on the table and held it out to me to take. The fact that he didn't look around the restaurant to double-check whether anyone we knew was nearby melted my heart.

With a smile, I wound my fingers through his. "I'd say spending more time together would be a good thing. Although, I'm not sure if I'll be at Prospect Glen after this year, so . . ."

"After what you've done with Music in Motion this year, your job is more secure than mine. And I have tenure." He popped a French fry in his mouth and offered me one.

Shaking my head, I chased a piece of pepper around on my plate and said, "I never thought I'd enjoy teaching. Especially after the way Chessie and the rest of the team acted when I first started this job."

"Which is why the work you've done this year is so remarkable. The students respect you. Not only that, they look up to you. Especially Chessie. I'm pretty sure she's going to Northwestern because that's where you went to school. The school wasn't even on her list before this fall. You're changing lives. That's important."

"More important than performing?"

"It's different and a lot more secure." Devlyn grinned.

"And it's not like you can't do both. There are lots of theaters around Chicago. I'm sure they'll be willing to work around your teaching schedule. Speaking of both, we should get back to the theater. I'd like to take another look at the stage. The band might seem cramped if we position them on the right like we'd originally discussed."

Just like that, the conversation shifted. Devlyn pulled his hand away to eat his meal while discussing spacing issues. No more romance. No more thoughts about the future and his assumption that I intended to stay at Prospect Glen and teach with him.

It wasn't until the waitress cleared away our plates—Devlyn's empty, mine still full—that Devlyn asked, "So if you weren't worrying about how to find the culprit behind the destroyed costumes, what's been bothering you?"

Feeling a bit like a coward, I decided to shelve talking to Devlyn about the audition. Instead, I said, "I think Chessie might know something about this morning's incidents."

Devlyn handed the waitress the bill and stood. "Chessie wants to win more than anyone else on the team, but I can't imagine her sneaking into the staging rooms and taking a knife to costumes."

"She's pulled all sorts of stunts in the past." Cooperating with a killer topped the list. Of course, at the time Chessie wasn't aware the person she was working with was a murderer. She was just interested in screwing with me. But still.

"Yeah." Devlyn put his hand on my back and guided me back into the sunshine. "But I'm pretty sure I saw Chessie in the lobby, attending the dance master class. I don't think she would have had time to hit all the teams and still attend part of her class. And while I think Chessie might go after the team she thought was her biggest competition, she would never have gone after all of them. Her ego would never let her believe that all the teams could give Music in Motion a run for their money."

He was right. Chessie believed our team was the best. While she wanted to take first place, she wanted to prove she was the best even more.

On the way back to the theater, Larry sent a text telling us that lunch was running late. We had a half hour until the team would be back at the theater, ready to work. Since the first of the team rehearsals was currently happening in the theater, we took the opportunity to sit in the back of the house and talk about the changes we'd need to make with our group.

While the choreography and music to our pieces weren't going to change, every new stage required us to adjust the spacing of the singers and the placement of the band. This was the biggest stage Music in Motion had been asked to perform on. While more space was better than less, it meant different adjustments to ensure the picture presented to the audience was balanced. In most of our competitions, the stage wasn't big enough for the band, which meant they set up in front of the stage. That placement put the conductor in an ideal position to not only direct the band but to cue the singers. This stage, however, was large enough to accommodate both the choir and the instrumentalists. The judges would take into account the overall production value of the team's performance. That included our nine-piece band's playing and appearance.

Scott's team was on the stage. Other directors and their

teams were scattered around the audience, observing their work. Three sets of risers were set in a straight line on center stage. On either side were chairs that indicated the placement of their band. The positioning would keep the stage balanced, but the conductor was going to have to stand near the front of the stage or maybe on the floor in front of it in order to be seen by all the performers.

"What do you think of putting the band on stage left?" Devlyn pointed toward the area next to where the risers were currently set. "We could adjust some of the blocking to create a nice balance."

Maybe. But, again, the conductor wouldn't be in a great position to see the singers. In a perfect performing environment, the conductor and performers could see one another at all times. Since young singers weren't the greatest at taking direction from the conductor, it was essential the conductor could see my team even if they couldn't see him.

"I think we should put the band in the center," I whispered. "Jim can be in the center, and the band's chairs can be set at an angle so the audience sees their profiles."

Devlyn nodded. "If we adjust the opening positions during the last song, I think we could make that work. And what do you think of shifting the lifts in the middle of "Ease on Down the Road" to either side, just off center."

I smiled. "We could also have the horns stand during their hits." It would make the band look like part of the performance instead of just the accompaniment for the singers.

"We need to get them something shinier to wear," Devlyn whispered as music played and Scott's team started to dance.

I thought about our band's black pants, black shirt, and white tie attire and nodded as the kids performed a stomping sequence. Devlyn was right. If the band was going to be front and center, they needed a bit more pizzazz. "Aunt Millie and Aldo should be in town soon. If you're willing to play chaperone with Larry and Jim tonight, Millie and I can do some power shopping."

"What you really mean is will I play referee between Larry and Jim," Devlyn said as the team onstage executed a simple but flashy lift with ease.

Scott's team was good. Better than good. They were serious competition.

"Jim and Larry have been getting along better these days," I said, leaning my elbows on the seat in front of me as I watched the team hit their final pose. The group wasn't singing full out, so I couldn't tell how powerful their vocals were going to be, but their tone and harmonies sounded strong and tight.

Ignoring the rehearsal onstage, Devlyn said, "That's because you've been around to keep them from going at each other's throats. Jim likes you."

"Jim also likes pizza and baseball," I said. "Order a large pepperoni for him and make sure ESPN is on the TV. I promise Millie and I won't take very long."

"I hope not." Devlyn's answering smile was slow and sexy. "I thought if we had time, we could meet in your room once the team is in bed to talk about our other project."

Devlyn. Me. My room. Just thinking about the combination was enough to make my pulse jump. "I think that can be arranged."

"Good." Devlyn winked. "It's a date."

Scott's team finished and left the stage and a new team appeared, along with the last person I wanted to see again—the now-familiar, finger-pointing LuAnn. On stage moving risers, LuAnn looked even more imposing than she did when accusing me of shredding satin. She stood taller and wider than almost all ten boys on this team. From the way they jumped when she snapped her fingers, they were more than a little intimidated by her personality. I had to give her credit, though. She didn't just stand by and wait for the kids to do the heavy lifting. LuAnn sat her purse down on the edge of the stage, rolled up her pink sleeves, and got to work. By the time they were done, the exertion had turned LuAnn's round cheeks the same shiny color as her shirt. The flush grew deeper when she put a hand over her eyes to look for something in the audience and found me.

"Get that woman out of here," she yelled.

All eyes turned toward the stage and then toward me.

Yikes. Heat flooded my cheeks. My muscles tensed, and I forced myself to stay in my seat instead of bolting toward the door. This was the second time LuAnn had singled me out, and I had no idea why. I was hurt, angry, and totally baffled.

"LuAnn," a pixie-like woman in dance clothes said, crossing the stage. "Rehearsals are open to other teams and their coaching staff. It's one of the rules all teams agree to when accepting a place at the competition. Now," the dark-haired woman said, taking LuAnn's arm, "if you don't mind, we need to get started."

Apparently, LuAnn did mind because she pulled her arm away and yelled, "Someone find Christine McCann. My daughter isn't stepping foot on this stage until that woman leaves this theater. I don't want to give her any other opportunities to sabotage this competition for our team."

"Christine warned you about making unfounded accusations." The dark-haired coach's voice rang with authority. "Now, if we don't want to lose our only rehearsal time onstage today, we have to get started."

LuAnn plopped her hands on her hips and glared in my direction. The dark-haired coach yelled, "Places. Cue music." But no one moved. The kids onstage watched LuAnn. I could feel the eyes of everyone in the audience watching me. Like a game of chicken, the observers were waiting to see who got out of the way first. The only problem was I was pretty sure no matter which way I jumped, I was going to get flattened. If I left, the kids could rehearse. LuAnn would feel victorious, and everyone would think that I had something to hide. Holding my ground would prove that I wouldn't be chased away, but it would fuel the strange grudge LuAnn had developed against me. Yep— both choices sucked. I was screwed.

My stomach clenched. LuAnn's face turned a shade of red that now matched her boots.

"Hey, maybe we should just get out of here," Devlyn said as the sound of "You Can't Stop the Beat" from *Hairspray* blared from the speakers. The dark-haired director yelled again. The kids onstage took the hint and hurried to their starting positions. LuAnn looked behind her at the kids, then back at me. Finally, in a huff, she stalked into the wings and the kids began to dance.

I let out the breath I hadn't been aware I was holding. "I don't get it," I said as one of the girls with a powerful voice nailed her solo. "Why does one of the other teams' coaches have it out for me?"

"I don't think she's technically part of the coaching staff." Devlyn motioned for me to follow him. Which I did. Gladly.

A few seconds later, we were standing in the lobby. Once the theater doors had closed, Devlyn explained, "The team currently onstage is Tapping to the Tunes. They're directed by Emma Harrod and Jake Wilder. LuAnn must be one of their parent volunteers. She did mention her daughter."

True. Which would explain why she was one of this morning's volunteers. The chance to size up other teams while currying favor with the National Show Choir Championships organization would be irresistible to some stage moms. "But what does she have against me?"

Devlyn leaned back against the lobby's brick wall. "She probably heard that Music in Motion is the team to beat and feels threatened. A lot of parents will go to any lengths to make sure their kids come out on top."

"Do you think she's going to harass the team, too?" I asked. Picking on me was one thing. Sticks and stones weren't going to hurt me. But if she started in on my kids, I was going to get mad.

"I doubt it. Especially not if there is any chance any of the judges could be around."

"Well, I guess I'll just do my best to steer clear of her during the rest of the week." I straightened my shoulders and nodded. "If I do that, I should be able to avoid any other trouble. Right?"

"Sure thing." Devlyn linked his arm through mine.

"Come on. Let's see if the kids have gotten back. We can tell them about the riser positioning—"

Yikes.

The sound of metal crashing and glass shattering echoed from the direction of the theater and sent us racing back toward the double doors. Devlyn reached them first. He yanked the door open. I followed behind and gasped as I looked at the stage. A black lamp bar and several canister lights were in the middle of the stage floor apron. Students were huddled near the wings, avoiding both the dented canisters and the glass. Twenty feet above the stage, a cable swung from the rafters. A tech must not have properly secured the cable that held the bar to the rail beam. It was just lucky no one was hurt.

Christine McCann raced onto the stage from stage left, verified that all the students were uninjured, and then peered up and said, "Someone please call 911."

And that was when I understood. First sabotaged costumes and instruments. Now a lighting mishap. Coincidence? Maybe, but the sick feeling in my stomach told me no. This wasn't an accident. Someone had rigged those lights to fall. The question was who?

Chapter 5

"The rest of today's rehearsals have been canceled," I announced.

"Are we going to get an extra rehearsal?"

"What happened to the lights?"

"Are they going to push back the competition?"

"This isn't fair."

While I agreed with that last sentiment, this scenario was preferable to the alternative. The last thing I wanted was my team to get squashed in a *Phantom of the Opera* moment. That wasn't the kind of history I was looking forward to making.

Holding up my hand, I waited for everyone seated on the staging room floor to quiet down and said, "I've called the hotel. No one is using the ballroom today or tomorrow, which means we can have it for rehearsal. Mr. O'Shea and I have come up with a different positioning for the risers than we normally use, and while this situation isn't ideal, it does give us an opportunity to spend more time than we usually would perfecting the new layout. The stage might not be cleared for us to rehearse, but that doesn't mean we're going to sit back and wait. The rest of the teams can do that if they want. We're going to work."

A couple of students cheered, easing the tension that had been building in the room. Thank God. My ability to work with high-strung, freaked-out students was chancy at best.

The students ignored Larry's request for them all to head for the bus and continued to talk over him. Larry yelled again. No one was paying attention. I was about to use my opera training to get the kids moving but stopped as I noticed the glint of jewelry sparkling from a hand perched on the frame of the open door. Several diamond-like jewels glistened in the light, along with a stone that from across the room looked as if it was colored a deep blue. I blinked and the pink-polished hand was gone.

Huh.

As Devlyn added his voice to the call to order, I weaved through the students, hoping to catch whoever had been lurking in the hall there before they disappeared. Why? I wasn't sure. But after everything that had happened thus far today, the idea of an unknown person eavesdropping outside our room wigged me out.

"Ms. Marshall, wait up." Unlike Larry, Chessie had no problems with projection. "I have a question," Chessie said as I reached the doorway and looked out into the hall.

Crap.

Kids filled the hall. A few teachers or parents were

giving instructions. At the end of the hall I thought I spotted a streak of pink disappearing through one of the doorways, but with all the commotion it was impossible to be certain. All I knew was that whoever had been standing outside our room listening to my instructions was gone.

Sighing, I turned and asked, "What's your question, Chessie?"

She beamed. "Jackie said her sequins were snagging on Brad's cummerbund during the last competition. We'll have time to practice with the costumes to make sure that doesn't happen again. Right?"

Sequins snagging. Lights falling. What next?

———

"We are a-here."

The Italian-accented announcement gave me enough warning to brace myself, but not enough time to get out of the way as my aunt and her boyfriend, Aldo, swept into the ballroom and made a beeline for me. A moment later, my aunt was squeezing the life out of me. Literally. In the last couple months, my aunt had been working out. Clearly, the upper-body exercises were working because I couldn't breathe. Help.

Finally, Millie must have gotten tired of squeezing because she loosened her grip. Hurray for oxygen.

Taking a deep breath, I yelled to my team, "You have five minutes until we start the run. If you need a drink, get one now." Then, taking two large steps back in case Millie decided she needed another hug, I asked, "How was the drive?"

"The drive was *perfetto*." Aldo stepped next to my

stylishly decked-out aunt and took her hand. "Spring is in full bloom. What could be better?"

Millie tugged to get her hand back. Aldo held tight. With his slight build, tufts of white hair just above and behind his ears, and slightly oversized plaid pants and white shirt, Aldo looked fragile and sweet. But while Millie had several inches on him in height (especially if you counted the sparkly pink stilettos she was sporting today), I'd learned the man more than matched her in sheer force of will. That was only one of the reasons I hoped Aldo convinced my aunt to marry him. The fact that the man could whip up an amazing lasagna without breaking a sweat was another. I liked good food. Sue me!

Sighing, Millie let Aldo tuck her well-moisturized hand into the crook of his arm and frowned. "We stopped by the performing arts center first, thinking we'd get there in time for your practice, and saw the police cars out front. Aldo tried to find out what happened, but the doors were locked and the sign said rehearsals were canceled for the day. When I couldn't reach you on your cell phone, I was worried something terrible had happened."

Oops. I pulled my phone out of my pocket. Six missed calls. Four from Millie. Two from a number I didn't recognize.

"I turned my cell to silent for rehearsal. One of the lighting bars above the stage fell today." I shoved my phone back into my pocket and tried to sound nonchalant despite my concerns about the reason the lights plummeted. "The head of the program is verifying that the theater is safe before we're allowed back inside."

Millie's eyes narrowed behind her sparkly, pink glasses. "How often do lights fall from the stage rafters?"

"It's been known to happen." During earthquakes. Hurricanes. The usual stuff.

Aunt Millie's broad shoulders slumped with relief. "Well, then I guess Aldo and I will check into our rooms. After you're done rehearsing, you can catch me up on everything that has happened since you arrived. I'd also like to talk about the styling choices I've made for the team. I think you're going to love them."

Giving my arm a pat, Millie turned and headed for the exit. Aldo stayed put. Once my aunt had disappeared through the exit, Aldo gave a lusty sigh and turned toward me. "My Millie insists we get different rooms while we are here. Your aunt is worried we will make a bad impression if the students know we are sleeping in sin."

I was pretty sure the sin Millie referred to didn't happen when they were unconscious, but I understood the point. "Aunt Millie doesn't want to do anything to distract the kids. She knows how hard they've worked to get here."

"And you." Aldo gave a toothy grin. "You do no' get paid for half of the work you do for this choir. If they win, it is because you give the students extra lessons and rehearsal time without a single penny more. Your aunt worries you work too hard."

"I know." And I was grateful. While I loved my parents and they loved me, Aunt Millie had always been the one to support my love of performing. It was her suggestion that I move into her house to save money while I taught at the nearby high school and waited for my big break. Neither of us had expected the murder cases I'd come in contact with or the harrowing experiences they'd led to. I had emerged from the adventures with a more high-profile name and my aunt . . . Well, since Christmas,

Millie had canceled two business conferences and had made arrangements with Larry to do hair and makeup at this competition without consulting me. In business, Millie was fearless. In her personal life, you just had to look at her reactions to Aldo and me to see that Millie didn't always have a handle on how to deal with the uncertainty that came along with love. As I spotted Devlyn walking through the door, I was forced to admit I wasn't any better on the love front than my aunt.

After telling Aldo I'd meet him and Millie later for dinner, I turned toward the stage we'd set and said, "Okay, everyone. Let's do this."

My phone vibrated as Larry took his position in the back of the room to assess the overall picture the band and the choir made. I looked at the phone display and frowned. It was the same number as two unknown missed calls. Once again, the caller didn't leave a message. Shrugging, I shoved the phone back in my pocket. Then I got to work adjusting the band's position while Larry yelled his opinion of how the whole thing looked. When we were satisfied with the setup, Jim lifted his hands, cued the band, and away we went.

Music filled the room. The girls twirled into the guys' arms and then spun out. After three steps downstage, they started to sing. Hmmm . . . the positioning of those on the steps wasn't exact. I made a mental note to run the opening sequence again and continued to watch for flaws. The tempo was a hair faster than I wanted, and the band was overenthusiastic with volume. If they played like this onstage, we'd be in serious trouble. The judges had to actually hear the singers in order to score them. Balance between the band and the choir was key.

When the number was over, I yelled, "Hold, please."

The best thing about that phrase was that it brought everything—actors, singers, dancers, instrumentalists, and conductor—to a halt. Talk about power. I had once wondered how stage managers could be content running the show instead of being in it. Making high school students freeze with just two words showed me just how much of a rush that job could be. Too bad that phrase didn't work on Millie's prized standard poodle, Killer. Then again, if it did, I might end up gaining several dress sizes. Having a dog intent on keeping you from the fridge was the best diet ever.

Larry and Devlyn walked over. After conferring, the two changed the team's starting marks while I talked to Jim.

"The kids look great," he said. "I can't hear them from back here, but I think I should be able to make it work."

"I hope so." I gave him a wide smile. "Having you and the band center stage will show the audience how important strong musicianship is to this performance medium."

Okay. That might have been laying it on a bit thick, but hey, desperate times called for desperate measures.

Jim straightened his shoulders and gave me a happy grin. "I'm glad to help. I've even asked the front desk to have my suit pressed. I want to make sure I look my best."

"You always look great, Jim," I said, and I meant every word. Jim's wife was a laundry fiend. Even his T-shirts were starched and ironed. And since she insisted on overseeing the packing of his competition attire, Jim wouldn't know a crease or a wrinkle if it smacked him in the face. His students, on the other hand . . . "But I do think I'm going to try and spruce up the band's look. We can talk about that later. Right now I need to work on making sure the musical balance fits the aesthetic one."

"Can I help?" Jim asked.

Oy. Jim was a gifted trumpet player and a very serviceable musical director. His powers of observation, however, were in need of work.

Widening my eyes a little to give me a deer-in-headlights, please-don't-flatten-me look, I said, "Up until now the band's placement has made it easier for the stage performers and the instrumentalists to work as one unit. This looks better, but . . ." I sighed. "The band sounds great, but I can't hear the singers. We need to keep the enthusiasm, but tone down the volume the way they did at sectionals."

Which involved my putting extra carpet under the drum set, bribing the bass player with a dozen peanut butter Twix, and channeling the time I played Shelby in *Steel Magnolias*. The tears worked on the audience as well as they did on Jim. I would rather not play that card again, but desperate times . . .

Jim frowned.

My smile dissolved.

Jim crossed his arms.

My lower lip trembled in what I hoped looked like sorrow instead of hours of practicing being able to isolate those muscles while killing time in my college dorm room.

Finally, Jim shook his head and sighed. "The acoustics are different now that we're on the stage. Okay. Let's rein in the volume and see what it sounds like."

Huzzah! Score one for my lack of a social life my sophomore year. "Thanks. If you have them play at mezzo piano while the team is singing, you'll really impress the judges when you bump up to forte during the dance breaks. The control they have over dynamics is quite possibly the thing that is going to put us over the top."

Turning, I heard Jim say to the players, "If technique is going to help win this thing, then let's show them everything we got. Mike, we might need to mute your bass drum if you can't bring down the sound."

Once Larry and Devlyn finished repositioning the singers, I signaled for Jim to start the music, and the opening notes of the first song in our set began again. The spacing was better, although I noticed Breanna and Franco bump into Chessie and Eric during the number. Thank God it wasn't before a lift or who knows what might have happened.

The kids struck their final pose. The brass performed the final hit. Jim looked across the room to where I was standing and lifted a brow in question. Continue? Or did I want to stop and fix?

My nod made Jim raise his hands. He cued the drummer, who played a rousing eight-bar solo as the singers took their next positions. The bass player was cued. The horns played a riff, and Megan opened her mouth to sing.

Crap.

Chessie was right about Megan's scratchy voice. I hadn't noticed during the last number because the sopranos as a whole were a strong section. But now that she was solo, I could hear the fatigue in Megan's tone. The way her shoulders raised as she took a breath told its own story. Whatever strain Megan was feeling was causing her to panic and change her singing technique instead of relying on it. Megan wasn't one of my voice students. Under normal circumstances, I would make a few minor suggestions and ask her instructor to work on it with her during their next lesson. But her teacher wasn't here, and the preliminaries began in less than two days. If I needed to replace her in the number, I'd have to make that decision soon.

I made notes about a shaky harmony and the final lift (the synchronization was slightly off), ignored the vibrating of my phone—again—and signaled to Jim to keep going. We would go back and fix the problems once we'd run the last number. Then we'd time it all once more to make sure we fit the ten minutes we were allowed. For every second over we'd be penalized. Not on my watch.

The final number was the strongest of the three. Chessie sounded great during her feature. She'd worked hard to have power without losing pitch, and as of now that lesson seemed to be paying off. As long as the excitement of the competition didn't throw her off her game, this number was going to make a great final impression. Especially if the kids danced and sang as strongly as they were doing today. Now I just had to whip the rest of the performance into shape and we'd be on track to do what we came to Nashville to do—make it to the finals and finish this year's season with a win. If this was going to be my last experience as a coach, I wanted to go out with a bang.

Devlyn and I worked with the kids and the band for the next hour with Larry yelling helpful advice from his spot in the back. By the time rehearsal ended, everyone was dripping with sweat. But the harmonies were fixed, the lifts were polished, and we could hear every note sung by the team. Things were looking up.

As the team and band filed out to get ready for dinner, I walked over to Megan. "Do you have a minute?"

When she turned, her overly bright smile couldn't mask the worry brimming in her eyes. "Sure, Ms. Marshall. What do you need?"

"Come with me." I headed toward the keyboard as my phone vibrated again. Same number as the previous half dozen times. Oy. "Could you give me a second?" I asked as Megan took a seat in one of the band's chairs. "I need to see who this is."

When Megan nodded, I walked toward the center of the room and answered the call.

"Is this Paige Marshall?" a low, whispery voice asked.

"Yes, it is." I turned to look at Megan. She swallowed hard, noticed me watching, and gave me a tenuous smile. The poor kid. "How can I help you?"

"You can meet me outside the performing arts center at nine o'clock. If you're even one minute late, you and your team will be very, very sorry."

Chapter 6

"Who is this?" I asked. No answer. I looked at my phone. Call ended. Damn.

I punched up the call log and dialed. No answer. Whoever wanted me to come visit them tonight wasn't interested in talking to me until then. Great. As if life wasn't exciting enough.

Since Megan looked content sitting across the room, I let my fingers do the walking and punched the mysterious number into my phone's Internet search feature. Unlisted caller. So much for that idea. Since I didn't have another that would give me the identity of my new friend, I shoved my phone back in my pocket, walked over to the electric piano, and took a seat on the bench.

"Is everything okay, Ms. Marshall?" Megan asked. "Did you get bad news?"

"Everything's fine." Or it would be when I had time

to perform a reverse call lookup. "I'm worried about you. How are you feeling?"

"I'm great." Megan swallowed hard, winced, and gave me a very large smile. "This is all so exciting. It's hard to believe the competition is almost here. Graduation will be here before we know it and then college and I can't tell you how much I appreciate everything you did to help me get ready for my auditions."

Between the high-pitched nervous giggle and the flush creeping into her cheeks, Megan was even worse at lying than Chessie. The two were going to need some serious acting classes if they planned to make a career out of performing.

"Megan." I leaned my elbow on the piano. "How does your throat feel?"

The fake smile faded, and tears threatened. "It's fine. A little tired." Another hard swallow. Another flinch. "I know today wasn't my best singing, but I'm going to rest my voice tonight and go to bed early. It'll be better tomorrow."

A tear fell.

My heart clenched.

I understood how important this week was to her. This was her final big performance of her high school career. She wanted this chance, and I wanted it for her.

"Tell me the truth," I said, resting my arm on the electric piano. "Does your throat hurt?"

Megan started to shake her head no but then sighed. "A little. But it's better than yesterday. It'll be fine by the competition. I promise."

Another tear fell. The despair in Megan's voice made

me want to cry, too. Being sick was hell on a performer, which is why we all had lots of tricks up our sleeves in order to get well. Or at least well enough so the show could go on. And we learned to carry our supplies with us.

"Here's what we're going to do." I stood and motioned for Megan to follow me toward the ballroom's exit. "I have some zinc lozenges in my room. Those will help with the swelling you have in your vocal cords. From now until tomorrow you're on vocal rest. No singing. No talking. Who are you rooming with again?"

"Chessie, Breanna, and Claire."

I smiled. Chessie would keep Megan quiet whether Megan wanted to be or not.

"We'll talk to your roommates so they know you need quiet. Drink lots of water. Get sleep. Take the zinc, and we'll see how you're feeling tomorrow. If your voice is still feeling strained, we'll have to let your understudy practice just in case your voice hasn't come all the way back by Thursday. Okay?" I looked at Megan as we crossed the lobby.

She gave a small sigh and nodded. "Okay."

On the way to my room I gave her a list of other tips that should keep her vocal cords from swelling further and aid in getting them back to normal. Armed with a fistful of strawberry-cream-flavored zinc cough drops and a warning to eat dinner before she consumed one—zinc never failed to seep into taste buds for a good long while and make everything immediately after taste like metal— I sent her out the door with a promise to check on her first thing in the morning. "And, Megan," I said as she opened the door to her hotel room. "Remember that even if you can't sing your feature on Thursday, there's still a chance you'll be able to do it on Friday. Take care of your voice. It's going to get better."

"Thanks, Ms. Marshall," she whispered. "You're the best." Then she disappeared into her room before I could lecture her on how bad whispering is for the vocal cords.

Oh well. She'd heard it before. And if she needed a reminder, I could talk to her after dinner.

"She's right, you know." My aunt's voice reached over my shoulder. "You've done a remarkable job with these students. I think they finally realize how lucky they are to work with someone like you. It's amazing how much can change over the course of a year."

Yeah. Back in August, I'd have never given a second thought to hopping on a plane and leaving Devlyn and Larry in charge of the team. I also would have never received a threatening phone call asking me to meet in front of a theater or else. Life had taken some strange turns.

"I'm not the only one who's changed this year," I said, closing my room door behind my aunt. "Look at you."

"What about me?" Millie asked, smoothing her low-cut, lacy mauve shirt. My aunt had performed a wardrobe change. The white capris were gone. In their place was a gray tulip skirt that showed off Millie's curvy hips and lots of leg. While Millie had upset Aldo by insisting that he book a separate hotel room, her outfit suggested she might not intend for him to stay there. Millie was sending mixed signals. No wonder poor Aldo was confused.

"You changed clothes," I said, taking a seat on the bed.

Millie looked down at her shirt and shrugged. "I freshened up. It was a long car ride, and I wanted to be comfortable."

Only someone who had undergone the Inquisition

would consider four-inch heels, a figure-hugging skirt, and a shirt that was wrapped tight enough to be a tourniquet comfortable.

"Aunt Millie, I know you've always avoided serious relationships."

"I'm married to my career." Aunt Millie started to sit on the bed, tugged on the hemline of her skirt as it rose up toward her hips, and stood back up. "It takes a lot of focus and energy to stay at the top of my field. I might even beat out Immojean Harley this year for the best sales in the country."

"Lots of people at the top of their fields get married."

"Yes, but most of the time it is the man who's at the top of his field, not the woman." Millie shrugged. "In my experience, it doesn't take long for a man to get tired of not being the center of attention."

"Then why do you insist I need to get married?" Millie was constantly pushing me into blind dates. The last one was a dentist who claimed gold fillings would help me sing better and glared when I picked up the dessert menu. Denying me chocolate cake might prevent cavities, but it wasn't going to score a second date. Much to Millie's disappointment. "If my performing career starts to take off, I'll have to travel."

"Yes, but you're on your way up," Millie insisted. "If you find someone now, they'll feel as if they're a part of it. The right man will understand how important it is for him to be waiting in the wings after the applause stops."

Maybe.

I thought about my earlier conversation with Devlyn. Would he be the type to build my career with me or get tired of not having me around all the time? I had no idea.

But I was sure about Millie's guy. "Aldo is a great accompanist. He understands that his talents are important and isn't afraid to share the stage with someone who gets more attention than he does. I've tried to stay out of your relationship." Because the last thing I wanted to do was encourage my aunt to take a more active role in matchmaking for me. "But I think you love Aldo and I'm certain he loves you. Maybe you should think about giving the two of you together a real shot. Who knows—with his support you might knock Immojean off her top salesperson perch for good."

Millie tilted her head to the side. "I could use some help beating Immojean. And Aldo does have a way with the ladies. That accent makes women forget their budgets. You should have seen him last weekend when I held a party for the North Shore Garden Club. He wore this sexy black silk shirt and had those women eating out of his hand and buying product as if it was going out of style. I guess it goes to show that sex sells."

As if my life wasn't complicated enough, I now had the image of Millie, Aldo, and sex in my brain. Help.

"So, how did rehearsal go?" Millie asked. "I would have stayed but I wanted to get Killer settled. You know how nervous he gets when he's left alone in the car for too long."

"Killer is here?" The dog hated me. Okay, "hate" was maybe too strong a word since I often found him hogging my pillow in the middle of the night. "I thought you were going to leave him at the doggie spa."

"I was, but he was unhappy when I tried to leave. He even bit the hostess to make sure he wasn't left behind."

Right. The bite had nothing to do with Killer's

disgruntled personality or his desire to do damage to anyone who wasn't a dog show judge or Millie.

"And really," Millie said, "now that I think about it, bringing Killer here is the best thing. He'll help distract the team. I know how nervous they get before a competition."

Running for their lives would certainly keep them diverted.

"Now." Millie yanked her skirt down and perched on the edge of the bed. "Tell me what's really going on down here. I know you're trying to keep your students from panicking, but lights don't fall from theater rafters without help."

Since Millie was going to find out anyway, I quickly explained the events of the day, complete with costume confetti, falling canister lights, and LuAnn's insistence that I was behind the problems. "I also got a strange call a little while ago from someone insisting I meet them outside the theater." Needless to say, this competition wasn't like any other I'd been to thus far.

Aunt Millie stood. "Well, if this LuAnn woman thinks she can make those kinds of accusations and get away with it, she has another thing coming. That woman doesn't know who she's dealing with. Just give me a couple of hours to track her down and she'll—"

"No!"

My aunt blinked.

Okay, that had came out more forcefully than I'd intended. But Millie and her dog had a lot in common. Both were impeccably groomed, wore lots of pink, and could be very, very scary when motivated. Emotions were running high enough at this competition. The last thing I needed was my aunt adding to the drama.

In a gentler tone, I said, "As much as making LuAnn apologize for her behavior would be fun, I want to set a good example for the students on the team. They need to learn how to ignore the LuAnns of the world and keep their focus on the performance."

"I guess you're right," Millie said. "But if that woman says anything about you around me, she's going to get several samples of that magenta lipstick that caused the test subjects' lips to swell."

"I thought you got rid of those." How my aunt had even gotten her hands on the defective product line of one of her competitors was beyond me. Changing subjects before Aunt Millie had a chance to educate me on the world of cosmetic warfare, I said, "I need to punch up the band's uniforms. Would you like to go shopping?"

"Does a fish like to swim?"

Leaving Aldo to deal with Killer and Devlyn, and Larry and Jim to supervise dinner and relocate instruments to my room, Millie and I headed out to explore the retail side of Nashville. Three hours and dozens of stores later, I'd learned that a person could purchase cowboy hats in every shade of the rainbow and that feathers, sequins, and rhinestones weren't just decorations—they were a way of life. Armed with a selection of sparkly ties and non-western-looking hats, I had just settled back in Millie's pink Caddy for the trip back to the hotel when I noticed the time.

Eight forty five.

My mysterious caller had asked me to meet at nine.

Between my chat with Megan and this shopping odyssey, I'd put the demand that I show up or be sorry out of my mind. Now that I'd remembered, I found myself curious enough to ask Millie to take a spin by the performing arts center. I wanted to know who'd called. More important, I wanted to know why.

Had I been alone, I wouldn't have considered making the trek, especially now that night had fallen. But now that Millie was with me, I was mulling the idea. The performing arts center was in a well-lit and heavily trav-eled area of town. On top of that, I seriously doubted that whoever was waiting for me expected me to arrive in a pink convertible Cadillac, so I'd have the element of sur-prise. Millie could do a quick lap of the building while I looked for whoever was lurking outside. Neither of us would ever step foot out of the car. This plan was as safe as safe could get.

Whoa! Horns blared. I grabbed the panic bar as Millie cut off an SUV and hung a right as she was instructed to do by her GPS. She narrowly missed a man hurrying through the crosswalk as she cruised down the street, talking about the pros and cons of glitter eye makeup.

"I don't want to overwhelm them with too much sparkle, but if we aren't doing the false eyelashes, a little extra punch might be called for." Millie spun the wheel, and we zipped into the empty but brightly lit parking lot of the theater complex. "Well, we're here. Now what?" Millie asked.

Good question. I had my aunt drive by the entrance. A sign was posted, informing us that tomorrow's classes and rehearsals would proceed as scheduled. That was a relief. The police wouldn't allow the show to go on if they thought there was a chance of foul play. Now I just had

to find out the identity of the caller who wanted to antago-
nize me, avoid the person like the plague, and focus on
the competition like planned.

Aunt Millie swung the car around the lot and drove
by the entrance again. There were three cars parked in
spots near the entrance. The cars were empty, and I
couldn't see anyone inside the lobby. The clock on the
dash read 8:56. Since there were still four minutes until
the caller's deadline, I told Millie to park at the far end
of the lot so we could wait.

Millie checked her voice mail while I watched the
parking lot for signs of movement. Nothing. So much for
my stakeout abilities. But I'd learned from the last time
I'd tried staking out a place. This time I wasn't trying to
hide in a car with the engine running. So that was something, right?

The clock struck nine. Millie made a call to a client
with a blusher emergency. By the time I'd learned how
to blend the cranberry cream to create a naturally rosy
flush, I was ready to leave.

"The caller must have been playing some kind of prac-
tical joke," I said as Millie eased the car out of the parking
spot. "Let's just—"

Holy shit.

Millie turned the wheel and slammed on the brakes
as a car sped by, narrowly missing us. The vehicle barely
slowed as it took a right and zipped out onto the street.

My heart slammed in my chest as I looked around the
parking lot for signs of where the car had come from. The
three cars from before were still parked out front. "That
car must have come from around back of the theater by
the loading docks."

Millie punched the gas. Yikes. I grabbed my seat and hung on for dear life as she rounded the corner of the performing arts center and made a beeline for the loading docks. The tires squealed as she hit the brakes. My seat belt prevented me from flying into the dashboard, but the ache around my midsection told me that this little adventure was going to leave a mark.

Ouch.

I was about to complain when I spotted something in the glare of the Caddy's headlights that made me forget what I was going to say. On the ground near the stage-left loading dock was a pair of bright red cowboy boots. And from the looks of things, the person wearing them wasn't going to be walking over me or anyone else again anytime soon.

Chapter 7

"Call 911," I yelled as I fought to unlatch my seat belt. When it finally came free, I threw open the door and raced across the pavement.

The boots still weren't moving. My stomach lurched as I realized why. LuAnn's bouffant, bleach blond hair was now streaked with red that oozed from a gash on her forehead. I was about to rip a piece of material off of my shirt to press against the wound when I noticed something much, much worse. LuAnn's darkly lined hazel eyes were staring up at the sky and her chest was still as a stone. LuAnn wasn't breathing.

Crap. Crap. Crap.

I knelt next to LuAnn's unmoving body and put my finger on her neck to feel for a pulse. Nothing. This was bad. But if the car that sped out of here had something to do with LuAnn's current state, there was still a chance.

Keeping that thought in my head, I gently lifted up

LuAnn's chin like the instructor taught us to do in the CPR class I took last fall. All Prospect Glen teachers were encouraged to take the class annually to make sure we could assist our students in the event of an emergency. I'd considered the class a waste of time since I planned on ditching the job the first chance I got. Good thing the instructor insisted I demonstrate what I'd learned then or I wouldn't be able to check whether LuAnn was breathing now that the airway was clear.

It was. She wasn't. Oh God.

Using my thumb and forefinger, I pinched LuAnn's nose, put my mouth to hers, and began CPR. Breathe. Breathe. Then, putting my hands on the slick red fabric on her chest, I pushed like the teacher had demonstrated. Come on, LuAnn. I pushed four more times. Still nothing.

Again.

Breathe. Breathe. Push. Push. Please. Come on, LuAnn. Please breathe.

"Paige."

I felt a hand on my shoulder, but I kept administering CPR. Another breath. Another set of pushes on her sternum as I willed the woman to live.

Sirens sounded in the distance. My aunt said that it was too late. I knew she was right. It had been too long. I tasted tears as I tried one last time. Nothing.

Emergency lights flickered. Sirens blared. Doors slammed and feet raced across the pavement as Aunt Millie helped me climb to my feet. The cavalry had arrived. But they were too late. I had tried to keep LuAnn alive, but my skill hadn't been enough. The weight of that inadequacy settled on my shoulders and after a few minutes the authorities announced what I had already accepted. LuAnn, with her red boots and larger-than-life, pain-in-the-ass attitude, was dead.

Millie and I stood next to the Caddy as paramedics stopped treatment and more cop cars arrived. My aunt dug a box of tissues out of the glove box. I had used almost the entire container by the time a small but firm-voiced policewoman who introduced herself as Officer Kira Durbin came over to take our names and ask if we were the ones who reported the accident.

Accident?

I blinked as Millie nodded and said, "My niece's show choir team is performing here this week. We were in the parking lot and were almost hit by a car speeding away from here."

While Millie gave her account of driving to the back of the theater and discovering LuAnn lying on the ground, I shifted to the side and watched several officers take photographs and document the crime scene. Was this an accident as the police officer talking to Millie suggested? If LuAnn was my unknown caller, she could have been waiting here for me to arrive. Whoever was driving the car could have panicked when he or she made contact with LuAnn and fled the scene. But if LuAnn wasn't the one behind the mysterious call . . .

I shook the thought free as Officer Durbin told Millie to take a seat in her car and then turned her attention to me.

Once she'd written my name, address, and phone number onto her report, she asked the same questions Millie had just answered. Yes, I saw the car that raced out from behind the theater. It was black (or maybe blue) with a large scratch along the passenger side. Or maybe that was just the glare from the parking lot lights. It was dark and everything happened so fast it made it hard to be certain.

Yes, we drove by the front of the facility and read the signs on the door.

No, I didn't notice anyone walking around the theater or cars driving in the parking lot other than the three that had been parked when we first arrived.

"There were three cars?" she asked.

I nodded. "One of those cars must belong to LuAnn," I reasoned since all of the cars back here aside from Millie's were equipped with emergency lights. Although now that I thought about it, I wondered why LuAnn would park her car in the front of the facility and then walk all the way back here to wait for me. Unless she crossed through the building, she would have had to have walked around the entire building to reach the road that led here from the parking lot. That appeared to be the only way for cars, trucks, or people to get in and out of this area. The rest was surrounded by a large wrought-iron fence.

"You were friends with the victim?" Officer Durbin asked.

"We met each other this morning," I said. "I don't even know her last name."

"So you don't know why she was here tonight?"

"No."

Officer Durbin closed her book. She must have been satisfied with my answer, but I wasn't. "I don't know if this has anything to do with what happened to LuAnn, but I got a strange call tonight." I pulled up my received call list, showed the number to the officer, and tried to remember exactly what the caller had said.

"Someone asked you to meet here tonight?"

"Well, not exactly here," I said. "They said the theater, which I assumed meant the front entrance. I didn't plan on coming, but when my aunt and I finished shopping, I asked her to swing by so I could see if anyone was waiting."

Officer Durbin's eyebrow arched. Yeah. Clearly, that wasn't the smartest idea I'd ever had. Since I'd already told her that much, I decided to tell the rest.

Quickly, I walked Officer Durbin through the events of today, including LuAnn's strange dislike of me, the ruined costumes, and the falling lights. It was entirely possible that the events were unrelated to LuAnn's death, but I figured it was better to be safe than sorry.

"So you think the person who called you tonight and asked you to meet him here was the one who was driving the car that hit the victim?" Skepticism dripped from every word.

As much as I wanted to be annoyed, I really couldn't blame her. It sounded stupid even to me and I was the one saying it.

"Probably not, but I dated a police detective in the past and he told me that more information was always better than less. So, I figured it was best to tell you about it in case it turned out to be important."

Okay, technically Prospect Glen Detective Michael Kaiser and I had never dated. In fact, since he'd attended *The Messiah* back in December, he and I had barely spoken. One moment he was dropping the "love" word into our conversations; the next he was too wrapped up in work to answer a phone call. Which I'd been telling myself was for the best. Aside from our mutual love of

French fries, we had very little in common. Still, I was fairly certain he'd agree that I'd done the right thing in sharing today's events.

After a couple more questions, Officer Durbin asked me to wait in the car with Millie and huddled with several of her fellow officers. Since Millie had her laptop open on the passenger seat and was borrowing the Internet signal from the Starbucks around the corner, I decided not to interrupt. Instead, I leaned against the hood of Millie's car, watched as LuAnn's body was being lifted onto a gurney, and felt a tear streak down my cheek. The woman might have been antagonistic and had tacky taste in footwear, but that didn't mean she deserved to die.

Closing my eyes, I pictured LuAnn standing onstage today with the team of high school students behind her. One of those students was her daughter. My heart ached as I thought about what this news would do to that teenage girl and the rest of the singers from that school.

Wait.

My eyes snapped open. I took a step forward and looked past the emergency workers pushing LuAnn's dead body from the scene. Where was LuAnn's purse? Earlier today, LuAnn was carrying a purse. A very large, very purple one. Where was it now? Most women I knew, especially ones who favored large handbags, rarely left home without their purses. Though I'd only met LuAnn today, the three times we'd come in contact, the woman had been carting around a large purple bag. It should have been with her now. But it wasn't. Did the cops pick it up or had it never been here in the first place?

I walked back toward the scene of the crime and tried to remember when I first spotted LuAnn on the ground.

Did she have the purse with her then? Not that I could remember, but I was pretty focused on other things like life and death. Accessories weren't exactly on my radar no matter how enormous or colorful.

"Excuse me," I said, stepping toward the area where Officer Durbin was conferring with colleagues. "Officer, can I ask you a question?"

She sighed, nodded at her coworkers, and strolled across the pavement. Ignoring that sinking suspicion that I was about to become the butt of several jokes, I asked, "Did you happen to find LuAnn's purse?"

"If the purse was here, one of my fellow officers will have found it." Officer Durbin gave me an overly bright smile. "You and your aunt are now free to leave. If I or the detective in charge of investigating the accident has any questions, we'll be in touch."

Not the most inventive of dismissals, but effective since it came with a badge. And since investigating LuAnn's death or the whereabouts of her purse wasn't my job, it was time to get out of here.

Millie was on another call when I climbed into the pink Caddy. Why anyone needed to talk about facial moisturizers at this time of night was beyond me. As I clicked my seat belt into place, I felt my phone vibrate. Oops. I'd forgotten to turn on the ringer.

Devlyn was wondering when I'd be back.

I typed, "Ran into an unexpected problem. Will be at the hotel soon," and hit "send." Technically, we weren't the ones who ran into the problem, but it was close enough.

When Millie wrapped up her call, I told her we were free to leave. She put the phone down and the car in gear.

Thank God Officer Durbin had her back turned or the way Millie hit the gas would have made her think twice about letting us leave without asking a few more questions.

Millie had to slow and wait for the police to remove the barrier they'd placed between the parking lot and the entrance to the loading dock. Once they let us through, I spotted a familiar blond figure climbing out from a black sedan.

"Pull over there," I said as Christine McCann hurried toward the barricade. "This will just take a minute." Before Millie could volunteer to come with me, I hopped out of the car.

"But I am the head of the competition that's happening at this facility this week," Christine said to the dark-haired officer who looked barely old enough to shave. Despite her bravado, I could hear the tremor in her words as she added, "I need to know what's happening."

"Christine." I waved.

Her eyes narrowed. "What are you doing here? Do you know what's going on? The facility manager told me the police were here, but he didn't give any more details." She turned back to the cop, who had one hand firmly planted on his hip near his weapon. "I have a right to know what's going on."

The guy behind the barricade didn't look impressed. I grabbed Christine's arm and tugged. Christine's day was already going from bad to worse. Harassing a police officer wasn't going to improve things for her. "Come with me."

Christine let out a huff as she followed me until we were out of earshot of Nashville's finest. Officer Durbin already thought I was nuts. I wasn't interested in perpetuating that belief any more than necessary.

"What's going on, Paige?" Christine demanded. Now that we were situated under one of the parking lot lights, I could see the pallor of Christine's face. She could benefit from one of Millie's blusher tutorials. "Why are you here? Are your students okay?"

"My students are fine," I said. Unless, of course, they had locked Larry in his room and were running through the streets of Nashville unchecked. "There was an accident involving a car in the back of the theater near the loading dock."

"A car accident?" Christine let out a laugh and a relieved sigh. "Well, why didn't the policeman just tell me that? I was worried it was . . . Well, the way the facility manager sounded on the phone I was certain it was something much worse. Thank goodness it wasn't anything more serious. I mean—"

"Christine—"

The woman in question wasn't paying attention. "After what happened with the lights, parents are understandably concerned, and—"

"Christine," I said louder, hoping to derail the train Christine was driving.

Nope. "We've been working hard to get the national media's attention. I know you understand how valuable that attention could be to some of these kids."

"Christine!" Okay, that was probably way more forceful than I'd intended, but it worked. Christine stopped talking. Vocal projection and power were two things I excelled at. I even had a master's degree to prove it.

Now that I had her attention, I lowered my voice. "LuAnn was involved in the accident."

"LuAnn?" Christine squinted toward the barricade. "LuAnn Freeman?"

Maybe.

"What was LuAnn doing here this time of night? If she's causing trouble again, I swear I'll kill her."

"You can't do that," I said.

"Why not?"

Eek! Now that I had Christine's full attention, I had no idea how to break the news. Since people always say the best way to tell bad news or remove a bandage is to get it over with fast, I took a deep breath and said, "Because LuAnn is already dead."

Christine blinked at me. "Dead?"

I nodded, glad that the worst part was over. Because after finding LuAnn and then having to break the news of her death, nothing could get worse.

Oops. I guess I was wrong, because a second later Christine's eyes rolled back in her head and she crumpled to the pavement.

Chapter 8

Yikes. I lunged forward, but was too late. Christine McCann hit the deck with a thud. Ouch.

The cop behind the barrier looked at Christine and then back at the road behind him as if trying to decide what to do. Remain at his post or run and help. I made the decision for him. "Don't just stand there," I yelled. "Get some water or call a paramedic."

Christine's groan and the opening of her eyes negated the need for the paramedics. Despite my urging to stay still, she struggled to a seated position and asked, "What happened?"

I would have thought sitting on the asphalt was answer enough. Still, I answered, "You fainted when I told you about LuAnn."

I was glad Christine hadn't gotten up yet. If a blackout had caused her to forget that information, the ground was a good place for this discussion.

Tears glittered in Christine's eyes. Her mouth trembled. Then, with a nod, she reined in her emotions and slowly climbed to her feet. When the young officer arrived brandishing water, Christine took the bottle from him and demanded, "Is it true? Did someone die in an accident behind that building?"

The officer glared at me.

I shrugged. No one had told me not to share with the class. As far as I was concerned, I was in the clear.

The cop must have thought so, too, since he dropped the attitude and politely said, "Yes, ma'am. There was an accident with a single fatality." With that the cop nodded and hurried back to his post.

"I don't understand." Christine unscrewed the cap on the water. "What was LuAnn doing here at this time of night?"

Good question.

"Maybe she was checking to make sure the facility would be open tomorrow."

Christine shook her head. "She was one of the first people I talked to after the police and the theater's technical team gave us the all clear. That was around six. There was no reason for her to be here."

Huh. By the time I'd left the hotel to go shopping with Millie, Larry hadn't received that kind of phone call. If someone hadn't been dead, I'd have been put out by the lack of notification. A body count put things in perspective.

Thinking about that body, I asked, "Do you know if she was the kind to carry only her keys and wallet? The police haven't been able to find her purse." I glanced around the lot. Two of the three cars that had been parked in front earlier were there now. The third was gone.

"LuAnn took that purse everywhere with her." Christine sighed. "It was something of a running joke at the local competitions. If any of the kids needed a Band-Aid or something to remove a stain, they looked for LuAnn and her magic bag. She would never have left the hotel without her purse. Maybe it got jostled by the accident and went under the seat of her car."

Considering the suitcase nature of the purse, that would have to be a really big seat. If the cops were going to check, they would first have to find LuAnn's vehicle. Since that was their job, not mine, I assured myself that Christine was steady on her feet and made a beeline for Aunt Millie's car.

Despite the fact the cops were on the case, I couldn't stop thinking about LuAnn and the scene of the accident we'd just left. If it was an accident. As much as I wanted to believe it was (because the other option was a whole lot worse), I couldn't get the problem of LuAnn's car and her missing purse out of my mind.

LuAnn's car wasn't in the parking lot of the theater, which meant she must have copped a ride. But if that was the case, she would never have left her purse behind. And more disturbing, why was LuAnn in the back of the theater to begin with? To meet me? Maybe, but then why was she near the loading dock instead of waiting in the front? There was something not quite right about all of this.

Perhaps it was the strange turn my life had taken in the last couple of months, bringing me in contact with Detective Kaiser, that made me think that LuAnn's death was more than just a terrible twist of fate. My stomach was tied in knots as Millie tooled her car into the hotel parking lot, and for once it wasn't due to my aunt's overly aggressive driving. It was because I thought I had once again happened onto the scene of a murder.

Oh help.

———

Millie and I carried bags of sparkly ties and other potentially useful accessories to my room. The hallway was strangely quiet (especially considering how many teenagers were in the surrounding rooms) when I opened the door and almost walked into a trumpet case.

Damn. I'd thought Devlyn, Larry, or Jim would have supervised the loading of the instruments back in my room. I'd assumed wrong.

Millie offered to help move cases, but I turned her down. As much as I appreciated the offer, I wanted to be alone. Besides, as much as my aunt acted as if she was unaffected by our adventure, I could see sadness and strain in her eyes. She needed time to recover. Thank goodness Aldo and Killer would be there to give her whatever comfort she needed.

After giving my aunt a tight hug, I sent her away and then stared at the pile of cases in front of me. Instead of getting to work, I leaned against the closet door and closed my eyes. The emotions I'd held at bay since being questioned by Officer Durbin stormed back. My throat tightened. Tears pricked the backs of my eyes. I could barely breathe as I remembered the way LuAnn looked as I tried to pump air into her body.

The sound of a key card sliding into the lock and the door handle being pushed made my eyes fly open. I didn't think. I cocked my arm back, turned, and let it fly. The bags in my hand swung around. By the time I registered the target was Devlyn, it was too late.

He tried to duck and failed, which was why the bags made contact with his head instead of his arm and shoulder. Oops. Luckily, the bags were filled with lightweight stuff. Devlyn had once told me he'd had several concussions during his football-playing high school days. I'd hate to be the one to give him another. I'd had a concussion recently, and it was zero fun.

"Sorry," I said, dropping the bags. "Are you okay? I forgot you had a key." I'd also just seen a dead body, but I figured I'd get to explaining that part later.

Devlyn rubbed his left ear and laughed. "I'm glad you didn't swing at me for leaving this mess in your room."

I looked at the instrument cases and went from apologetic to bummed that I'd dropped the bags in two seconds flat. "This was intentional?"

Devlyn leaned against the exit door and grinned. "Well, the kids piled the instruments like this on their own, but I let them. I figured helping you restack them gave me a great excuse to spend time in here with you."

Okay, that was kind of sweet.

Devlyn pushed away from the wall, stepped around the trumpet case, and gave me a smile that normally made my toes curl. Tonight, it made my bottom lip quiver and the tears start to flow. To Devlyn's credit, he didn't say anything when I wrapped my arms around him, put my head on his chest, and started to sob. The more I tried to stop crying, the harder the tears fell. Tears for LuAnn. Tears for her daughter and her family, who had to have heard the news of LuAnn's death by now. And a whole lot more sniffles and sobs for the kids who knew and worked with LuAnn. No matter whether they liked her or not, they were going to feel the echo of her death in their lives.

And yes, there were tears shed for me. I'd tried my best to save LuAnn, but I felt guilty for not being able to do more. And I couldn't help wondering whether if I had reported the strange phone call to the police earlier today, that could have prevented what had happened. I doubted it. Officer Durbin's reaction to the call had been pretty telling. Still, I wished I had tried.

The right side of Devlyn's shirt was wet and my nose was running when the tears finally ran their course. I was also incredibly embarrassed. A really sexy guy had come to spend time with me and I had just cried all over him for no reason. Okay, I had a great reason, but he didn't know that. He must have thought I'd come completely unhinged.

Keeping my head down so Devlyn wouldn't have to see my red, blotchy face and my leaking nose, I apologized and made a dash for the bathroom.

Crap. I cracked my toe on the trumpet case, tripped, and went flying. Ouch. I smacked my arm on the doorframe to the bathroom, but at least I wasn't flat on my backside. That was something, right?

Rubbing my elbow, I looked at the floor to make sure there weren't any other obstacles and grabbed a tissue from the bathroom.

Yowzah.

A glance in the mirror told me I was right about one thing. I was a mess. My nose was drippy. My eyes were red and swollen, and even Millie and her talent with cosmetics couldn't erase the blotchiness from my skin. Unhinged was a bad look for me.

"Hey," Devlyn said from the doorway. His eyes met mine in the mirror, and I could see the concern in them. Yep, I was a wreck. "What's going on? Did you and Millie have a fight?"

I dabbed at my eyes and swiped the tissue under my nose to catch any wayward drips before turning toward Devlyn. "Millie and I found a dead body."

"You're kidding." Devlyn smiled. When I shook my head, the smile faded. "You're not kidding? How did you run into a dead body?"

"Technically, we didn't run into her. Someone else did. Or maybe they didn't." The more I thought about it, the more I wondered whether the car was the only contributor to LuAnn Freeman's death.

"I'm confused."

Of course he was. "Sorry," I said, taking another tissue. "Why don't we sit down and I'll tell you about it."

Conversations about death were creepy. Holding that conversation in the bathroom took the strange factor to a whole new level. Of course, I wasn't sure chatting in what currently looked like a mismanaged warehouse was a better idea.

"On second thought," I said, "why don't we rearrange these cases while I talk."

It turned out that despite my swollen toe, the crappy instrument storage by the band was a good thing. Shifting and stacking cases made it easier to tell Devlyn about the night's events.

When I was done, Devlyn stopped stacking a drum

case and stared at me. "LuAnn Freeman? The same LuAnn who accused you of sabotaging the other choirs?"

"That's the one."

Devlyn stacked the last two instrument cases in front of the bed by the window and said, "Well, it's a good thing the cops don't know about that or they might not have been so willing to rule her death an accident." He slapped the dust off his hands, turned, took one look at my face, and sighed. "You told them?"

"If I didn't, someone else would have," I said, taking a seat on my bed. "Now when someone else mentions it, the police won't wonder what I was trying to hide."

"I hate that you have a point." Devlyn sat down next to me and linked his fingers through mine. "I also hate that you can talk so calmly about the cops interviewing people and potentially looking at you as a suspect."

Devlyn had a short memory considering I'd just had a massive meltdown fifteen minutes ago. I leaned back on the pillow and closed my eyes. "So far, it appears that LuAnn's death was an accident. Besides, I was with Aunt Millie when it happened. I couldn't have a better alibi."

People remembered pink cars. Millie had a stack of tickets to prove it.

"Well, it's a good thing this was an accident and you won't need it. Right?" Devlyn's fingers tightened on mine. I opened my eyes to find his watching me with a steely intensity. "You don't think this was an accident."

"I think that a lot of unusual things happened today and it would be a pretty big coincidence if LuAnn was involved in all of them." I was, too, which was something I was having a hard time ignoring.

"Well, it's good the police are investigating," Devlyn said, sliding his arm around my shoulder.

"That's the thing," I said as Devlyn placed a kiss on my neck. "The officer I talked to wasn't interested in hearing anything that suggested LuAnn's death wasn't an accident. I mean, I know that my getting a phone call from an unknown number telling me to meet them at the theater or else could have been a high school prank, but—"

"You got a what?"

Oops. I'd missed that part. "I got the call when I was talking to Megan. Then Millie came to talk to me and I forgot about it until we were driving near the theater. We decided to drive by just in case the call wasn't a joke."

Devlyn pulled his arm back and stood. "You and your aunt thought it was a good idea to meet someone who threatened you at an empty theater after dark?"

When you put it that way . . .

"We didn't plan on getting out of the car."

"You didn't plan on finding a dead woman, either." Devlyn raked a hand through his hair and paced the rug. "Look, I know that you have a hard time staying on the sidelines when something unusual happens, but we aren't in Prospect Glen and Mike isn't here to bail you out if you tick off the cops."

"I don't need Mike to bail me out."

"I hope not, because the team and I need you to stay focused on what we're here for."

The implication that I wasn't focused stung. While this wasn't the job I'd dreamed of my entire life, the past few months had taught me two things. One, I liked it more than I expected. And two, I was damn good at it.

"The team doesn't have to worry and neither do you. Now, if I'm going to teach a master class and keep the team on track tomorrow, I guess I should get some sleep." I brushed past Devlyn and opened the door.

Devlyn stood there for a moment. Then he sighed. "Look." He glanced down the hall before brushing my cheek with his hand. "At least promise me you'll talk to me before you do anything crazy."

When I didn't say anything, he brushed his lips against my forehead and waited as if giving me one last chance to let him stay. Part of me was tempted to close the door and let him help me forget LuAnn's sightless eyes and the nagging sense of guilt I felt over her death. I had a feeling Devlyn would be very good at making a girl forget. But if our relationship had any hope of a future, we couldn't take that kind of step now. Not under these circumstances. I had to stand on my own two feet tonight. It was time for Devlyn to go.

"Don't forget to leave my key," I said.

Devlyn put his hand in his pocket, pulled out the blue card key, and placed it in my outstretched hand. With one last kiss on the cheek, he whispered, "I'm just down the hall if you need me." Then out the door he went, leaving me alone with two thoughts.

First, I really hoped LuAnn's death was an accident. Second, seeing her stomping around in her boots one minute and dead the next reaffirmed one thing: You had to take opportunities when they came or there might never be a chance for them to come again. Tomorrow, I'd tell Devlyn and Larry that I had been offered an audition at the Lyric. More important, no matter what happened with the competition, I was going to take it.

Chapter 9

Of course, to have that discussion, I needed not only to get them alone but to get a word into the conversation. Larry had gotten a wake-up call from Christine McCann this morning informing him of LuAnn's accident. She assured him that LuAnn's death would not affect the competition schedule from moving forward. From the way Larry's hair stood on end, the two distinctly different colors of his socks, and the stutter in his voice, it was clear that Larry hadn't been sufficiently reassured.

"Devlyn said you told him y-y-you found LuAnn. Are you okay? You l-l-look tired. Maybe you should cancel the master class," Larry said, stabbing some of the hotel's buffet breakfast pancakes with his fork. "After everything that h-h-happened yesterday with LuAnn, you should keep a low prof-f-file."

"Why don't I check with Scott and see what he says about the master class?" So far, Larry and I were the only members of our group in the hotel's breakfast area. The rest would be joining us soon. If I was going to tell him about Friday, now was the time. Taking a deep breath, I said, "But you might be right about keeping a low profile. You know, my manager called and there's an audition—"

"I still can't believe LuAnn Freeman is dead." Larry waved his fork, sending bits of food flying. "Did you know that she single-handedly kept this competition going the last couple of years?"

I blinked. "I thought Christine McCann was in charge of this competition." The bio I'd read said she'd taken the helm five years ago.

"She is." Larry poured more syrup on his pancakes. "But the competition was in a huge financial hole. There were lots of rumors that the whole thing was going to fold. A bunch of longtime coaches made noises about pitching in with fund-raisers, but nothing came of those. So LuAnn went out and found sponsors who were willing to keep the competition financially afloat."

Wow. "I didn't realize you knew her."

Larry shook his head. "Just by reputation. People said she was a force to be reckoned with."

After watching her in action yesterday, I could see why.

While Larry was sipping his coffee, I picked up a piece of bacon and steered the conversation back to my audition. "Larry, you know I love working with this team, but—"

The rumble of a low growl made the hair on my neck stand on end. The growling grew louder and the click-click-click of nails on the polished gray tile told me the source was coming near.

Slowly, I turned and came nose to nose with the fluffy white bane of my existence—Aunt Millie's award-winning standard poodle Monsieur de Tueur de Dame. Translated into English: Mr. Lady Killer. Millie intended the name to be cute. I thought it was prophetic because the dog lived up to the shortened, more commonly used version of his name—Killer.

Killer bared his teeth and growled again, sending a waft of dog breath in my direction. Ick. Killer hadn't brushed. The dog moved his snarling snout closer, nipped the bacon out of my hand, and devoured it before I had a chance to complain.

"I love that the two of you are such good friends." My aunt appeared behind Killer and patted the dog on his fuzzy head. Killer looked up at Millie with adoration and let out a burp. Killer now had bacon breath.

"Did you sleep okay, Aunt Millie?" Every time I'd closed my eyes, I'd seen LuAnn's face. That image hadn't made for a good night's sleep. My eyes felt grainy and had required more than a little cosmetic assistance to make me look as if I hadn't been on an all-night bender. Millie, however, looked as if she'd spent time in a spa. Her rosy cheeks matched the color of her pants and light-weight spring sweater.

"I slept like a baby." My aunt's eyes sparkled with happiness, and the smile that spread across her face as Aldo appeared next to her spoke loud and clear as to the reason why. I'd gone to bed alone last night, but Millie had not. While I was happy for her, I couldn't help feeling a twinge of jealousy. Despite her protests to the contrary, Millie had found someone to love who loved her back. I wanted that. More than I had realized.

"I'm glad to hear you're okay," Larry said. "When P-P-Paige told me you were with her last night . . . Well,

I know how I felt after I walked into the theater at the beginning of the school year and saw Greg Lucas dead. I didn't s-s-sleep well for weeks."

Being a murder suspect and getting kidnapped probably had more to do with that, but what did I know.

The sound of giggles and shouts to "wait up" announced the first arrivals of our team. Leaning close, Larry whispered, "When do you want to t-t-tell them?" Whispering was a good plan. Too bad when Larry stuttered, he tended to project his voice more than intended.

"Tell us what?"

Crap.

Chessie walked up to Killer and scratched his head. I started to tell Chessie to be careful and got into position to shove her out of the way if and when Killer snarled or snapped. But the dog just plopped his pompon butt on the floor and nuzzled his head under Chessie's hand for more attention. I wasn't sure whom I considered the biggest traitor.

"We want to talk about the things that happened yesterday," I said before Larry could answer. For a guy who had worked with teens for twenty years, he was bad at subterfuge.

"Oh." Chessie stopped petting Killer's head. "Well, I guess I should get some fruit before everyone else arrives."

"Fresh fruit sounds like a wonderful idea," Millie said. "Paige, would you take Killer's leash? I don't want to take him too close to the buffet. You know how excited he gets when there's bacon around."

Before I could object, Millie shoved a pink, rhinestone-encrusted strap into my hand and followed Chessie to the breakfast display. With a lusty sigh, Aldo followed, leaving Killer and me to fend for ourselves. Killer walked to the table, sniffed my baconless plate, and bared his teeth. Yep, this was bad.

Thank goodness Larry either thought my stories about Killer's personality disorder were exaggerated or was too distracted by LuAnn's death to care about missing digits as he held out a link of sausage. In Killer's world, pork took precedence over torturing me. Hurray.

By the time Larry ran out of sausage links, Millie had returned to retrieve Killer so he could snack off of her plate. Millie and Aldo scored a table across the room, which meant I didn't have to worry about canine intimidation tactics as I considered how best to break the news of LuAnn's death to the team.

My heart skipped when Devlyn walked into the room. For a minute, he just stood in the doorway. His head turned in my direction and his eyes met mine for a moment before he sauntered over to the buffet. I waited for him to join Larry and me at our table. Instead, he took a seat with Jim and some of the band kids.

Hurt bloomed in my chest. Yes, I'd asked him to leave last night, but that didn't mean I didn't want him to be concerned about me today. A contradiction? Perhaps, but I'd tried and failed to keep a woman from dying last night. A little latitude might be in order.

Ignoring Larry's curious look and the queasy turning of my stomach, I smiled and tried to be cheerful as I greeted the rest of the kids who staggered into the breakfast area.

Chessie was seated at a table for two. When her boyfriend walked in, I waited for her to wave Eric over to join her. Instead, she feigned intense interest in her yogurt cup as he piled eggs, pancakes, and bacon onto his plate and sat on the other side of the room.

Uh-oh. This wasn't good.

I thought it was an even worse sign that, while Chessie pretended nothing was wrong, Eric didn't bother to hide his concern as he watched her while shoveling in food. Meanwhile, the rest of their friends looked baffled to see the two sitting apart. In my experience, teenage couples didn't just break up. They imploded. Breakup drama typically involved Facebook posts, text messages, and phone calls to their closest friends. The fact that no one seemed to understand what was happening told me Chessie and Eric had either managed to avoid the drama (which, considering Chessie's nature, seemed highly unlikely) or they hadn't broken up.

My speculation on which scenario had occurred was cut short when Breanna slid into the seat across from Chessie. The room grew strangely quiet as the petite strawberry blonde asked, "Is everything . . . you know . . ." She looked across the room to where Eric was sitting, then back at Chessie. "Okay?"

"What?" Chessie's eyes widened for a moment. Then she laughed. "Oh, it's fine. I asked to be left alone this morning so I could save my voice." As if to prove the point, she smiled at Eric and gave him a wiggly finger wave.

Eric looked startled. After a moment, he waved back.

Taking that as a sign that everything was normal, the group went back to their chatter. But the nervous glances Eric gave Chessie made me pretty sure more was going on here than met the eye. And when I thought back on the strange way Chessie had behaved after the discovery of the damaged costume, I couldn't help but be worried at the reason why.

Larry nudged me and raised an eyebrow. I did a quick count of the students scattered throughout the room. Everyone was here. If we were going to break the news about LuAnn, this was as good a time as any to do it.

Standing, I brushed some wayward crumbs off my gray slacks and said, "I'd like to have your attention for a few minutes. The theater was inspected after yesterday's accident. According to the head of the competition, the theater has been cleared. Classes and rehearsals will go forward as scheduled. So, please make sure that you're ready to go when it's our time to take the stage. We only have today's rehearsal to make sure we are ready for the preliminary competition. After what happened yesterday, I've also decided to keep our costumes and instruments here at the hotel until tomorrow. If there are any costuming problems, we'll deal with it then."

A couple of the boys threw bits of bacon toward Killer. The dog barked his gratitude and sucked them off the floor as fast as they fell. If I didn't hurry things up, I was going to be seriously upstaged by a dog.

"Also," I said a little louder, "last night, there was an accident outside the theater. One of the parents with the team from Memphis was hit by a car. She didn't survive." Bacon stopped flying. The teens' expressions turned from amused to dismayed. Killer whined and played the starved, pathetic card, but he'd lost his audience. Even Millie ignored his pleas for more as I continued. "There are going to be a lot of kids who knew or worked with LuAnn Freeman. I ask that you all be extra sensitive as you attend master class and share the theater today."

Larry stood. "The buses will be ready in ten minutes. So eat fast."

No one seemed to be interested in finishing breakfast. Killer was able to beg several more pieces of bacon and sausage from the kids before it was time to leave. It was a good thing Killer didn't travel with this team often or he'd gain too much weight to compete at the dog shows he and Millie both loved. Although, judging from his happy dog yips, I doubted Killer would agree.

I walked back to my room to get my purse and my audition book, just in case I found time to squeeze some practice in for myself. With the Lyric Opera appointment forty-eight hours away, I needed to pick audition songs and give them a little polishing. No matter how many times I'd sung a piece, there was always something to be tweaked or acting choices to rethink.

After shoving my purse in my blue duffel bag, I swung the strap over my shoulder and checked the time. The bus would be leaving in four minutes.

I double-checked to make sure the door was latched, then turned and almost bumped into Devlyn.

"Hey." He shoved his hands in his back pockets. "I wanted to apologize. You had a rough night. I was surprised and overreacted. Which is pretty pathetic when you think about it. I mean, I should be able to deal with situations with more maturity than the students I teach. Don't you think?"

The apology combined with Devlyn's humor about his own shortcomings made me smile. "Maturity?" I teased. "I didn't know that your gender understood the definition of that word."

"Oh, we understand it." He smiled back. "We just have

trouble putting it into practice. Especially when we had a plan about how the night would go and it doesn't turn out the way we'd hoped." He looked to make sure the coast was clear and then reached for my hand. "I really am sorry. Did you get any sleep? You look tired."

I laughed. "Thanks. That's exactly what a girl wants to hear."

Devlyn grinned. "You're always beautiful, but I've looked into those blue eyes enough to know when they're tired. Are you sure you're okay?"

A door opened down the hall, and Devlyn stepped back. Sigh. "I'm fine. Honest. But Larry might change that if we don't make it to the bus on time."

"You're right," Devlyn said as an older couple walked past. "Let's go."

The atmosphere in the theater's lobby was subdued. Gone was the high energy of yesterday. Kids stood in groups. Some were talking in hushed tones. Others were crying. News of LuAnn Freeman's death had spread. Larry, Devlyn, and I herded our kids through the red-carpeted space toward the doors that led to our staging room.

"Ms. Marshall." Christine McCann waved and hurried over on tan heels that made her stand four inches taller than my five-foot-seven. "Do you have a minute? I'd like to have a word."

I had no idea what she wanted to talk about, but the steely look in her eyes said she wasn't about to take no for an answer. After sending Devlyn and Larry off to supervise the team and give them the room assignments for the master classes, I followed the head of the competition back through the lobby. She led me to the theater and asked me to take a seat.

After sliding into the one next to me, she turned toward me and said, "The competition is in trouble."

Whatever I expected her to say—that wasn't it. "Trouble? Did the police rule LuAnn's death a murder? Are the students in danger?"

The idea of my kids being at risk made my pulse spike.

"The last I heard, the police are still leaning toward accidental causes."

For some reason that didn't make me feel any better.

"The thing is . . ." Christine shifted in her chair. "I have some doubts about whether or not LuAnn's death was truly an accident. LuAnn was a forceful personality. She helped me keep this competition afloat when I first took the helm. But while her tactics were successful, they often rubbed people the wrong way."

"I got that impression."

"Yes." Christine looked toward the empty stage. The risers and piano must have been moved to the wings while the techs and police looked for the reason the lights fell. "I hope LuAnn's behavior yesterday won't deter you from helping me now. She took issue with the publicity angle I pitched to the press. She thought the attention you might receive could give your team an unfair advantage in the preliminary round."

I could see why that would set LuAnn and the leaders of the other teams on edge. After all, the story wouldn't exactly be a story if my team didn't make it past the first phase.

"It's due to what I learned while researching the publicity angle that we're having this conversation." Christine turned away from the stage and focused her attention on me. "Our biggest sponsors have learned about the damaged costumes, the lighting mishap, and LuAnn's death. Several are talking about pulling their sponsorship. They don't want to be associated with a program that is unsafe for the participants. Which is where you come in."

"Me? You want me to talk to the sponsors?" If I was the opera star I hoped one day to be, that might make some kind of sense. But something told me the moneymen wouldn't be impressed by a woman who currently taught kids how to do jazz squares.

"Of course not."

Oh good.

"I want you to track down the person who's behind the destroyed costumes and turn them in to the authorities. Once you do, the sponsors will have no concerns about safety, and the financial future of the competition will be saved."

Wait. I must have just hallucinated. Because Christine couldn't possibly have said what I'd thought I'd heard.

"I'm not a private investigator." Or an investigator of any kind. My foray into murder investigations was a fluke and, despite Devlyn's concern, not something I wanted to do again anytime soon. "If you want to find the person behind the damaged costumes and lights, you should hire a professional." Someone who had a clue what they were doing might be a good place to start.

Christine shook her head. "A stranger asking questions could cause a panic. You, however, belong here. And since everyone knows you helped the police catch Greg Lucas's murderer, they won't be surprised when you ask questions about the costumes or LuAnn's death now."

"But I have a master class to teach and students to supervise. I don't have time—"

"Donna Hilty was able to return sooner than expected. She'll be teaching the master class with Scott as was originally planned. Which gives you time to help me get to the bottom of this." Christine stood, smoothed down her gray skirt, and started up the aisle toward the exit. "The directors of the team LuAnn's daughter belongs to are in their staging room right now. I'd suggest you talk to them first."

"Wait." I jumped up and hurried after Christine. "I can't do this."

Christine stopped, turned, and gave me an unfriendly smile. "Unless you want the judges to send your team home after the first round, I strongly suggest you find a way that you can."

Chapter 10

What the hell had just happened?

I watched the theater doors close and shook my head. Had the head of the National Show Choir Championships just blackmailed me? I wanted to believe I'd misunderstood, but I was pretty sure I hadn't. If I didn't discover the person or persons behind the damaged costumes and instruments and turn them in to Christine or the authorities, my team was going to get cut in the first round.

Yep. This officially sucked.

And while I was pretty sure what she was doing was wrong, there was very little I could do about it. If I told anyone about this conversation, it would be Christine's word against mine. It didn't take a rocket scientist to figure out who people would believe.

Well, the joke was on Christine, because I had no idea how to go about finding the identity of the saboteur.

Despite what the papers had written about my involvement in the murders I'd had the misfortune to be involved with, I didn't have an innate skill for pointing to a killer. Hell, my lack of understanding as to who the killer was had actually gotten me a bullet in the arm. I had the scar and the wound to my ego to prove it.

The one difference between those cases and this one was that I had some idea of who the players were. None of the teachers or the students here was familiar to me. It would be almost impossible to pinpoint the perpetrator before tomorrow when my team took the stage for the preliminary round. Which meant my team was going to get eliminated through no fault of their own.

This wasn't fair.

In a small corner of my mind, I realized that though this scenario totally gypped my team, it could potentially solve one of my problems. If Music in Motion was eliminated in the first round, I could go back to Chicago for my audition without worrying that my departure would hurt my students' chances in the final round. Yet, while that was true, I wasn't willing to let my team take a hit just so I didn't have to feel bad for focusing on my career. They deserved the chance to perform and be judged based on the same criteria as everyone else. If after that they didn't make it to the final round, well, that was the way it was meant to be. Performing didn't always reward the ones you thought were the most talented or prepared. Personal taste and vision had a lot to do with who got cast and who didn't. As did who you knew and what you'd done in the past. Which was probably why LuAnn had felt threatened by Christine's push for publicity using my story.

I knew it was wrong to think ill of the dead, but when the woman was alive she'd been a menace. Between her reaction to the ripped costumes and her anger at me before the light beam fell, one would think those things had happened just so she could draw negative attention to me and my team.

That was crazy. Right?

Or maybe not. Eliminating the competition was a tried and true method of coming out on top. LuAnn's first reaction after finding the costumes was to call for my team's ejection. She'd reinforced that sentiment when she'd yelled at me in the theater. And LuAnn now might get what she had been campaigning for. Unless, of course, I found a way to track down enough evidence to convince the sponsors not to bail.

The idea that LuAnn might be behind those events at least gave me a place to start asking questions. Even though the thought of doing so made me a little queasy. I might not have liked LuAnn, but hadn't she already been through enough? She was dead. The only factor that made me feel better about attempting to prove LuAnn was behind the incidents was the possibility that her demise wasn't an accident. If that was the case, there was a murderer on the loose and the students, including LuAnn's daughter, could be in danger. Asking questions could be a good way to help them avoid potential danger.

Rationalization complete, I headed for the exit, looking for people who would talk to me about LuAnn Freeman. Christine had suggested I start with people from LuAnn's school. Logical, but not something with which I felt comfortable. At least, not now. Though they were the ones who knew LuAnn the best, they'd also be mourning her loss the hardest. I wasn't going to go to their staging room and ask them a bunch of questions. For now, I'd take another tack and hope it would give me the answers I needed.

I checked my watch. Twenty minutes until master classes were scheduled to begin. Teams were still arriving. The lobby and staging room hallways were filled with activity. Which was why I headed downstairs, hoping to chat up my former master class partner and longtime show choir coach, Scott Paris.

Taking a shot that Scott liked to be prompt to his teaching engagements, I headed to the greenroom. The sounds of "Don't Stop Believing" accompanied my descent down the stairs, telling me someone was early enough to be playing the piano. When I turned the corner, I was surprised to see a woman with bright red hair seated at the baby grand. Scott was nowhere in sight. Bummer.

I was about to head upstairs when the woman looked up from the piano keys. "You wouldn't be Paige Marshall, would you?"

I wouldn't? Smiling, I said, "As a matter of fact, I am."

The woman's expression went from happy to horrified in less than a second. "Oh, honey, I'm so sorry. Christine told me that she'd let you know I'd returned in time to run this class with Scott. She promised you'd be okay with changing back to the original schedule. Knowing you came to teach and found me here just breaks my heart."

Ah. This must be Donna Hilty—Nashville singing sensation turned show choir coach. "Christine and I talked a little while ago. I'm just glad that the emergency that would have prevented you from teaching wasn't as bad as you anticipated. The kids will be thrilled to have the opportunity to work with you."

"So, you're really not upset?" Donna stepped around the piano. For the first time I had a clear view of her outfit. Between the ruffled white skirt and the fringe-lined baby blue shirt, Donna Hilty looked like a country-style china doll.

"I'm really not," I assured her. Since Donna could be a good source of information, I added, "In a way, I'm relieved. After what happened last night, the kids need to be around people who knew LuAnn. I just met her yesterday. And being the one that found her after she was hit by that car—"

"Oh my gosh, honey." Donna walked over, put her hand on my arm, and gave it a squeeze. "You found her? I can't imagine what that was like. I would have taken one look at LuAnn and fainted dead away."

Something told me Donna was made of sterner stuff. Especially when you considered that I no longer had any circulation in the arm that she was holding. Yeouch. Donna might look small, but she had one hell of a grip.

I tugged on my arm. Donna held fast as she lamented the death of one of show choir's biggest supporters. "I honestly don't know what we'll do without her enthusiasm. Bless her heart."

Donna started to sniffle. Tears leaked from her eyes and streamed down her face, sending a trail of mascara down with it.

Okay, maybe it was insensitive of me, but the emotional outburst was a relief. The tears gave me the excuse to yank my arm away so I could grab a Kleenex out of my purse. Any longer and my arm would have gone numb.

Donna took the tissue with a nod of thanks and dabbed at her eyes. The more she wiped, the more tears appeared. And the sound of feet on the stairs and chatter coming down the hall told me that kids were on their way.

This was bad. The worst thing a teacher could do was demonstrate lack of control. It was a lot like working with dogs. You had to show you were the alpha in order to earn respect and get them to pay attention. At the first sign of weakness, all bets were off. Clearly, I hadn't learned this lesson before dealing with Killer. This was why I lost my bacon. The last thing I wanted was for Donna to lose hers.

Handing her another tissue, I whispered, "I think some of the kids are early for class. If you want a minute to go to the bathroom or get a drink, I'm happy to supervise until you return."

Donna snuffled, eked out a thank-you in between sobs, and raced into one of the dressing rooms to the right. Just in time. The door closed behind Donna, and several girls walked in. I told them to take a seat and watched as more kids filtered in. Chessie, Breanna, and Megan arrived along with several of the Music in Motion boys. When they spotted me, they walked over to say hello. I let them know about the change in instructors and asked Megan how her throat was feeling. The way her cheeks flushed when she answered told me she wasn't as fabulous as she claimed. I warned against singing or speaking during the class and then sent the group to find their seats. Meanwhile, I watched the dressing room door for signs that Donna had recovered from her crying jag.

"I didn't expect to see you down here." Scott's warm

baritone voice rose over the teenage chatter. I turned to find him standing behind me, wearing a shiny silver dress shirt and a wide smile. "Did Donna get called away? It wouldn't be the first time her manager pulled her from a commitment. Teaching is important, but she has a bigger career to think about. You understand all about that, right?"

"Donna's here," I said, pointing toward the bathroom. "She just needed a minute to pull herself together. She's taking LuAnn's death pretty hard."

"I doubt it." Scott stepped closer and lowered his voice. "Donna didn't much like LuAnn."

"LuAnn and Donna didn't get along?"

"Not in this lifetime." Scott chuckled. "Just last month they ran into each other at the Louisville Invitational. The show onstage was nothing compared to the one the two of them put on in the back. I was working with my team in our staging room so I didn't see it. But the way Donna tells it, she went toe-to-toe with LuAnn about having her removed from her position with this competition, and LuAnn tossed out the cliché that it would only happen over her dead body."

The door to the dressing room opened, and Donna walked out looking as if she'd never shed a tear. When she spotted Scott, she waved. Scott gave her a warm smile and whispered to me, "Seems like Donna got her wish. I guess I shouldn't be surprised. When it comes to winning, Donna always does."

Chapter 11

The master class started. I watched from the doorway as Donna welcomed the students and gave them a pep talk. Once she was done talking, she gave a nod to the piano player, who promptly launched into the intro of "Someone to Watch Over Me."

Donna's voice had a country twang and a rich timbre that gave her rendition of the song a different quality than I was used to hearing. Her voice was unique. Not only that, she had flair. I could see why her singing career had taken off and had to wonder what she was doing here in this greenroom instead of touring the country. Did she like teaching that much? Scott seemed to imply that her main focus was her personal performing, but I wasn't sure how much stock to put in his testimony.

The students applauded. A bunch in the back stomped their feet and screamed more loudly than the rest. It was easy to see that Donna's students not only won competitions under her direction; they loved her.

When the first student got up to sing, I headed for the stairs. Listening to high school kids sing from *Wicked* and *Hairspray* wasn't going to help me figure out who was behind the costume-shredding. However, learning more about Donna and LuAnn's relationship might.

Donna hadn't been here yesterday. Aside from Music in Motion, hers was the only other team not affected by the sabotage. If Donna and LuAnn's animosity was as well-known as Scott suggested, it was possible one of Donna's team had decided to take matters into their own hands. If that was the case, the student or students were smart. Had they targeted only LuAnn's team, someone might have guessed the reason why. But by targeting so many groups, they'd concealed any additional motive. Of course, I could be completely wrong, but a girl had to start somewhere.

Heading up the stairs, I sent a text to Larry asking him to meet me in the lobby. Our team hadn't been at the Louisville Invitational, but Larry loved gossip. If people were buzzing about LuAnn and Donna's fight, Larry would know.

The lobby was filled with high school students. Crap. I'd forgotten a master class was also assigned to run in here today. Acting Musical Theater Scenes was currently in progress. Several kids glanced in my direction and began whispering among themselves. The instructor up front gave them a stern look, but the kids didn't seem to notice. Or if they did, they didn't care.

Not wanting to disrupt the class any more than I already

had, I walked over to the far side of the lobby to wait for Larry. I was thankful when he arrived a few minutes later, looking out of breath and a little wild around the eyes.

"Is everything okay? Did s-s-someone else get hurt? Why aren't you teaching?"

Oops. I'd assumed Christine McCann had told the other teachers about the master class instructor change. I'd assumed wrong. "Everything is fine. Donna Hilty got back earlier than expected and was able to teach the class as originally scheduled."

"That's not fair." Several kids glanced in our direction at the sound of Larry's distressed and fairly loud protest. "Our students were looking forward to watching you work with other singers. The least Christine could have done was allow you to teach the class alongside Donna and Scott. Now people are going to assume you were too freaked-out by your discovery of LuAnn Freeman to handle your teaching duties. What will the judges think if they hear that kind of speculation?"

That I was human? Call me crazy, but finding a dead body would make any sane person flip. Someone who didn't get upset in that situation would be far more concerning. Larry was too overwrought to appreciate the distinction.

"I wouldn't worry about the judges," I said. "They'll have more important things to deal with." Like evaluating the performers instead of the teachers. I hoped. "Besides, if people talk about anyone falling apart, it will be Donna. I talked to her before the master class. She had to go to the bathroom in order to pull herself together. LuAnn's death hit her really hard."

Larry cocked his head to the side. "Are you sure you're talking about Donna Hilty?"

"Blond hair. White high-heeled cowboy boots. Lots of fringe?"

"That's her." He frowned. "But I'm having a hard time believing she was upset about LuAnn. I've never seen any of their fights personally, but they're legendary."

I shrugged. "Maybe the two of them decided to bury the hatchet."

Larry shook his head. "Unless Donna had a personality transplant, the only place she'd bury the hatchet was in LuAnn's back. Donna thought LuAnn's interaction with the sponsors for this competition caused her team to be held to a different standard than others. A couple of weeks ago, Donna filed a formal complaint when Central Memphis High School was invited to attend this competition. I think I mentioned that to you a while back."

He had talked about being copied in on a complaint about one of the participating teams. Apparently the heads of all the programs also invited had received the e-mail directed to Christine McCann. Knowing how cutthroat the theater and show choir world could be, I hadn't paid attention to the parties involved or the claims being made. Getting my own team ready had taken priority then. But I was interested now.

"Why did Donna file the protest?"

"Central Memphis only took two first-place trophies this year. And those were in the first two competitions they attended. Since then, they haven't placed higher than third." Larry shrugged. "Donna felt they didn't measure up to the rest of the field and that other teams more deserving were overlooked. All because of LuAnn's influence over the sponsors."

"I'm guessing that didn't go over well."

Larry laughed. "Scott Paris threatened to pull his team out of the competition. He was working hard to convince other directors to do the same, when suddenly he changed his mind and Donna withdrew her complaint. Christine must have found a way to smooth things over with both of them, but I haven't heard how she managed it. Whatever she said must have been really persuasive, because Donna was threatening to go to the media with her concerns and Scott was right there with her."

Huh. "Are Scott and Donna friends?" Because their actions, while separate, sounded coordinated. And the way Scott had talked about Donna this morning made me think they knew each other from more than bumping into each other at competitions.

Larry shrugged. "It's hard to tell. Donna likes to flirt, so there have been whispers about her and just about every male director she's ever talked to. Why do you ask?"

"Just curious," I said, hoping Larry couldn't hear the lie in my voice. The last thing I wanted was for him to learn about Christine's threat. Larry had finally stopped stuttering. I didn't want to make him start up again. "It sounds like a lot of the opposing directors weren't wild about LuAnn."

"Not just the opposing ones." Larry nodded toward the two instructors demonstrating how to make an arc cross. One of the teachers was the diminutive, dark-haired woman I'd seen when LuAnn was yelling at me from the stage.

"LuAnn didn't get along with the directors from her school?"

"Not from what I've heard."

"Then why would they allow her to be so involved with the team?" It wasn't like she was on staff or being paid by the school district to work with the kids. Parent volunteers were essential in any program, but it was easy for well-meaning parents to cross the line, turning their assistance into interference. Stage moms and dads were common in this business. We had a number of them who would be arriving to watch the preliminary competition tomorrow. Which would add a whole new layer of drama to this event. But Larry and Devlyn excelled at setting boundaries for our parents, even the ones on the school board who held positions of power.

"Got me. All I know is that she's been wreaking havoc on the show choir scene for years and that I've counted myself fortunate that our schools don't normally compete against each other. Oh." Larry snapped his fingers. "Did Devlyn talk to you about the staging idea he had last night? He thought it might be a good idea in the second number to move the couples on the left and right downstage for the first lift. It's a more complicated move than the other teams are doing, so he thought we should give the judges a better view."

It was a good idea. Especially considering Christine's threat. If I didn't finger the crazy costume-cutter, my team was going to need every extra point they could get.

"Devlyn and I will redo the spacing on that number when we get onstage. Do you know where he's at now?" I wanted to enlist his help with Christine's task. Maybe if he turned on the charm, he could convince Christine to back off and let my team be judged on their merits instead of my unskilled detective work.

"I think he was going to do a walk of the stage to look at spacing options. He might still be there."

Well, there was only one way to find out.

Leaving Larry to watch the scene from *Chicago* currently being acted out by two master class students, I headed in search of Devlyn. I found him in the stage-right wings, looking up into the rafters.

"Is something wrong?" I asked, stepping onto the stage.

Devlyn glanced at me and then back up into the space above the stage. "I just talked to the lighting designer for the competition."

"And?"

He frowned. "I was assured that yesterday's mishap wouldn't happen again and that a member of the theater staff will be standing in the fly rail whenever the building is open to make sure of that."

I squinted into the dimly lit wings for the ropes and pulleys that raise and lower set and light battens from the rafters down toward the stage. I spotted the locking rails and arbors for the fly system against the far wall stage right. "The lights that fell were attached to the fly system?"

"That's what it sounded like."

I walked past the curtains into the wing space for a closer look. Leaning against the back wall near the fly rail was a gray-haired guy in jeans and a T-shirt. His eyes narrowed. He pulled a cell phone out of his pocket and watched as I took another step closer. This must be the staff in charge of watching to make sure the fly system was secure.

Changing directions, I walked up to the man and smiled. "I just wanted to say thank you for guarding the fly rail and keeping my students safe. Knowing that someone accidently unlocked one of the operating lines and caused a batten to fall to the stage yesterday is kind of scary." I held out my hand. "I'm Paige Marshall, the head coach for Prospect Glen's Music in Motion team."

The wariness faded from the security guy's eyes as he took my hand and shook it. "Thomas Pluck. I'm sure whoever freed the operating lines didn't understand the implications of what they were doing. Teenagers can be too curious for their own good and forget their actions have consequences. I should know. I raised three of my own. Don't worry." He grinned, which gave me a great view of whatever bits of Tom's breakfast were still clinging to his teeth. Ick. "We're going to make sure that no one without authorization will come near the fly rail for the next couple days."

"You have no idea how much better I feel knowing that. Thanks again," I lied. With one last look at the fly rail, I headed back toward Devlyn, feeling far worse than when I'd walked over. Was I grateful someone was guarding the rail so no other lights fell? You betcha. But hearing that it wasn't a broken cable but operator error that caused the batten to fall made me queasy.

I supposed it was possible one of the high school kids was messing around backstage and somehow accidentally released the batten, but I doubted it. Most of the kids at this competition were upper classmen. They'd spent a great deal of time in theaters. Most if not all would understand at least in theory how a fly system worked. Would they risk all the work they'd done to get to this competition by playing around with the rail? I guessed it was possible. Still . . .

"I know that expression." Devlyn crossed his arms over his chest.

"What expression?"

"You think the falling lights are related to LuAnn Freeman's death."

"No." Maybe. After all, the Central Memphis team had just left this stage when the lights fell. Devlyn and I weren't here when it happened, but now I wished I had been to see where LuAnn was standing when the lights plummeted to the ground. Was she safely in the wings or had she been crossing the stage? Was the dropping of the batten an accident or had the person manipulating the operating line been aiming for a specific target? No one but the person responsible could answer the last question, but I was pretty sure I could find someone who could tell me where LuAnn was when the light bar fell.

I noticed Devlyn still watching me. "You don't believe me?"

"I know you." He took a step closer. "Something is going on in that beautiful head of yours. Are you going to tell me what it is?"

"As a matter of fact, I am." Or at least part of it. Taking Devlyn's hand, I led him onto the stage so Tom the tech security guard couldn't hear our conversation. After glancing around to make sure no one else was in sight, I shared my conversation with Christine.

"She said what?"

"Shhh." I looked into the wings where Tom was busy picking at his teeth. Too bad he didn't have dental floss. He could use it.

Thank goodness Tom didn't notice or wasn't interested in Devlyn's outburst. Christine hadn't told me to keep her request to myself, but I didn't want word to spread about what I was doing. "Look, I don't like it any more than you do, but the only way I can guarantee our team gets a fair shake from the judges is to help Christine and the competition keep their sponsors from dropping out. Unless, of course, she can be convinced to back off."

"Christine McCann is known for doing whatever it takes to get her way. It's one of the reasons she not only got this job but kept it."

"Then I have to find a way to solve her problem, or someone has to talk her out of this." I smiled. "Maybe someone like a handsome theater teacher I know."

"Are you asking me to flirt with Christine?"

I had been going to say yes, but there was a note of hurt in Devlyn's voice that made me instead say, "No." Upsetting Devlyn wasn't on my agenda, but if he volunteered, I wouldn't turn down the offer.

Sadly, he didn't. Bummer.

"The thing is," I said, "Christine seems to think my involvement in the two murder cases means I'm qualified to get the information she needs. It might help if someone reminds her that my lack of investigative skills almost got me killed." Near-death experiences weren't good résumé builders.

"I don't know if anything I say will help." Devlyn shoved his hands in his pockets and rocked back on his heels. "But I'll give it a shot. In the meantime, what are you going to do about Christine's demands?"

"What I have to do. If I don't at least make an effort to do what she wants, the team will suffer. They've worked too hard not to be judged on the merits of their work." I waited for Devlyn to protest. When he didn't, I let out a sigh of relief and explained, "So far, I've learned that LuAnn had a serious run-in with Donna Hilty at a recent competition and that she didn't even get along with her daughter's instructors."

"Wait." Devlyn held up a hand. "Are you investigating the damaged costumes or LuAnn's murder?"

I wasn't entirely sure. "LuAnn was the one who discovered the sabotaged costumes, and Donna Hilty's team was one of the few who didn't have any damage done to their possessions. I'm not sure if either detail is going to lead me to the person who's behind it, but I have to start somewhere."

"Well, if you're asking questions about LuAnn, you might want to talk to some of the people who work on this competition. I was walking by the registration office after the kids headed to their master classes, and I overheard one of the staff say that karma had a way of kicking people in the ass and that LuAnn had earned exactly what she got."

While I appreciated the sentiment, karma wasn't the one behind the wheel. But after all that I'd learned about my fellow coaches, I couldn't help wondering whether one of them was. And since investigating the shredded costumes for Christine McCann seemed to be yielding more information on motives for murder than sabotage, there was a good chance I'd stumble over the answer to that question whether or not I wanted to. If that was the case, I just hoped I didn't end up on the wrong side of a gun this time. In the movies, dodging bullets looked thrilling. In real life, it sucked.

Changing the subject, I asked Devlyn to explain the new layout for the lift that Larry had mentioned to me.

Devlyn walked downstage to show the change of position. I nodded and tried to pay attention to his reasoning, but in my head I was making a list.

Donna Hilty.

Scott Paris.

The competition's organizational team.

And Central Memphis High School's head show choir director.

All of them might have reason to want LuAnn dead. So far, the police weren't ruling the death of LuAnn Freeman a murder, but if they did, those four would top my suspect list.

Four potential killers. All of whom I had to question if I wanted my team to have a chance to win. And as I heard the shouts and laughter of students telling me the first group of master classes had let out, I realized there was no time like the present to start.

Chapter 12

The hallways were filled with excited teenagers as Devlyn and I navigated our way to our staging room. Larry and our students were supposed to be waiting to receive any additional news or instructions before lunch. I started to follow Devlyn through the door to our room but then noticed the director for Central Memphis High School walk by. Since she was headed toward the lobby instead of down the hall to her school's assigned room, I decided to follow. This might be the only time I'd catch her away from her team.

"Excuse me," I said, hurrying across the expansive red carpet.

A couple of kids ran past, but I dodged them without losing my balance. At the start of the school year, I would have ended up on my backside. If nothing else, this job had given me new skills. "Excuse me," I called louder, wishing Larry had remembered the director's name.

When the dark-haired woman stopped in her tracks and turned, I waved and picked up the pace.

"I was hoping to catch you alone to offer my condolences," I said as I hurried over. "I'm Paige Marshall."

She crossed her arms over her chest and tapped her foot. "I know who you are."

From her tone and body language, I guessed she wasn't interested in being best friends. She and LuAnn had that in common. Now I just had to find out what else they might have shared. "I wanted to tell you how sorry I am about LuAnn and to find out if your kids and, more important, LuAnn's daughter are doing okay."

The director cocked her head to the side and studied me. She must have decided I was sincere because the stiffness in her shoulders eased and she held out her hand. "Nikki Boys. I'm sorry I snapped at you. I'm a little on edge."

"I understand."

She gave me a sad smile. "I bet you do. I heard you found LuAnn. I can't imagine what that must have been like."

I was thankful Nikki didn't ask for details, because I didn't want to relive LuAnn's death. Letting out a sigh, she said, "The kids are upset. LuAnn started helping with this program long before I became the team's coach. She showed up to most of our rehearsals and made a point of getting to know each and every student personally. Some stayed at the hotel with LuAnn's daughter, Kristen. Her aunt wanted to come and drive Kristen home, but Kristen insisted on staying to compete. She said her mother would want it that way. She's right. LuAnn wouldn't have wanted her daughter to miss this competition. Although, I doubt she could have ever foreseen this happening." She laughed. "LuAnn thought she was unbeatable. I guess the driver of that car proved her wrong."

Yikes. The satisfaction in Nikki's tone was scary.

"I heard you and your aunt were in the theater parking lot when the accident happened and that you watched the car drive away." When I confirmed that, yes, Aunt Millie and I were almost sideswiped by the car in question, Nikki asked, "Did you happen to see the driver?" When I didn't answer immediately, she hurried to add, "I was just wondering because knowing why the accident happened and who was behind it would help Kristen and the rest of the kids. A sense of closure would aid the healing process."

Closure was a good thing. But the intent look in Nikki's eyes made me think she had another motive for asking. Too bad I hadn't a clue what that motive was. "The car was moving really fast," I said. "I only caught a momentary glimpse of the person behind the wheel, but I did get a good long look at the car."

Not good enough to identify the make and model or even the color, but Nikki didn't need to know that. Nikki spreading the word that I could identify the car used in the accident might panic the guilty party enough to make them turn themselves in to the police. Of course, they'd only do that *if* the hit-and-run really was an accident. If it was something more, maybe the killer would be made nervous enough by my potential eyewitness account to make a mistake that would give away his or her identity.

Nikki's eyes widened. "It's lucky you were around. If you hadn't been there, who knows how long it would have taken before LuAnn's body was discovered. I don't know how well Kristen would have dealt with the idea of her mother lying on the ground alone all night."

"I doubt that would have happened," I said. "Kristen or someone else from Central Memphis would have noticed LuAnn wasn't back. Right?"

"I'd like to think so." Nikki shifted her feet and sighed. "But none of us even knew that LuAnn was gone. LuAnn wasn't happy with the way yesterday went."

"I don't think the falling lights or the destroyed costumes made anyone very happy."

Nikki frowned. "LuAnn was more upset that Christine McCann ignored her demands to have you and your team disqualified. She left Christine dozens of messages after the lights fell insisting that you had something to do with the whole thing, even though we all know you weren't near the fly rail. Christine had to come to our hotel and talk to LuAnn in order to get her to stop calling."

Wait. "Christine saw LuAnn last night?" Christine mentioned talking to LuAnn after the police gave the all clear at the theater, but she didn't say that she went to LuAnn's hotel to deliver the news. Or that she made the trip because LuAnn was pushing her to oust me and Music in Motion.

"Yeah. When LuAnn snapped her fingers, Christine came running. Had Christine known that LuAnn's offers of assistance came with strings, she might have decided to seek help elsewhere. Nothing LuAnn did was out of the goodness of her heart. There was always a price to be paid. And more often than not it was a lot higher than anyone expected it to be. I think Christine finally figured that out."

"Why do you say that?" I asked.

"Because last night I heard Christine tell LuAnn that she was through living with LuAnn's threats. That she wouldn't give in to LuAnn's demands anymore. When LuAnn started screaming about going to the sponsors and the press and ruining Christine and the competition, Christine told LuAnn to do her worst because it would be the last thing she'd ever do." Nikki lowered her voice. "To tell you the truth, when I heard that LuAnn was dead, I assumed Christine was involved."

Wow. "You really think Christine McCann wanted LuAnn dead?"

She shrugged. "I know she wanted to remove LuAnn's involvement in this competition. I appreciated that sentiment since I felt the same about LuAnn's involvement in my program. Especially since LuAnn put in an application to be the assistant coach for our show choir. If she'd gotten the position, I would have had to turn in my resignation. As a volunteer, LuAnn was a pain in the ass. Worse, she thought she and her kids had more talent than they did and insisted I didn't know how to coach them to their fullest potential. She tried to have me fired at least three times that I know of. There was no way in hell I'd work with her in an official capacity." Nikki laughed. "And now it sounds as if I had a reason to kill her. Thank God this whole thing was an accident or most of the coaches in this building, myself included, would be at the police station instead of in the audience tomorrow. She had that kind of effect on people. Hell, even you had a reason to kill her."

"I'm not the killing kind," I said. Then I steered the conversation to the true puzzle I had to solve. "I'm also not the ripping-up-costumes or dropping-lights-from-the-rafters kind. Do you have any idea why LuAnn pointed the finger at me?"

Nikki waved at a blond-haired woman across the theater. "With LuAnn it's hard to say. I know she was threatened by you and your team. The videos we've seen are impressive. And Christine's press release for the competition mentioned you by name. When LuAnn found the damaged dresses, she probably thought making an accusation was her best chance of getting rid of your team and the threat they pose." The blond woman pointed at her watch and Nikki nodded. "I have to get going."

She started to walk away and I called, "Wait! This might sound strange, but after everything you've said about LuAnn I was wondering . . . Is it possible LuAnn was behind the ruined costumes and damaged instruments?"

Nikki stopped and turned. "With LuAnn, anything was possible."

With that pronouncement, Nikki strode away, leaving me thinking about what I'd learned. As one of the volunteers for the competition, LuAnn could enter any of the staging rooms without raising suspicion. By pointing the finger at me, LuAnn might have been trying to deflect attention away from the real reason she was in Scott's staging room.

My gut told me I was on to something. Now I just had to find people who saw LuAnn going into other rooms yesterday morning. While that wouldn't be definitive proof of wrongdoing, this wasn't a court of law and I wasn't a police detective. I just needed to show Christine there was a strong chance LuAnn was behind the sabotage. Christine could take it from there. My team would be able to compete free of Christine's threat and things could return to normal. Three guys walked by in bright blue tights and puffy white sequined shirts. Okay, maybe normal was pushing it, but at least things could go back to the way they were supposed to be.

With my plan in place, I headed back to Prospect Glen's staging room to remind my students we had two hours for lunch. Then we had rehearsal onstage. I was hopeful that, during those two hours, Devlyn would help me find enough evidence to show that LuAnn was to blame for the costumes.

Or maybe not.

"Christine isn't going to be happy if you find out LuAnn was behind the problems," Devlyn said after the students went in search of the nearby Subway for lunch. "Have you thought about what the sponsors will say when they hear that the person who convinced them to support this contest was working to sabotage it?"

No, but now that Devlyn had asked the question, I was concerned. The last thing Christine would want was for LuAnn to be behind the contest's troubles. Even if I could prove it, I doubted she would be grateful and Music in Motion could still suffer. Crap.

"Well, what do you suggest I do now?" I asked. "I can't accuse someone else just to make Christine happy." How icky would that be?

Devlyn shoved his hands in his pockets and frowned. "I guess the only way to really find out what happened is to keep asking questions. Maybe we should be asking how damaged the costumes were for LuAnn's team. With the number of people she upset and what happened to her last night, there's a good chance someone she ticked off was behind the whole thing."

If so, whoever was behind the ruined costumes was smart. Targeting so many teams made it almost impossible to tell which one was the true focus of the attack. Or if they were all targeted equally.

Since I'd already had a heart-to-heart with the head coach from LuAnn's high school, I asked Devlyn to take a whack at finding the extent of the costuming issues. "Maybe you can flash a couple of smiles and offer to help with repairs. Nikki didn't look like she was headed back to her staging room, but maybe someone else is there now."

"You want me to do this now?"

"There isn't a lot of time to waste. Tomorrow is the preliminaries."

"Okay," he sighed. "But as soon as I get back you owe me lunch. Deal?"

I smiled. "Deal."

With a wink, Devlyn disappeared out of the door and I sat down to try to decide what I should do next.

"Hey, Paige. Do you have a minute?"

Scott Paris stood in the doorway.

"Sure. How did the master class with Donna go?" I asked.

"Not bad. We weren't able to pull off some of the special surprises I was hoping for, but the kids seemed to enjoy the experience." Scott strolled into the room and closed the door.

With everything that had happened at this competition thus far, I'd rather have had the door open. But Scott clearly wanted privacy. I guessed I would just have to wait for him to tell me why.

"You have some very talented students. One of yours—I think her name was Chessie—has a real star quality."

"Chessie has a powerful instrument," I agreed. "We've been working to improve her technique so she has a better control of dynamics." Chessie often confused being loud with sounding good. Unfortunately, the louder she sang, the less pitch control she had. Off-key singing wasn't exactly the stuff successful careers were made out of.

"Well, I was impressed. I just wish we would have had time to have some of your other singers perform." Scott shrugged. "Donna was pretty intent on showcasing a lot of her own students, especially when a couple of the judges snuck into the back to watch. If you haven't figured it out, Donna's incredibly competitive."

"And yet she's friends with you." At least, that was the impression he'd given me when we first spoke about my stepping up to cover the master class.

The wide, bright white grin against the tanned face made him look a deranged game-show host. "Donna's one of my best friends in the business. I can't imagine what I'd do or how this competition would continue if anything like what happened to LuAnn Freeman happened to her."

If this was "Let's Make a Deal," I wasn't trading the money in my purse for whatever Scott was offering behind door number two. Otherwise, I was pretty sure I was going to get zonked.

"I thought LuAnn was the one who saved this competition from financial ruin. She's the one who lined up the sponsors. Right?"

"LuAnn made an incredible contribution by bringing together Christine and some of the state's best patrons of the arts." Scott's smile grew even wider, which I hadn't thought possible. Now he resembled the clown doll my grandmother gave me when I was six. The thing scared the hell out of me. I was forced to put it in a place of honor on my bed whenever my grandmother came to visit and had nightmares for days after she left. Until, of course, I realized that despite what the movies claimed, a doll couldn't come to life and attack me. Unfortunately, the same couldn't be said for Scott. The man was alive and taking a step in my direction.

"Donna and I have been worried about the threats LuAnn was making. This program means too much to both of us to see it go down because of LuAnn's demands, which is why we've lined up several new potential sponsors. They'll be at the final round of the competition on Friday evening. As long as the competing teams perform well, the program won't experience any ill effects from losing LuAnn or her influence."

Wow. That was cold.

Despite my shock at Scott's insensitivity, I couldn't help wondering why he was telling me this. We weren't friends, and I wasn't a long-standing member of the show choir community. So what was up?

"Have you told Christine about the new sponsor opportunities?" That would make more sense than sharing with me.

"Donna and I are going to tell Christine this afternoon. I trust you'll keep it confidential until then. I wouldn't want anyone thinking we're doing this to give our teams an unfair boost. That kind of talk could hurt both our students' feelings and their performance scores. You can understand not wanting to have your students penalized for something that's out of their control, can't you?" Before I could answer, Scott headed for the door. Hand on the knob, he looked over his shoulder and added, "And I'm sure your students will appreciate having your full time and attention on them instead of on other matters that have nothing to do with you."

As Scott disappeared out the door, I realized that not only did Scott know I was asking questions about the sabotaged costumes; he wanted me to stop. The question was—why?

Chapter 13

"That's great news," Devlyn said as we walked out of the theater to find lunch. "If new sponsors are already lined up, Christine won't need you to act like Sherlock Holmes and our team will get a fair shake from the judges. End of story."

"Maybe. Unfortunately, there's no guarantee those sponsors will sign on. Especially not if whoever was behind yesterday's incidents strikes again."

"There haven't been any other problems today," Devlyn argued.

No. But the day was only half over.

"Besides." Devlyn gave me a smile. "If whoever was behind the sabotage wanted to ruin Central Memphis's chances in the competition, they've already gotten their wish. According to their assistant director, most of their costumes are beyond repair. The school was going to next-day ship a bunch of their other costumes, but so far they haven't arrived. They're hoping they'll be here by tomorrow."

And what then? Would the new costumes get targeted or would the person responsible for the chaos be content now that LuAnn was dead? And what about the other teams who'd had their belongings ruined? Were they making sure someone was watching their staging room at all times? Or would Christine frown on those kinds of security precautions since they could attract the notice of both the old and potentially new sponsors and raise questions she might not want to answer?

More than that, I couldn't help but still wonder whether these issues and LuAnn's death were connected. If so, someone capable of killing was on the loose and my students could be in danger.

I stopped walking and looked across the parking lot at the performing arts center.

"What's wrong?" Devlyn asked.

I thought about confessing my worries, but remembered our fight last night and instead said, "I forgot that I told Millie to meet me here with the new hats we bought for the band. I want to use them during rehearsal today. Would you mind bringing me a sandwich when you come back from lunch? If I ask Millie, she'll bring an entire buffet."

While most of what I'd said was pure fabrication, the part about Millie and the food was the truth. The last time I'd asked her to drop off a sandwich was when I was helping out with musical rehearsals. She brought not only the requisite bread and lunch meat but also three kids of pasta salad, two liters of water (sparkling and flat), a spring mix salad with several selections of nonfat dressing, and a chocolate torte, all packed in an enormous white wicker picnic basket. What Millie lacked in culinary skills she more than made up for with style and a caterer on speed dial.

"I could stay—"

"No," I said, hoping I sounded casual instead of desperate to get Devlyn off the premises. Smiling, I added, "At least one of us should get out of this building and recharge for a while. If the rehearsals run over, we'll be here for a whole lot longer than we originally planned."

Devlyn sighed. "Okay. I'll be back in an hour with extra salt for your French fries. If you need anything before then, call."

He glanced around and then leaned toward me. I waited for his lips to brush mine. Instead they touched my cheek. Then Devlyn turned and headed toward the street.

For a minute, I watched him go. The light breeze blew his hair, which had gotten longer than he normally wore it. He'd been too busy to get it cut. Personally, I liked it better this way. It looked freer, sexier, and slightly more rugged than his usual style. That was probably why he'd already made an appointment to have it trimmed. He had to keep up appearances.

Not for the first time, Devlyn's need to pretend to be what he wasn't chafed. As much as I understood why he'd created the pretense when he'd started at Prospect Glen, he had tenure now. More than that, he had a reputation as a talented, engaged, and dedicated teacher never accused of even a whisper of impropriety. With the right explanation—heck, probably with no explanation at all—the two of us could date in public. Especially since I had no plans of teaching at Prospect Glen next year. According to Larry, the school board was known to frown on teachers getting involved with each other. However, even with that known, two Prospect Glen teachers had gotten married last year. So even with Devlyn not knowing about my Lyric audition and my plans to leave teaching behind, there shouldn't be a problem. So why was there? He'd given me his explanation, but the longer I was a part of his teaching world, the less it made sense.

Since standing here wasn't going to give me any insight into that problem, I walked back across the asphalt determined to find answers to the other questions I had. After a quick call to Aunt Millie to request she bring the hats for the band—because while that excuse to Devlyn was polite fiction, it was also a good idea—I opened the door of the performing arts center and strolled back inside.

Devoid of teenagers hopped up on sugar and caffeine, the lobby was eerily quiet. Huh. Now that I was here with no one around to see what I was up to, I had no idea what I should be doing. Yes, I wanted to talk to Christine, but I wasn't sure where to find her. On top of that, with almost everyone gone, this seemed like a good opportunity to snoop around for other information.

But what?

Devlyn had confirmed that the majority of costumes for Central Memphis High School's team were damaged beyond repair. But how about the others? Remembering the fabric strewn around the staging room for Scott's team, I veered toward the stage-right hallway. It was empty, but I could hear the murmur of voices from an open door nearest the backstage entrance.

I looked at the names of the schools on the closed staging room doors as I walked down the corridor with my shoulders straight and my head held high. The best way to look as if you weren't doing something covert was to look as if you belonged where you were. At least, that was what my acting coaches always told me. Since the technique had worked well in the past, I decided to use it again to check out Scott's staging room. Scott and I had been together when LuAnn screamed her discovery of the ruined costumes. Because of that, I assumed he wasn't involved. But that wasn't necessarily true. He and I had run into each other as I was leaving the greenroom master class. He had just come downstairs. Where he had been and what he'd been doing just before that was anyone's guess.

Someone laughed in the staging room next to Scott's. To keep up impressions, I knocked. No one answered. Scott and his team weren't inside. Or if they were, they weren't answering.

I knocked one more time, wrapped my fingers around the handle, and turned the knob. Eureka. The door was open.

Poking my head in, I called, "Scott?" as if I was fully expecting him to be here. When he didn't answer, I opened the door the rest of the way and took a step inside.

As expected, no one was there. On one side of the room were two long racks filled with sparkly costumes. On the other were tables with mirrors surrounded by lights. Along the back wall, instruments were neatly stacked. Cleary, the band members in Scott's group were better at playing Jenga with the black cases than mine were.

"Huh," I said aloud, hoping to add authenticity to the

moment. "I wonder if there's anything to write with around here."

I glanced over my shoulder at the open doorway behind me. No one was there, but whoever had been laughing and talking until moments ago was quiet. My little monologue had probably bought me a few minutes before they came to see what I was up to. Time to get moving.

Since the costumes were in plain view and the main thing I was curious about, I made a beeline for the racks. The red and gold satins and silver and blue lamé dresses were hung with care. I examined three of each. If I looked closely, I could see where the seam on one of the skirts had been repaired. But other than that, the dresses looked great.

I glanced at the doorway behind me to make sure no one was coming and hurried to the back rack where the pink tulle skirts were hung. Of all the pieces I saw on the floor yesterday, the tulle ones were shredded the worst.

Or maybe I'd hallucinated that. Because the ones I was currently looking at were in perfect condition. No tears. No rips. No shredded anything. Which shouldn't have been possible. The only way these costumes could look this pristine was if they had never been damaged in the first place.

The sound of footsteps had me turning toward the door. Plastering a smile on my face, I called, "Scott?" When no one answered, I stepped out into the hallway and almost ran smack into a woman with deep brown skin and an unhappy expression.

"This isn't your staging room," the woman said.

Putting on the wide-eyed ingénue expression I'd had

to use in dozens of shows, I said, "I was looking for Scott. He and I . . ." I looked down at the floor as if embarrassed. "Well, he asked me to come by to talk to him."

In the nine months I'd been a part of the competitive show choir world, most of the teachers I'd met had been hardworking and good role models for their students. But here and there a few of the male teachers I'd encountered made it clear they would be interested in sharing choreography ideas in a private setting. From the overly flattering language he used when we first met, I thought Scott might be one of them. If I was right, I was banking on his reputation to help me get out of here.

After several long moments, the woman's frown curved into a knowing smile. "Don't feel bad, honey. Scott's not known for being the most reliable man around. He probably got caught up with another . . . meeting."

The innuendo in her voice and the knowing gleam in her eyes made my cheeks burn. Wanting this woman to believe I was a Scott groupie and being made to feel like one were two totally different things. Note to self—next time come up with a better cover story. Either that or get better at hiding the blush I could feel heating my face.

Giving the woman a weak smile, I said, "Would you do me a favor and not mention that I was here? I mean . . . or if you do . . ."

"Don't worry, honey." She patted me on the arm and then walked to the door of the staging room and peered in. When she saw everything was as it should be, she closed the door and nodded. "I won't tell anyone, but if you don't want your heart broken, steer clear of Scott and his flattery. Word on the street is that he's taken. Only he doesn't always remember that."

Huh. Back in the lobby, I thought about what I'd just learned. Unless Scott and his team had created and brought with them an entire duplicate set of costumes for the team, it was impossible to think they'd be ready to go today. The idea that they'd whipped up a second group of identical outfits "just in case" seemed far-fetched at best. Finding the perfectly repaired costumes was the most damning evidence I'd found thus far and strongly suggested Scott's involvement in the costume caper. Unless, of course, something like yesterday's sabotage had happened in the past. Then he'd have a reason to bring a set of duplicate costumes. If that were the case, I'd be back to square one. I guessed I'd better find out.

Since I wasn't sure how many of the coaches had a long history of attending this competition, I decided to go to the source I knew would have the answer—Christine McCann. Of course, to talk to her, I'd first have to find her. A task that was easier said than done.

None of the three older ladies in the registration room had seen her recently. Drat. Worse, none of them seemed to know when she'd be back because she wasn't answering her cell phone. Double drat.

I was about to leave when I saw a familiar dark-haired woman in the corner lift her hand. The large, very sparkly rings she wore caught the light and made me stop in my tracks.

"Can I help you with something else?" she asked when she caught me staring.

I smiled and held out my hand. "I just realized how rude I've been. We've never officially met. My name is Paige Marshall. I'm the coach for the Prospect Glen Music in Motion choir."

Since I'd given the woman no choice, she put her hand in mine, which gave me a closer look at the rings on her hand.

"Kelly Jensen. I'm the school liaison and assistant director for this competition."

I remembered getting e-mails from a Kelly Jensen. Most of them involved local hotel information, rehearsal schedules, or lists of restaurants within walking distance of the performing arts center. Others contained releases that had to be signed in order for the competition to be filmed and the media to take photographs. The messages were fun and chatty and made me conjure up images of a blond, fresh-faced college girl with wide-eyed enthusiasm and a cheerful smile.

Boy, was I wrong. The black dye job and shocking blue eye shadow made it hard to gauge the woman's age, but I was guessing it was somewhere around sixty. Of course, I could be mistaken. The neon orange flowers decorating the maxi-dress she wore made it hard to concentrate.

"Thanks for all your work. Christine and the rest of the organization are lucky to have you on their team," I said, trying not to look obvious as I studied the jewelry on her manicured, pink-polished left hand. Except for her thumb, every finger was decorated. The largest ring was on the middle finger—edged with shiny clear gems was an enormous blue stone. I'd seen only the bedazzled hand of the mysterious eavesdropper outside my team's staging room for a few seconds, but I was pretty sure that this was the same jewelry.

After Kelly finished giving me a song and dance about how pleased she was to serve such a worthwhile organization and help today's students prepare for tomorrow, I said,

"I really liked your outfit yesterday." I gave her what I hoped was my most vapid smile. "I have a thing for pink. You *were* wearing pink, right?" At least, that was the color of clothing I saw when I tried to learn the identity of the mysterious lurker.

"Why, yes." She let out a laugh that sounded more confused than lighthearted. "Pink is very popular at this competition."

So the signage indicated.

But while show choir kids and staff alike gravitated to shades on the fuchsia side of the color wheel, not everyone had glitters like the ones Kelly was sporting. I'd bet the money in my checking account (not a lot, but all I had) that Kelly had been hovering outside our team's staging room doorway yesterday, listening to what we were saying.

While that was suspicious, it was the vanishing act she'd performed immediately afterward that really raised my interest. What had Kelly hoped to achieve by eavesdropping? It wasn't like she was coaching a team and was going to steal choreography secrets. Hell, even if she was coaching, she wasn't going to learn anything she couldn't find on YouTube. Our competition numbers had been videoed and posted online at least a dozen or more times that I was aware of. So what would Kelly have to gain by the intrigue? And since Kelly was an employee of the competition, was Christine aware of the extracurricular activities? While I was thinking about it, I couldn't help wondering whether Kelly was aware of Christine's less than professional blackmail behavior.

"Do you know if LuAnn's death is going to affect the sponsors?" I asked. "I overheard her telling someone that she was close personal friends with the people who helped finance this competition. She was worried they were going to bail and the competition would come to an end."

Kelly's eyes flared, and her cheeks flushed with anger. "This competition will live on long beyond LuAnn Freeman. My husband and I were on the board that founded this organization. As terrible as the tragedy of her death is, I can honestly say that alive or dead, it would take a whole lot more than a woman like LuAnn Freeman to bring it down."

Yikes.

My phone buzzed before I could come up with any other questions to ask. Aunt Millie had texted. She was in the lobby with a load of sparkly hats, ready for me to show her where they belonged. Fun times.

Unfortunately, Millie wasn't the only one waiting. The minute I stepped through the double doors onto the lobby's plush red carpet, my hair stood on end at the sound of a low, angry growl.

Killer.

"There you are, Paige." Millie waved and hurried over as fast as her four-inch strappy sandal heels would allow. Decked out in a rhinestone collar and sparkly leash, Killer trotted along beside her with his mouth open and his tail wagging. Some people would probably say that he looked adorable. I thought he looked scary. Especially when he plopped his pompon butt down on the carpet and let out a loud bark.

"Hush, Killer. That's not how you behave in a theater." Millie tugged at the leash. Killer went mute. It was an amazing trick that never worked for anyone but my aunt. With a grin, she said, "He's just excited. I'm pretty sure he thinks he's here for a dog show."

I was pretty sure he thought he was looking at dinner. But hey, I could be wrong.

"Thanks for bringing these." I took the three bags from my aunt. Killer stood and grumbled. Millie tugged on the leash a little harder than she had before. Killer whined and sat back down. Score one for theater etiquette. Now, if only there were a way to silence cell phones during a performance in the same manner.

Millie turned that steely glance at me. "So why did you really ask me to come down here?"

"I told you—"

"The hats. And rehearsing with them is a great idea, but something else is bothering you. Is it the woman we found last night?" Millie gave my arm a squeeze. "Thinking about her has given me several bad minutes. Have the police found the person who was driving the car?"

"Not that I know of." No doubt I would have heard. "And I'm fine, Aunt Millie." Or I would be if Christine called off her threat to have my team blackballed in the opening round.

"Well . . ." My aunt sighed. "I guess if anyone would be able to handle finding a dead body, it would be you."

The sad thing was that Millie was right. What did it say about my life that I had practice finding corpses?

Millie's eyes narrowed behind her pink frames. "So, if it isn't the dead body that's causing those frown lines, what is? And don't think you can fool me with one of those stories you used to spin when you were a little girl. I can tell when you aren't telling the truth."

Sadly, this was mostly true. Though I'd taken lots of acting classes, using my skills on Millie always felt . . . well . . . icky. I was better at withholding the truth from her than creating an entirely new version of it. Unfortunately, the look Millie was giving me now was the one she used in business when her more affluent clients claimed they couldn't afford to place a new order unless they got a discount. The last time I saw Millie use that expression, the client not only paid full price but ordered twice the amount she'd intended.

Which was why I found myself pulling Millie over to the side of the lobby and quietly explaining my predicament and Christine's use of blackmail to enlist my help. When I finished, I braced myself for Millie's reaction. The last time someone had threatened me, my aunt was ready to call everyone from the principal of Prospect Glen to the chief of police in order to fix the problem. (How the chief of police was going to convince the school board not to fire me from my show choir job was still a mystery to me.)

Millie's jaw clenched. Her eyes narrowed. I waited for the explosion. Instead, she let out a sigh and said, "Well, I don't like her tactics, but I can't blame the woman for enlisting your help in this mess."

I blinked. "You're not upset?" I felt like I'd stepped into the *Twilight Zone*. Millie's impassioned defense of me was something I'd not only expected but had come to rely on.

"The aunt in me is furious, but the businesswoman understands." Killer inched toward me. Millie barely glanced his way as she yanked the leash. "When someone's threatening your business, the head of that business is required to use the resources available to her to fix the problem. If she had more time, I'm sure she'd have come up with a different solution. But the competition starts tomorrow. She needs someone who is here and has the skills to help. That's you."

Skills? What skills? I had a master's degree in opera performance. That wasn't exactly the stuff private investigators were made of.

"So, what's your plan and how can I help?" Millie asked.

Plan? There was no plan.

"I need to ask Christine whether the contest has a history of sabotage in the past. If not, then I have a suspect." Scott was involved in something. The question was what. "The person I think is involved told me he and another coach are orchestrating a meeting between Christine and some new sponsors. If that happens, Christine won't need me to investigate."

"But that doesn't mean you'll stop." Millie plopped a hand on her hip. "If you don't know who the perpetrator is, how can you make sure they won't strike again? Your team could be next."

The same thought had crossed my mind, which was why I'd considered asking Aldo and Killer to hang around the staging room once our costumes were loaded in. I'd have asked Millie, but she actually knew how to control Killer's impulse to behave like his name. With Aldo in charge, Killer would be free to do his worst. Typically that behavior was reserved for me, but I was happy to share the fun with whoever was behind the costume catastrophes.

Unfortunately, Millie wasn't done raining on my parade. Giving me a sad shake of the head, she said, "Christine won't be willing to risk losing her current sponsors no matter what promises those directors make about new ones. Negotiating deals with sponsors takes time. Discussions over the terms could take weeks if not months."

I had twenty-four hours.

Well, crap.

"So much for that idea." I sighed and looked down at Killer. His puffy tail wagged with delight at my plight. Watching me suffer was almost as good as gnawing on me. "I just don't want my team to pay the price if I can't figure this out in time."

"Well, maybe that's where I can help." Millie smiled. "Why don't you let me talk to the head of the program? I know people who are looking for ways to support the arts and education. I can't promise that they'll be willing to write checks, but I can guarantee they won't consider sponsoring the competition if your team isn't treated fairly."

I shook my head. "She might think that you're bribing her to give my team an extra advantage in the competition."

Getting a low score we didn't earn would suck, but so would being awarded an inflated one. I understood that in show business, who a person knew was often more important than talent. Hell, despite my desire to get by without using personal connections or networking, my role in *The Messiah* was in part due to Aunt Millie. Had I known that when I accepted the role, I might have done something stupid—like turning it down just to prove a point. I'm glad I hadn't been given the chance to make that mistake. But while many of these kids would figure out the benefits of networking along the way, right now I wanted them to learn about the payoff hard work and execution received.

Millie frowned. "I'd never use blackmail to cheat high school kids."

"I didn't think you would." Blackmail was too obvious for my aunt. Despite the color of her car and her shoes, Millie knew how to be sneaky.

"Good. Because all I intend to do is make sure that Christine knows other options are open to her in case you can't find the person responsible before the preliminaries start."

If that was all Millie was going to do, I had no reason to object. "The teams are at lunch now. Christine should be around when rehearsals begin. I'll introduce you to her then."

"It'll be best if Killer and I introduce ourselves. That way she understands you have nothing to do with the discussion. It will be just between us two business-women."

Fair enough.

Millie gave a satisfied nod. "If the conversation goes as I believe it will, you won't have to feel guilty when you need to step away from the investigation to focus on your team or go to your audition on Friday morning."

My stomach lurched. "How do you know about the audition?" I'd wanted to mention it to Millie last night, but after discovering LuAnn's body, discussion of audition logistics seemed frivolous.

"When your phone was going to voice mail, your manager called the house number. He wanted to make sure I told you to call him immediately, since he was worried you wouldn't be able to juggle your schedule and make this opportunity." She gave me a stern look. "I assured him you'd be there even if I had to drive you to the stage door myself."

Auditionees didn't go through the stage door. They

went through the front just like anyone else who hadn't been hired to perform in the show. Still, I appreciated Millie's point if not the slick coat of guilt I felt at the thought of my students' reactions when they realized I had to leave Nashville.

"You do plan on going to the audition, right?" Millie let the leash go slack, and Killer took it as a sign he was allowed to get up.

I took a step back, just in case. "My flight is tomorrow night after the preliminaries."

"Good." She smiled. "After *The Messiah* I knew it was only a matter of time before you got your next big shot. Alan sounded very positive about this audition. You should be, too. Have you decided what you're going to sing?"

"I haven't had a lot of time to think about it."

"The director will love you no matter what you sing."

Maybe. Maybe not. "I just feel guilty leaving. The kids have worked really hard to get here."

"You've worked hard, too. You deserve your chance. I'm sure Devlyn said the same thing when you told him."

"Told me what?"

My heart sank as Devlyn strolled up next to me with a McDonald's bag in one hand and a large Diet Coke in the other. I sent Millie a look warning her that I hadn't shared my news with Devlyn, but she either misread the expression or didn't care because she said, "We're talking about the audition Paige has on Friday with the Lyric Opera in Chicago."

Devlyn went still. "You're leaving in the middle of the competition to go to an audition?"

The disappointment in his eyes made my palms sweat.

"I'll be here for the preliminary round and then fly back in time—"

The McDonald's bag dropped to the ground. Killer lunged for it as Devlyn walked away without a backward glance. Millie let out an exasperated sigh. Killer chowed on the still-wrapped cheeseburger. I watched Devlyn go, wondering whether his departure meant I'd just lost a whole lot more than my lunch.

Chapter 14

"Chessie, make sure you set yourself directly in front of the second set of risers." I nodded as she shifted her position. "Does that look good to you, Devlyn?"

I looked out into the audience and cupped a hand over my eyes in an attempt to locate his position in the back of the theater.

"It looks good from here, Paige," Larry yelled. "If you're happy with it, we should start running the program. We only have thirty minutes to work out any problems before tomorrow's preliminary competition."

"Let's run it," I yelled back, pushing my annoyance at being ignored by Devlyn into the background. If he wanted to be unprofessional, so be it. I, for one, was going to do my job. "Places, everyone. Megan . . ."

She turned and looked at me. I could tell she was still struggling vocally, but I could also see how badly she wanted to do this rehearsal. If I pulled her in favor of her sister, I had a feeling she would fall apart. Not something I wanted for her in this last rehearsal of her senior year.

"You can dance the numbers, but I don't want you to sing," I said. Megan's mouth spread into a delighted smile as she nodded and took her position. "Claire?"

"I'm back here."

Claire stood up from her seat in the middle of the house. "Could you stand in the wings and sing Megan's part? It'll help me determine if we have the right balance between the choir and the band."

Claire hurried down the aisle and climbed the stairs to the stage. By the time she was standing next to one of the curtain legs, the choir was in their opening poses, ready to go. I hopped down from the stage and stood in the front row as Jim raised his baton. The band lifted their instruments. Their hats sparkled in the stage lights. Jim counted off the tempo and motioned for the music to start.

The opening notes filled the theater. The kids began to twirl. I watched as they sang, shimmied, and strutted through the first song. Then the second. Finally, they performed the lifts of the last number and hit their final poses. Breathing hard, they waited for the band to cut off before dropping their positions and looking to me for what I thought.

Not perfect, but not bad. Exactly what a dress rehearsal should be. Performing in front of an audience always provided an adrenaline burst that gave the choir more energy and spark. If they sang this well tomorrow, there was no doubt in my mind that Music in Motion would make the finals on Friday. Unless, of course, Christine told the judges to score us down. I could only hope that either Millie worked her magic or I managed to single out the costume culprit before then.

"Everything looks good." I checked the clock on my cell phone. We still had fifteen minutes of rehearsal time. Good. We needed another run. This time with Megan's understudy. "We're going to go through the program one more time. Megan, could you take a seat? I want Claire to run it just in case."

Megan's shoulders slumped as she walked to the escape stairs. Claire took her sister's place on the stage next to Megan's partner. Her face was a mask of determination when I yelled for Jim to cue the band.

As always, Claire performed her dance steps flawlessly. In that area, she was more gifted than her sister. No matter how many dance classes Megan took, she still wasn't confident in that area of performance. I hoped Megan would find the confidence she needed when she went away to college. The one thing she didn't need help with, however, was letting her personality shine through when she was onstage. Megan's smile and bubbly nature were huge assets for our team. Her sister—well, I'd been working on Claire's facial expressions. The good news was she no longer looked as if she wanted to kill her dance partner. The bad news was that smile I'd finally convinced her to wear looked slightly unhinged. With luck, Megan would be able to go on tomorrow. If not, I only hoped some of the judges found the deranged look appealing.

When the music ended, I climbed back onto the stage. Larry and Megan followed. I waited a minute to see whether Devlyn would join us. When I didn't see him walking down the theater aisles toward the front of the house, I turned back to the kids. Out of the corner of my eye, I saw a shadow shift in the wings stage right. Had Devlyn gone backstage? Nope. Devlyn was in the middle of the house, standing with his arms crossed. Huh.

I stopped closer to the stage-right wing and squinted into the dimness beyond the curtain legs. There. Someone was back there, watching us from backstage. The fly rail was on the other side along with the security guard, so I knew it wasn't him moving from behind the leg to the exit.

Drat. He was gone. Oh well.

Turning, I said, "Our program is in great shape." Relieved smiles spread across the team's faces as they gave one another high fives and whispered excited comments.

Holding up my hand for silence, I continued. "But, we have some little things I'd like to iron out tonight after dinner. Claire—I'd like you and your partner to run the transition into the second lift a few times. It looks a little awkward. Also, Chessie, on the third song you and Eric looked like you had some trouble making it to the other side of the stage in time to start the second verse. What happened?"

As the band began putting away their instruments, Chessie and Eric talked about the traffic pattern problem they had.

"Okay," I said, "we'll take a look at that back at the hotel. The bus will be leaving in thirty minutes from the front of the theater." From what I'd heard, the police had given the okay for people to use the loading docks, but the one on our side of the theater had yet to be repaired. At least that was the excuse I was using for having the kids load and unload the buses up front. Truth was, I didn't want them wandering around the area where LuAnn Freeman had been killed. And face it, I wasn't all that interested in seeing where I'd tried and failed to save her again anytime soon.

The clang of the theater doors opening announced the next team's arrival. I saw Donna Hilty in her white cowboy boots sauntering down the aisle toward us and told my team that it was time to vacate the stage. It was Donna's team's turn. And I was curious to see how they'd perform.

"I'd like everyone to help the band carry their instruments and store them in my room. You'll then have time to rest—and when I say rest I mean it—before dinner. Once dinner is over, we'll run things one last time."

Under Jim's direction, the kids worked fast to get the instrument cases off the stage and move them to the front of the lobby. Larry promised to keep an eye on both the instruments and the students as they waited for the bus to arrive, which left me free to duck back into the theater and watch from the back as Donna's team took the stage.

They had rearranged the risers so that their band was situated on stage right. The instrumentalists were talented. The singers even more so. The dancing . . . Well, unless the choreography got more complicated in the next two songs, I wasn't worried about them outscoring us.

From my spot in the back, I watched as Donna called a halt to the performance, fixed a spacing issue, and told the kids to reset and do it again. They ran the number a second time. Another stop and fix. Then a third. Donna sounded more disinterested with every correction, and each time through, I noticed the kids making more mistakes than the last. The students' smiles were tense as they went through it a fourth time. I glanced at my watch. Only ten more minutes until the next team arrived. They'd have to run the three required songs straight through if Donna planned on giving her kids the chance to rehearse all the numbers onstage.

"Let's stop here."

So much for getting the opportunity to dance and sing through all the numbers. Shoulders tensed and hands clenched as Donna picked apart the routine, shifted positions, and made the kids run the number again. They barely had a chance to execute the first sixteen bars (which now looked stiff and riddled with missteps) before Donna yelled hold and started reworking the staging again.

My heart went out to the teens. I desperately wanted to ask Donna what she thought she was accomplishing with this rehearsal. If this practice had been held a week ago, I might understand picking the steps apart until it was perfect. But the competition was tomorrow. I hadn't been doing this job long, but my years of performing had taught me that changing too many things could confuse the singers onstage.

As a professional, I was used to a show changing and evolving through previews and even through the early weeks of performance. But once the steps were set, the only changes made were to polish numbers that had gotten a little sloppy or rework something to accommodate a new actor taking over a role. Students at this level didn't have the experience to deal with these kinds of changes mere hours before one of the biggest performances of their lives. More important, all of these changes and criticism were taking a very large chomp out of the students' confidence. One of the most important ingredients in a great performance was confidence. A performer who felt secure in the material and his or her execution of it had more fun. If the singers onstage had fun, the audience did, too. When performers looked tense or uncertain, the audience felt it. Donna should know that.

Two girls bumped into each other. An exasperated Donna called a halt again, making one thing very clear— this team was in serious trouble.

"Scoping out the competition?"

The sound of the baritone voice made me jump. I turned to see Scott Paris standing five feet away. So intent had I been on what was happening onstage, I'd missed hearing him come in. But I was glad he had.

"Actually," I said, turning away from the stage where the students were finally taking positions for the second number, "I was looking for you."

"Me?" Scott laughed. "My team doesn't rehearse for another hour. You should have checked the schedule."

"I did." At least, I had earlier. Since Scott was one of the few teachers I'd met, I'd noticed that his team was scheduled several slots after mine. "But I figured since you came to watch our rehearsal, you were probably doing the same for everyone."

Scott's smile disappeared. "You're mistaken. I wasn't in the theater for your rehearsal."

"Not in the house. I saw you backstage." Before Scott could lie again, I added, "I guessed that you didn't want me to think you were spying on my team, which is why you left while I was giving notes instead of waiting until the rehearsal was finished. Unless, of course, there was another reason you were hanging around in the shadows."

Scott stiffened. The theater door that led to the aisle

behind him clanged open. A new group raced in as Scott said, "You can't possibly be implying what I think you are. I always knew Christine's judgment was flawed. First she teamed up with LuAnn. Now you. Christine might have wanted to cut the strings that LuAnn had attached, but at least she was able to deliver on her promise. You're not the private investigator the press releases Christine sent to the media make you out to be. If you were, you'd know I'm not the one behind the lights falling or the destroyed costumes. I mean, why would I destroy my own team's chances of winning this contest?"

"You wouldn't."

Scott ran a hand through his hair and let out a sigh. "Well, at least you understand that I'm not insane enough to spend my time slicing and dicing fabric."

"Oh, I think that's exactly how you spent your time yesterday morning." I smiled as the new team reconfigured the risers. "It's the only way to explain how your costumes were ripped on the seam and easily repaired while everyone else's were a total loss. You were smart to include your own team's attire in the attack, but not smart enough."

Okay, maybe goading Scott and tipping my hand wasn't the best option, but I'd had it up to my eyeballs with men today. I couldn't help myself. Satisfied my words had hit their mark, I turned to leave.

Ouch. Ouch. Ouch. A hand grabbed my arm and yanked me backward. I stumbled and tried to pull away, but Scott had a viselike grip and wasn't letting go. His face was red, and the vein in his neck looked ready to pop. Fear streaked through me even as the voices coming from the stage told me I had nothing to worry about. Scott might be angry, but he wouldn't do anything in front of two dozen or more witnesses. Right?

Scott's fingers dug deep into my forearm. "I don't know what you're playing at, but if you repeat these unfounded suspicions to Christine, you'll be sorry. I suggest you worry about your own team and I'll worry about mine. Otherwise, I might have to start paying more attention to your team. And I'm pretty sure you won't like what happens then."

With one last glare, he let go of my arm and stalked down the row to the aisle. As I watched him go, I couldn't help wondering at the expression I saw as he stormed toward the exit door. I expected anger. Instead, there was fear.

Chapter 15

What did Scott have to be scared of?

I rubbed my aching arm as the theater door clanged shut behind him. Though the perfectly repaired costumes looked suspicious, they wouldn't be enough to prove Scott was behind it all. If I talked about my suspicions to Christine, the most that would happen was his team pulling a low score from the judges Christine had influence with. That might not make Scott happy, but the threat of losing the competition wouldn't have caused the terror I saw on his face.

So what did?

"You're wasting your time."

I jumped, spun around, and saw Donna Hilty seated in the audience ten seats down from me. If one more person snuck up on me without my hearing them, I was going to go to a doctor and have my hearing checked. Either that or I'd deck them. My nerves couldn't take much more of this.

"What do you mean?" I asked.

"You batting your eyelashes at Scott." Her lips curled into a less than happy smile. "Scott prefers a lady who allows him to pursue. Women who throw themselves at him are a turnoff. Especially when the woman in question has an agenda that has nothing to do with his body and everything to do with winning a competition."

"Excuse me?"

Music filled the theater as the next choir began their run-through.

Donna uncrossed her legs, got up from her velvet blue seat, and sauntered down the row. "You obviously know about Scott's connection to the judges. LuAnn tried the same thing you're doing, you know. Trust me, honey. It didn't work for her, and I can promise that it certainly won't work for someone like you."

"You've got this all wrong . . ." I started to say, but Donna wasn't interested in listening.

"No. You're the one who has this wrong. If you're smart, you'll keep your distance from Scott. Unless, of course, you want to end up just like LuAnn."

Donna gave me a satisfied smile and then strolled away, accompanied by an enthusiastic arrangement of "Don't Worry, Be Happy." Standing in the theater, surrounded by the sights and sounds that were so familiar, I was struck by my outsider status. I knew theater and music, but I didn't understand these people, their relationships, or their motivations. And I needed to if I was going to keep my kids from getting hit by unfair scores or from being affected by whoever was behind the incidents that had happened yesterday. It was time to get more information on the key players. And when my cell vibrated and I read the text from Larry telling me the buses were out front, I knew who my first source of information would be.

"Are Scott and Donna Hilty together?" I asked Larry as we stood on the sidewalk, watching the kids climb onto the bus. Devlyn was already on board.

"Together?" Larry blinked. "As in dating?"

Or sleeping together. The two didn't always have to go together.

"Have you heard whether or not they're together?" I asked. "Donna said something earlier that made me wonder if they were."

Larry stepped a couple of feet away from the buses and waited for me to follow. Quietly, he said, "A couple of the directors I spoke to this morning said that Donna and Scott have been spending a lot of time together. But that doesn't really mean anything. I saw them having lunch today, and I didn't see sparks flying. People just like to gossip. I mean, look at you and Devlyn. You're together all the time, and it's not like you're dating or anything."

So much for counting on Larry's powers of spark observation.

"Donna also said Scott had some kind of connection to the judges. Do you know what she was talking about?" I asked as the last of our team climbed up the bus's steps.

Larry frowned. "The judges aren't supposed to have a personal connection to any of the schools or the personnel. That's part of the rules and regulations."

That Larry believed rules were in place to be followed instead of broken made me want to give him a big hug. Unfortunately, I knew that reality didn't wear his rose-colored glasses and that life often didn't play fair.

"Are you coming?" Larry asked as he started to climb onto the bus.

I looked up and saw Devlyn watching me from the second passenger window. Our eyes met for a brief second before he turned away. Tears stung the backs of my eyes, and I took a deep breath. As much as I wanted Devlyn to support me, I knew that there was nothing I could do to change how he felt. That was up to him. For now, the only thing I could do was help myself and my team.

"If you're okay handling the kids on your own for a while, I'd like to hang around here a little longer," I called. "I'll catch a lift with Aunt Millie or call a cab to get me back in time for our run-through. Okay?"

"Sure thing." Larry gave me a thumbs-up as the door to the bus closed behind him. I stepped back from the curb and watched the bus pull away, all the while watching Devlyn's window. I was sure he would turn to look at me. He never did.

With a sigh, I watched the bus disappear down the street. Then I headed back into the theater in search of Christine McCann. It didn't take long to realize I wasn't the only one looking for her. Several coaches in need of extra rehearsal time, the theater manager, and Kelly the sparkly school liaison were all in search of the head of the competition. They hadn't found her and were now meeting in the lobby, trying to decide whether they should be angry or concerned. After LuAnn's death last night, concerned seemed to be winning out.

Bedazzled Kelly walked to the other side of the lobby, pulled out her cell phone, and dialed. After several moments, she shoved the phone back into her purse.

Walking over, I asked, "Christine isn't answering her phone?"

"No." Kelly frowned. "And no one's seen or heard from her since she left for her eleven thirty lunch meeting. It's not like Christine to be out of touch. Especially not on competition week. She insists all of us be reachable by phone no matter what the hour. Last night she called me at two in the morning to talk about our problems with the sponsors and how the police—" She shook her head and straightened her shoulders. "This just isn't like Christine."

"Who was her lunch meeting with?" I asked. "Maybe they'll know where she was going next or if she got called away."

"Don't you think we've thought of that?" Kelly snapped. "If we knew who Christine was meeting with, we would have contacted them. But we don't. So all we can do is wait around and hope she turns up or starts answering her phone. Now, if you'll excuse me, I'm going to check in with some of her family and see if they've heard from her."

Kelly pulled out her phone and stalked away. Meanwhile, I walked toward the other directors to see whether they had any information. Donna and Scott weren't among those gathered here. According to one director, the two of them had cleared out as soon as Donna's group had loaded their instruments into their room. Scott's team would be back in less than an hour for their allotted stage time. Until then, it was anyone's guess where they were or what they were up to.

Huh.

Since no one in the lobby had any information, I did

a lap of the theater building in search of someone who did. But other than the team rehearsing onstage and the teens killing time in their staging rooms, waiting for their turn, no one was around for me to ask questions.

Since I'd hit a dead end, I placed a call to my aunt and asked her to pick me up near the back of the theater. Sliding my phone in my pocket, I headed toward the loading docks.

A workman was tinkering with the stage-left door. Glancing at me, he said, "If you're looking for the boxes that were here, I moved them." He pointed to five small cardboard boxes that were stacked against the wall to the right of the large door.

"No. I was just seeing if the door was fixed. Thanks." With a wave, I walked around to stage right, and exited on that side.

The loading docks and back parking lot looked different in the bright afternoon sunshine. Or maybe it was just that I was standing here when there wasn't a body lying on the ground with the life draining out of it. That kind of thing tended to freak me out.

The cops had done a great job of cleaning up the backstage area. Not a single cigarette butt or empty gum wrapper remained on the ground. But despite their attention to detail, there were reminders of what had occurred here less than twenty-four hours ago. A piece of yellow police tape fluttering from the edge of one of the Dumpsters and the dark stain of dried blood on the cement pavement clearly marked the place where LuAnn had died.

As I looked at the stain, the emotions from last night came storming back. The desperation. The desire to keep LuAnn alive no matter what. And the sense of failure and sorrow that threatened to overwhelm me when I realized she was gone. Nothing I had learned about LuAnn since her death made me like her any better than I had when she was alive, but that didn't stop me from wanting justice for her. A driver who didn't expect someone to be standing back here had hit her and then panicked and driven away.

At least, that was the last verdict I'd heard from the police. Maybe things had changed. There was one way to find out.

Pulling out my cell and the card that Officer Durbin had given me last night, I dialed the officer's direct line.

Voice mail. Drat.

I considered leaving a message, but hung up after the beep. Giving me an update on LuAnn's death probably wasn't going to be high on Officer Durbin's to-do list. I looked at the card again and then dialed the general precinct number.

A deep male voice on the other end asked me where I wanted my call directed. Hmmm . . . good question. "I was one of the witnesses for the case of the hit-and-run death of LuAnn Freeman. It happened last night. Do you know if the detective in charge of that case is around? I'm afraid I was too frazzled to remember the detective's name."

Technically, the detective had been too busy dealing with the first responders, getting photographs taken, and alerting the next of kin to talk to me. But I figured the guy answering the phone didn't need to know those details. After I'd been put on hold and subjected to country music Muzak for ten minutes, there was a click and a chipper female voice said, "This is Detective Martin.

Detective Christopher isn't in the precinct right now. I was told you were a witness on last night's hit-and-run. Have you remembered something new to add to the investigation?"

I wished I could say yes. Unfortunately, for me and LuAnn, nothing I'd learned today would lead the police to the driver of the car. But I hoped Detective Martin would be able to tell me whether the police truly believed LuAnn's death was caused by a terrible accident or whether they felt there was something more behind last night's hit-and-run.

With that in mind, I said, "My name's Paige Marshall. I was the one who called 911 and performed CPR on the victim until the paramedics arrived." The memory made my throat go tight and my eyes start to tear. "There's been a lot of talk today from people who knew her. Some are saying that LuAnn Freeman's death wasn't an accident. I know you can't give out the specifics of your investigation, but I was the one who saw the car speed off and I guess I'm feeling a little unsettled. I mean, if someone intentionally killed her and they know I saw them . . ."

I let my words trail off and cringed at how melodramatic I sounded. Improvisation wasn't always my strongest suit. I needed to brush up on my technique.

Lucky for me, Detective Martin wasn't a stage critic. "I'm not the lead detective, but I can assure you, Ms. Marshall, that you don't have to worry. The evidence thus far suggests that the incident last night was target-specific. Since you didn't see the person behind the wheel or—"

"Wait." My stomach lurched. Target-specific. For that to be the case, then . . . "LuAnn's death wasn't an accident."

"That hasn't been officially determined."

"But unofficially?"

"Look," Detective Martin sighed. "I can't tell you much more than I already have. For now the case is open and active. If you remember anything more about last night, please contact Detective Christopher or me. And rest assured that if we have any other questions or feel your safety might be compromised, we'll be in touch."

Too bad that assurance did nothing to make me feel better. The good news was the question I'd asked had now been answered. The police believed someone had intended to kill LuAnn Freeman. And that person was still out there. Would they come after me or attack someone else at the competition? I had no idea. But it was a risk I couldn't afford to take. Up until now, I'd only truly been worried about my students not getting a fair shake from the judges. Now Christine McCann was missing and there was a chance my students' lives were at risk. And there was only one thing I could think to do about it.

Millie arrived. Minutes later, I was strapped in and being glared at by an angry poodle because I'd gotten to ride shotgun. I didn't care. Threats from a pampered pet weren't on my current priority list.

Larry and Devlyn must have gotten the texts that I sent en route because they were waiting for me in the lobby when I stepped through the doors. Devlyn barely glanced at me as I crossed the tan tiled floor and announced, "We have to pull out of the competition. And we have to do it now."

Chapter 16

Larry and Devlyn looked at me as if I'd sprouted feathers and was clucking like a chicken.

"Are you kid-d-d-ding?" Larry choked out. "We have parents arriving tonight. We can't just leave. What would everyone think?"

"That we believe their children's safety is more important than winning a show choir competition." I looked from Larry to Devlyn. The anger I saw in his eyes took my breath away. Turning back to a sputtering Larry, I explained, "I just talked to a detective with the Nashville Police Department. She said LuAnn's death was no longer being ruled an accident. They think she was targeted."

Color drained from Larry's face. "B-b-but that doesn't m-m-mean she was attacked because of the comp-p-peti-tion. Maybe someone wanted her jewelry."

Mugging by vehicular homicide wasn't exactly the easiest way to score glitters. Although, LuAnn's missing purse made the theory sound less ridiculous than it otherwise might have. Still . . .

"Christine McCann is missing."

Larry's mouth dropped open, and the anger simmering in Devlyn's eyes faded.

Well, that had gotten their attention. Since I had it, I hurried to explain. "After you both got on the bus, I talked to the staff of the competition. No one can find Christine. She isn't answering her phone. No one wanted to say it, but I could tell they were worried something bad had happened."

"Maybe this is all a misunderstanding. I don't want to pull the kids out of the competition, not after all their hard work. But if there's a chance they're in danger . . ." Larry pulled his cell phone out of his pocket. "I'm going to call Christine. Maybe her staff forgot that she was getting a massage. It's been a stressful week."

And as far as I could tell, it wasn't going to get any less stressful. Larry walked around the lobby, searching for a signal, and I looked at Devlyn. He had his arms crossed. His normally sexy mouth was pursed in a tight line. I waited for him to say something. Anything.

Finally, I couldn't stand the tension and said, "I wanted to tell you about the audition. My manager called on Monday night. He set up the audition without my knowing it and—"

"She's fine," Larry yelled from the other side of the lobby. He hoisted the cell phone in the air as if it were a trophy and hurried across the tile toward us. "Christine had a meeting with the detective in charge of LuAnn's case and thought she'd turned her cell to silent, but turned it off instead. She apologizes for the concern she caused.

She also assured me that the she asked the detective whether there was any reason to be concerned about the safety of the students and adults involved in the contest. He said no."

No reason? I pictured the shattered lights on the floor of the stage. Was he kidding?

"Did Christine tell him about the fallen light bar and the destroyed costumes?" As far as I was concerned, those incidents combined with the hit-and-run were enough to merit nagging doubt if not full-out worry.

"I asked. She said the police are reviewing everything. So far, they haven't turned up any evidence that links the incidents. But Christine understands completely if we think the students are in danger and want to pull them from the show."

My stomach unclenched at Larry's words. "So now what?"

"Now I call Principal Logan and give him an update on what's going on here in Nashville. He'll be the one to decide whether we keep our students here or go home."

"What's your recommendation going to be?" I asked. Larry was invested in the students he taught. He was also the head of the music program and the top authority for our team here at this competition. Because of that, Principal Logan listened to and respected Larry's opinion.

"Well . . ." Larry suddenly developed an avid fascination with his scuffed loafers. "It's understandable that you'd be worried about what LuAnn's death could mean. Especially after what you've been through this past year."

I blinked. "What do you mean?"

"Well, you've seen a lot of death." Larry looked over at Devlyn. "And Devlyn pointed out earlier that after your two recent brushes with murder cases, it's only natural you'd jump to conclusions and see danger around every corner."

I went still. "You think I'm making this up?"

"No." Larry shook his head so hard, it looked as if it might fall off. "It's just that your perspective is different. You've been shot and had to protect our students from a murderer in the past. If I were you, I'd be freaking out, too."

Okay. Now I was starting to get angry.

Before I could defend myself to Larry, he said, "Let me call Principal Logan. If he thinks we need to leave, we'll leave. I'll let you know what he decides."

Phone pressed to his ear, Larry went in search of a cellular hot spot. I, however, didn't need to look for one. I was already feeling the heat, and the man next to me was the reason why.

"You told Larry that I'm crazy?"

Part of me thought Devlyn would feel upset or guilty at having the less than kind words he'd spoken come out into the open. Boy, was I wrong. "No, I told him you might have a skewed perspective. What I should have said is that you had a completely different agenda."

"What's that supposed to mean?"

Devlyn scoffed. "I'm talking about you looking for any reason to ditch the contest and go back to Chicago for your big audition. You've been searching for a way out of this job since the first day you took it. Now you have one and you're willing to sacrifice all the hard work these kids did in order to get what you want. Well, I hope that audition for the Lyric Opera on Friday is worth screwing over a bunch of performers who would do anything to make you proud. They won't forgive you for letting them down. And neither will I."

The words punched into my gut, taking my breath away. I'd seen Devlyn's disappointed anger directed at students during rehearsal. It never failed to motivate them to learn the lines or blocking they hadn't spent enough time working on. But this was different. Devlyn wasn't using his anger as a tool to get me to study a script. He was using it to wound. And, wow, he had hit his mark.

Yes, I had an audition to attend.

Yes, I'd bought a plane ticket that would get me back to Chicago.

But never once had I taken my audition into account when considering whether my students should stay at this contest. They'd worked too hard for that.

My hands shook as I pressed them to my stomach, trying to still the flutter of nerves and nausea. "I would never hurt these kids."

"What do you think leaving in the middle of this competition will do?" Devlyn yelled. Several of the hotel staff behind the counter glanced our way, but Devlyn didn't appear to notice. "You made them rely on you. You made them care. Now, just like that, you're planning to up and bail. Well, two can play that game."

Without another glance, Devlyn turned and stalked away. I started to follow but then stopped myself. Devlyn wasn't in the mood to talk rationally about this. And neither was I.

Tears burned behind my eyes. One streaked a path down my cheek. I brushed it away and looked over to where Larry was giving me a happy smile and a thumbs-up. He then hurried out of the lobby with a spring in his step.

Principal Logan must have said it was okay for the team to stay and compete.

Part of me was worried. The other part wondered whether Devlyn and Larry weren't on some level correct about my past experiences clouding my ability to see LuAnn's death clearly. If so, I was glad the team would be staying. Of course, they would still take the stage with the threat of being lowballed if I wasn't able to give Christine the name she was looking for. The only way I'd be able to fix that problem was if I put aside the hurt and disappointment swirling inside me and focused on finding the answer. Too bad that was easier said than done.

"Ms. Marshall?"

Chessie. Oh, great. This was the last thing I needed.

Taking a deep breath, I plastered a smile on my face and turned. "Is there something I can do for you, Chessie?"

Chessie was wearing an oversized Prospect Glen T-shirt and a pair of shorts. The wet condition of her hair told me where she had just come from. The pool. I waited for her to say that Megan's voice had gotten worse or to report some sort of injury that had occurred poolside.

"He was wrong."

Her words were so quiet, I wasn't sure I'd heard right. "Who was wrong?"

Chessie's face turned bright red. She shuffled her flip-flop-clad feet and looked around us at the empty lobby. "I didn't mean to overhear, but Mr. O'Shea was wrong to say what he did."

Oh, crap. Chessie knew about the audition. That meant soon the entire choir would know.

"I was coming to get change for the vending machine

and heard you, Mr. DeWeese, and Mr. O'Shea talking about the competition. So I stayed in the hallway over there and listened."

She pointed to a spot twenty feet away, and I sighed. From that location she would have heard every word. I was ready to tell her that she didn't have to worry, that the team would be competing tomorrow as planned, when she asked, "Do you really have an audition at the Lyric Opera?"

I waited to see the same anger Devlyn felt reflected in her eyes. But there was excitement. Choosing my words with care, I said, "My manager called Monday night to tell me he'd arranged an audition with the artistic director of the Lyric for Friday morning. I asked if we could reschedule, but the director is leaving town. I know the team will be disappointed if I'm not here, so—"

"Mr. O'Shea is wrong." Chessie frowned. "The team won't fall apart if you're not here, standing in the wings. We'll miss you, but we'll be fine. The only way we wouldn't be is if you missed this audition because of us."

For a minute I was speechless. It was hard to believe this was the same girl who tried to get me booted on my first week or tried to strong-arm me into giving her a second solo during the winter concert. "Are you sure?"

Chessie smiled. "My parents hate that I'm going to major in musical theater. Megan's and Jacob's parents feel the same way. They think we're setting ourselves up for a life of rejection and failure." She tossed her wet hair and shrugged. "Maybe we are. But we have to try. Right? And maybe if you end up with a really great role at the Lyric, our parents will stop freaking out and see that sometimes dreams really can come true."

Wow. My heart swelled with pride. Chessie had grown and changed a lot this year. It was amazing to see the difference and know that I might have had a small part in helping her mature.

"And if you end up as a big star, I'll be able to ask you to help me get an agent and land important auditions. It's all about who you know in this business, right?"

Okay, maybe Chessie hadn't changed as much as I was giving her credit for. In a way, I was glad. It was her fierce determination to do whatever it took to succeed that would help her in this business. Networking and taking advantage of connections had always been something I was bad at, much to my various managers' dismay. Having a personal connection to someone—the director, music director, choreographer, or other member of the production staff—was sometimes the only way to get your foot in the door. Granted, that only got you in the door. After that, how you performed was what got you cast.

"You're right." I smiled as part of the weight I'd felt since Devlyn had stormed off lifted. "A lot of this business is who and what you know. It's also about taking advantage of opportunities when they present themselves."

"Which is why you have to go to Chicago and take that audition."

I nodded. "But I plan on being here when you walk on the stage. I'm taking the last flight out tomorrow, and my plane back should land hours before the final round."

"Did you tell Mr. O'Shea that?"

"He didn't give me the chance."

"Boys." Chessie rolled her eyes. "Sometimes they just don't understand."

"What's Eric not understanding these days?" I asked. "I noticed that the two of you have been keeping your distance since yesterday afternoon." Not long after the discovery of the ruined costumes. I'd noticed the gleam in Chessie's eye yesterday while Larry and I were talking to the team about the incident. I'd even planned on speaking with her just in case she'd had something to do with the destroyed costumes. But between the falling lights and the hit-and-run, I'd forgotten about that moment. Until now.

"Oh, you know Eric." She shrugged.

I did. The all-American boy was completely devoted to Chessie. The only thing he was more devoted to was his passion for the law. Ever since he'd been questioned as a potential murder suspect, Eric had ditched his desire to go into music education and replaced it with a passion for righting wrongs. If Eric was upset with Chessie now, my guess was it had something to do with her doing something he felt was legally questionable. And I had a sinking suspicion I knew what that something was.

"Chessie, what do you know about the ruined costumes?"

"Nothing."

The flushed cheeks and clenched hands were a dead giveaway. The girl was lying.

"Chessie." I put my hands on my hips and gave her the Aunt Millie look I had practiced for months in my mirror.

"I don't know anything." Her eyes flashed with a combination of fear and defiance. "Honest."

I crossed my arms over my chest and waited for several beats, trying hard to mimic the way my aunt made her eyebrow twitch upward. I waited for Chessie to cave, but she just stood there, looking at me. My Millie look needed more practice.

"Chessie," I sighed. "Don't make me find Eric and ask him what he knows. It'd be better if I heard whatever this is directly from you."

Eric still believed he owed me for helping keep him out of jail. Between that and his respect for authority, Chessie's secret would be out in the open in no time.

Chessie must have come to the same conclusion because she dropped the defiant pose and said, "I didn't have anything to do with ripping up the costumes."

"But you saw who did."

She bit her lip and nodded.

"And Eric knows you saw them. Does he know who it is?"

Chessie shook her head. "Eric wanted me to tell him so he could report it to you or Mr. DeWeese."

"Which is why the two of you aren't speaking."

"Eric doesn't understand that a performer has to take advantage of every professional opportunity."

Okay, now I was confused. What kind of opportunity could witnessing a fabric-shredding session yield? Wait . . . The only way Chessie could turn witnessing the costume cutting into a professional opportunity was if the person doing the shredding was in some way connected to the performance world. And there was only one person at this competition I could think of who fit that description.

Nashville's own country music sensation—Donna Hilty.

Chapter 17

"You saw Donna Hilty defacing the other teams' property?"

Chessie let out a dramatic sigh. "Yes. I mean, I didn't realize it was her at first. I got bored at the dance master class and asked if I could go to the bathroom."

Oy. The bathroom break trick was the oldest excuse in the book. Hell, I'd used it more than once in my time to get out of class. The beauty of the excuse was that even if the teacher believed the student was faking the need to pee, the request couldn't be turned down. Not without a really good reason. What teacher wanted to be responsible for a bulging bladder? And even more problematic was that there was no way to set a time requirement on a bathroom break. Some things just couldn't be rushed.

"I take it you didn't go to the bathroom?"

"Well . . ." Chessie hesitated for a moment, clearly remembering the times she claimed she had to pee during

Music in Motion rehearsals. "Not exactly. I mean, I was going to use the bathroom in the hallway by our staging room. The ones in the lobby can get really crowded."

And hell was the perfect place to build a ski resort. However, as much as I wanted to call Chessie on her creative storytelling, there were bigger issues at work here.

When Chessie realized I wasn't going to question her miraculous control over her kidneys, she gave a bright smile. "Anyway, I went through the doors into the hallway and was going to stop in our staging room really quick when I heard a noise from the room next to ours."

"What kind of noise?"

"It sounded like fabric ripping, kind of like when I got my heel caught in my rehearsal skirt doing that backwards hitch kick during the run of the musical last week."

I remembered. The sound of Chessie's dress ripping echoed through the theater loud and clear. So did the sound of Chessie's backside hitting the wooden floor.

"Anyway, I decided to find out what made the sound. The door to the room next to ours was closed, but I could hear more ripping coming from there. I thought about opening the door, but I figured whoever was inside had the door closed for a reason. So I went back to our staging room and waited for them to come out. When I heard the door open, I waited a minute and then peeked around the corner and saw the back of a woman walking in the other direction. There was something familiar about her so I snapped a picture with my cell as she went into the room two doors down. That's when I decided to take a look in the room next to ours. I mean, it seemed pretty obvious that she was up to something. And that's when I found the ruined costumes. I took a picture of those, too. Just in case."

Just in case of what, I wasn't sure. What I was sure of was that Chessie's story had a lot of holes in it, which told me more had happened in that hallway than what she was saying. And the stubborn look in her eyes told me I wasn't going to find out what that something was. Chessie must have been up to something, but at the moment I was less concerned about whatever that was. I wanted to see the photographs.

"Do you have your cell phone with you?" Do pigs like mud?

Chessie pulled out her cell, pushed buttons on the screen, and handed the phone to me.

"The woman in this photo is a brunette." Which, other than her curvy backside, was the only thing I could tell about her.

"She was wearing a wig. I was able to get a profile shot of her coming out of the second room. It's a little crooked because I had to stick the phone out of the door and snap the shot without looking, but you can tell it's Donna Hilty. See."

She handed the phone back to me. The photo was off center and a little fuzzy, but the face in the middle of all that brown hair was unmistakable. As far as evidence goes, the photograph was circumstantial. There was no law against wearing a wig or going into rooms that belonged to other teams. The date stamp and time of the photo was more damning. Not only was it the same period in which the sabotage took place; it was also the day that Donna claimed to have been called out of town due to a family emergency.

"Why didn't you tell Mr. DeWeese or me about what you saw?"

Chessie flushed and my stomach sank.

"You told Donna that you saw her. That's why she picked you to sing at the master class this morning." I didn't need to see Chessie's nod to know that I had hit the mark. Scott mentioned Donna mostly selected her own students to perform. Scott had sounded surprised at Chessie's power and polish. At the time, I'd taken his astonishment as a slight against my teaching abilities. I should have realized he was saying something more, but I didn't know the guy well enough to understand the subtext. I did, however, know Chessie. She wasn't the type to let Donna off the hook with just a master class solo.

"What else did you get Donna to promise you?"

Chessie sighed. "She promised to land me an audition with her manager and to let me rehearse and maybe sing with her backup singers for one of her concerts this summer."

I shook my head. "The woman ruined the costumes for most of the teams competing against hers and you're taking her word that she'll keep her promise?"

"Of course not." Chessie straightened her shoulders. "I insisted she call her manager in front of me and arrange the audition. After she left, I looked up his website, called the number listed, and confirmed the audition. I meet with him in two weeks. I also had my mother call him and confirm so that we didn't make travel arrangements to New York City for nothing."

Chessie might be a lot of things, but stupid wasn't one of them. I found myself both horrified by her powers of manipulation and proud at the way she covered all her bases. Too bad I was going to throw a wrench into those plans.

"I'm going to need to borrow your phone."

"What?" Chessie clutched the yellow-cased phone to her chest. "No. You can't let anyone know that I told you about Donna and the costumes or she'll cancel my audition."

Chances were she'd cancel it anyway. Donna didn't strike me as the type who liked to share. Especially not with a girl half her age.

"I have to let Christine McCann know about the photos. It's the right thing to do." It was also the one thing that would guarantee our team would be scored fairly tomorrow. I held out my hand and waited.

Chessie's lip trembled as she put the cell in my hand.

"You never know," I said. "Donna's manager might still give you an audition. If not, that's okay. You have college to get through. I'm betting a lot of opportunities will present themselves then. And you'll be even better prepared to take advantage of them. Now, go tell Eric that you talked to me. He's going to be really proud of you."

Making your boyfriend happy wasn't exactly the same as getting an audition with a big-time manager, but hey—sometimes you had to take what you could get. Chessie gave the phone in my hand a wistful gaze before hurrying off to find Eric.

For a minute, I just watched her go. I couldn't help wondering whether if I'd had her desire to succeed at all cost, my career would have taken off years ago. If so, I would never have needed to move in with my aunt or take this teaching job.

As strange as it was to admit, I was glad I'd had this

chance. No matter what happened in the future, I'd learned a lot from this job. I'd always thought that teaching was for those who couldn't make it on the stage or got tired of the endless rounds of rejection and auditions.

I was wrong.

Teaching didn't get applause, but it did bring a sense of deep satisfaction. No matter what happened in my career, I would know that I'd mattered to people like Chessie, Eric, and Megan. I'd made a difference. It wasn't Broadway, but maybe Broadway and the Lyric weren't the only important things out there for me. I still wanted to perform. Nothing could make me give up that dream. But maybe . . . just maybe . . . the dream could be expanded and changed so that I could do even more. Maybe not this, but something . . .

Well, before I could contemplate what I was going to do with my future, I needed to worry about the present. I texted Larry, asking for Christine's phone number. A few minutes later, I was dialing.

"Christine McCann speaking."

I let out a sigh of relief at the sound of Christine's voice. Though Larry said he'd talked to her, part of me had still remained concerned. She was safe, and I now knew the identity of the person behind yesterday's sabotage. Both made me feel better. There was still LuAnn's death to worry about, but I'd think about that later. For now there was only one thing on my mind.

"It's Paige Marshall. I know who sabotaged the costumes yesterday, and I even have proof."

"That's great news, although I admit I was about to call to say not to concern yourself with the favor I'd asked."

Christine and I clearly had different definitions of the word "favor."

"You see," she continued, "I had a meeting with a new sponsor. He's already signed papers of intent, which will be formalized after the competition closes this weekend. I'm sorry I wasted your time."

"Congratulations on the new sponsor. That's great. And you didn't waste my time." Not really. "I feel a lot better knowing the identity of the person behind the instrument and costume damage. Now no one will have to worry about leaving their staging room unguarded for the competition. And I'm sure if you talk to Donna—"

"You think Donna Hilty was responsible?" Christine laughed. "I sincerely hope you haven't repeated that accusation to anyone else, seeing as how Donna wasn't even in town yesterday. She was called away on a family emergency."

The laughter irked me. First she blackmailed me into investigating. Now she was laughing at my conclusions without giving me a chance to explain. I guess it shouldn't come as a surprise that I sounded put out when I explained, "I know Donna claimed she went out of town. But she lied. And I have the picture of her coming out of one of the staging rooms yesterday to prove it."

"You're mistaken." Christine's voice cracked like a whip. "Donna's a celebrity. Her career doesn't depend on how her team ranks nationally, so she has no reason to impair the chances of the other teams. Besides, if she'd been in the performing arts center yesterday, someone would have recognized her and made me aware that she had returned."

"Not if she was wearing a disguise." I took a deep

breath. "Look, I understand that Donna Hilty's an important name in show business. You wouldn't want to accuse her of wrongdoing without proof. But you wouldn't want people to realize that you turned a blind eye when you were informed of Donna's actions. So, why don't we meet? Then you can see the photograph and decide for yourself."

"Is that a threat, Ms. Marshall?"

Threat? "No, of course not." Although, now that I thought about it, maybe it was. Turnabout, after all, was fair play. "I just want to make sure nothing else happens to ruin this experience for the students. They've worked hard to get to this point and shouldn't have to look over their shoulders because they're worried about what might happen next."

Christine let out a loud sigh. "Fine. I have to meet some of the board members for dinner tonight. But just so you're aware, I've known Donna Hilty for years. She would never stoop to the kind of behavior you're accusing her of."

Experience told me that rarely was anyone aware of what some people were truly capable of. I only had to look back to the murders of Greg Lucas and David Richard to know that.

Christine asked what hotel I was staying at and agreed to meet there at eight. I should be finished rehearsing with the students by then. If not, Christine would simply have to wait.

After hanging up, I slipped both my phone and Chessie's into my purse and headed to my room. After the day I'd had, I needed a shower and a few minutes to think. Despite the mounds of poorly stacked instruments, my hotel room felt like an oasis of peace and tranquility. After rolling up my sleeves, I stacked the cases against the far side of the room and felt a spurt of pride that the chore took me only ten minutes. A little more practice and I'd be ready for a gig as a roadie.

Now that I had a clear path to the bathroom, I grabbed a change of clothing and a towel and headed for the shower. As the hot water eased the tension out of my shoulders, I thought through the events of the day.

As much as Donna Hilty irritated me, I, too, was astonished to learn she was the one behind the ruined costumes. Donna wasn't a superstar, but she had a strong career. Why put that at risk in order to play Edward Scissorhands? The press would have a field day with the story. Hollywood stars got away with bad behavior on a daily basis, but country music fans tended to be less forgiving of their singers. Especially those whose stars hadn't risen all the way to the very top. Why take the chance of being discovered? Did winning mean that much to her? And what about Scott Paris? Where did he fit into this whole thing? The miraculously repaired costuming and his close relationship with Donna suggested he was involved in some way. Maybe if I learned more about them, I'd be able to see how the pieces of this fit together.

Once my hair was dry and I had changed into a pair of jeans and a fitted black T-shirt, I headed to the hotel's business center in search of the information I needed. It was time to surf the World Wide Web.

Or it would be when the curly-haired guy sitting in front of the computer finished printing his boarding pass, checking his e-mail, and logging in to his Facebook and Twitter accounts. When he logged on to eBay, I cleared my throat and shifted my position to remind him that I was waiting for my turn. The guy turned, looked at me, smiled, and placed a bid on an ugly brown glass lamp. When he finally pushed away from the desk, he had placed bids on six more items that ranged from collectable quilting plates to a state-of-the-art weed whacker. Did this guy know how to have a good time or what?

Once he was gone, I settled myself into the still-warm chair and let my fingers do the walking. First up—a search for all things related to Donna Hilty. A click onto her personal website and I was treated to a glamour shot of Donna with big makeup, even bigger hair, and a whole lot of white fringe. Her bio talked a lot about her family's struggles to make ends meet and the way being discovered by her manager and landing her first recording contract helped lift them all out of poverty.

Following that uplifting story was a list of her accomplishments, including her Grammy nomination for best new artist and a host of other award nods and wins. Also documented were the release dates and titles of her ten solo albums as well as a number of live performances and the year that she took time away from her busy concert schedule to coach show choir. That was three years ago. According to the archived press release, Donna wanted to give back to the type of high school program that taught and nurtured her passion for music. Maybe she did, but after seeing her teach today, I wasn't sure I bought the public explanation. She didn't look like a teacher driven to push her students to improve. And she certainly didn't have the connection with her kids that I saw from the other directors I'd met this season. It was easy to see the difference in the teachers who cared about their students and the ones who were just going through the motions. Which made me wonder—if Donna didn't like teaching, why was she doing it? It wasn't like she had my reasons and needed the money.

I thought I might have found the answer when I clicked on an article about Donna snubbing an autograph-seeking young girl on crutches. Donna pushed the pen and paper away hard enough to throw the girl off balance. Thanks to her father, the girl didn't fall. But Donna's popularity did. The story was picked up by several news outlets, and lots of blog posts were dedicated to encouraging a boycott of Donna's concerts and albums. I wasn't a huge country music fan, so the story had never made it onto my radar, but the furor must have been great enough to push Donna into canceling several of her appearances. Several weeks later, an article appeared announcing Donna's acceptance of a teaching position at a local Nashville high school. The story included a photograph of Donna in dance clothes enthusiastically rehearsing with high school students. Many of whom were quoted as saying that working with Donna was one of the best experiences of their lives.

The angry articles about Donna's diva disposition dissipated. Stories were written about her willingness to give up the money she would have made touring in order to help the next generation of singers. A new album was released to a smattering of acclaim, and Donna's singing career was back on track. Hurray for the power of public relations.

So why ditch all that work repairing her public image to win a competition she wasn't invested in? Scott said she was competitive, but no one could want to win that badly. Right? It didn't make any sense.

Putting aside that question, I looked to make sure there

wasn't anyone waiting for computer time and then typed in my next search—Scott Paris. Eek. There were at least two dozen people named Scott Paris on Facebook. I added the name of the high school he taught at and searched again.

Ha! Found him. Scott didn't maintain a website of his own, but he did have a page on the one run by the high school. Scott was in his eighth year of directing the choir program. He also worked on the musicals and had not only instituted the show choir program but had taken his team to this final competition in their first year. Go Scott.

Not only had Scott made his mark as an instructor, according to several websites; he was also an up-and-coming show choir music arranger. The rates he charged made me wonder whether I shouldn't have paid better attention in music theory class. Four-part harmony. A couple of dance breaks. A key change at the end. How hard could that be? Clearly, it must be harder than I thought or more people would be doing it.

Most of the links were about the competitions his choir performed in. More often than not, his team won. I was about to give up after surfing through several pages of links when one of them caught my eye. It was a review of a small, dinner-theater production of *Guys and Dolls* from ten years ago. The critic didn't like much about the show, but he did like Scott Paris's delightfully rollicking rendition of "Nicely Nicely" and predicted big things for Scott's performance career.

Well, either the critic's crystal ball was broken or Scott had his fill of performing, because not long after that he hung up his character shoes and devoted himself full-time to teaching. At least, that was what it looked like from the articles in the archives of the school newspaper. Although, I'd known more than one teacher in my time who swore they gave up the dream of the bright lights of Broadway for the love of teaching, when in reality they still harbored the hope that someone would discover their talent and take them away from parent-teacher conferences and grading papers.

I clicked around the other links, looking for more information about the man. According to the write-ups, he grew up in the Atlanta area, attended the University of Memphis, and graduated with a double major in musical theater and music education. As far as I could tell, Scott had never been married. His work was his life, which showed in the number of accolades he received for his direction and mentoring of the students at his school. Despite his smarmy attitude, there didn't appear to be a hint of impropriety attached to Scott's dealings with his students.

I was struck by this fact for reasons that had nothing to do with my investigation. Devlyn wore pink and hid our relationship because he claimed it was the best way to avoid come-ons from overenthusiastic high school girls and potential misunderstandings. Past experience had made Devlyn overly cautious, which I understood. When he was first starting out, he'd seen a teacher brought down by a girl's false claims of sexual impropriety. And, as he said more than once, a single man who spent lots of time around his students was a perfect target for overeager teenage fantasies and parental paranoia.

Scott was single. As far as I could tell, he was straight. Eight years into teaching he was well respected and sought after for show choir workshops and special master classes. And he wasn't the only one I'd seen on the competition circuit who wasn't married and had managed to avoid scandal. Devlyn was smart. He was attractive and talented and really good at making me feel as if I was doing something important by teaching jazz squares and triple turns to these kids. If it hadn't been for him, I would never have survived a week at this job.

Closing my eyes, I could still picture Devlyn in the audience of the Merle Reskin Theatre during opening night of *The Messiah*. The minute the last notes were sung, I sought out his face in the audience and saw the pride and affection he felt for me. Aunt Millie was the first person on her feet applauding, but Devlyn was right behind her. Mike Kaiser had stayed seated even as the rest of the audience had given us a standing ovation. I thought Devlyn's response was a sign of his support and that all of the stolen moments since then were leading to something more permanent. This week had shown me how wrong I had been. Devlyn wanted someone who fit into the world he had constructed for himself. Someone who would accept the limitations he placed on his life.

Someone who wasn't me.

I brushed a tear off my cheek, pushed aside thoughts of Devlyn, and went back to the task at hand. Donna had mentioned that Scott had connections to the judges. If that was the case, I was hard-pressed to see what they could be. And since I didn't have a list of the judges for this competition, I couldn't look them up. So I did the only thing I could think of. I typed in the name of the person Donna claimed was trying to use Scott's association with the judges—LuAnn Freeman of Memphis, Tennessee.

Wow. There was more than I expected.

Not only did several sites list her home address; there were photographs from both the street level and above views of her house. I wasn't sure whether property values in Memphis were in any way comparable to those in Chicago, but it was clear LuAnn and her family weren't hurting for cash. That house was huge. So was the acre or more of land it sat on, complete with flowering trees and an Olympic-sized pool.

More than a little creeped out at how stalkerish I felt looking at a dead woman's house, I clicked on an article about a dispute with a local water company. I wasn't surprised to see LuAnn was the one leading the complaint. The woman had had a forceful personality and hadn't been scared to use it. However, I was surprised to see the article list her as a former social worker. LuAnn's disposition seemed far more abrasive than the kindhearted type I typically associated with the job. The house wasn't what I'd expect, either—unless social workers got paid better in Memphis than they did in Chicago. She must have won the lottery or she married someone with lots of cash. Regardless, according to what I read, LuAnn had decided to step away from social work eight years ago. Instead of kicking back and taking some time off to relax, LuAnn opted to fill her time volunteering for her children's activities. LuAnn was listed as an assistant soccer coach, a troop leader, team mom for the traveling baseball squad, and the president of the show choir boosters. Her life made me tired just reading about it.

After several more clicks and no new information, I typed "Kelly Jensen" into the search window. The woman's eavesdropping behavior outside our staging room and her less than favorable relationship with LuAnn made me curious. According to the competition's website, Kelly had begun working with the organization just before Christine came on board. Her bio talked about her family's long-standing passion and dedication to helping expand the influence of the arts in today's youth. Yay for Kelly's family. They sounded like people I'd love to meet.

I clicked on the next article and felt my heart drop. Unless I kicked the bucket, I wouldn't be meeting Kelly's family anytime soon. They were dead. According to the article dated almost six years ago, Kelly's husband, daughter, granddaughter and close family friend were on their way to this very competition, which the Jensens had helped found, when they were hit by a truck whose driver had fallen asleep at the wheel. Kelly had planned on making the trip with them, but had come down with the flu and insisted her family enjoy the show without her.

Poor Kelly. That kind of loss had to be devastating. I admired Kelly's ability not only to keep going, but to do so in a job that worked to continue the type of performance her family had been on their way to see. The woman had to have a spine stronger than steel.

Still bummed for Kelly, I typed in the last name on my list, and information on the head of the United States Show Choir competition filled the screen. I scanned the information on the monitor as one of the hotel patrons appeared in the business center doorway, waiting for his turn at the computer. Quickly, I read the highlights of Christine's life. The first part had been high-powered. After graduating with her MBA, Christine went on to serve as head of marketing for not one but two different Fortune

500 companies. Then, suddenly, she left her seven-figures-a-year job to run this competition.

Huh. One had to wonder why. Did she have a long-buried passion for singing and dancing, or had something gone wrong in her corporate gig that made working with stage moms sound like a good idea? Too bad the guy behind me was doing a dance that signaled he either needed to pee or he was getting impatient. Whatever else I could learn from the Internet would have to wait until I could ask my questions when Christine and I met later tonight. Maybe the answers would help me understand why she was so reluctant to believe in Donna's guilt or was less concerned about the students competing than in the cash that funded it.

When I got there, the ballroom smelled like a combination of tomato sauce, pepperoni, and chlorine. The attitude of the kids was upbeat as they scarfed slices of pizza and downed gallons of soda. Some of my team members' parents had arrived early and were joining the festivities. I made the rounds, greeting parents. Once I was done asking about their trips and assuring them that the students didn't appear emotionally scarred by the events of this week, I settled into a seat next to Aunt Millie and Aldo with a plate of pizza. Thank God Killer was taking a nap in Millie's hotel room, which meant I could eat my dinner in peace.

Killer wasn't the only one absent. Devlyn had opted to skip mealtime or find sustenance elsewhere. On the happy front, Chessie and Eric seemed to be back on good terms. They were seated next to each other, holding hands. The handholding made for awkward pizza eating, but it didn't look as if either of them cared as they talked with Chessie's parents. The only thing that made Chessie pout was when I said she couldn't have her phone back until later tonight. But that frown was quickly turned into a smile when Eric complimented her willingness to sacrifice her needs for the good of the team. Score one for truth, justice, and a boyfriend who knew how to placate his girl.

All in all, everyone was having a good time. Strike that. There was one person sitting at the far end of one table with her eyes firmly fixed on the untouched food in front of her. An overly bright smile was plastered on Megan's face, but I'd lay odds that there were tears in her eyes. After taking one last bite of pizza, I wiped my hands on my napkin and pushed back my chair. It was time to play teacher.

"Megan, can we talk?"

The stab of panic in her eyes made my heart hurt, but I kept my smile pleasantly neutral as she stood and followed me out of the large room and into the hall.

"How are you feeling?" I asked, even though I was pretty sure I knew the answer.

"I'm great." Megan smiled. "The vocal rest is helping."

I could tell how much she wanted me to believe her, and I hated that I didn't. "Sing the opening of the first song for me."

Megan swallowed hard. "You want me to sing?" Her speaking voice sounded better than yesterday, but the deeper timbre and slight rasp in the sound told me that Megan had yet to recover fully.

I nodded and listened carefully as Megan sang the

opening notes to our competition set. "That's enough." I sighed. "Claire will do the run-through after dinner, and as much as I hate to do this, I'm going to have her compete with the team in the preliminary round."

"No. I'll be okay by tomorrow. I promise."

The trembling lip almost made me cave. "Yes, but if you sing tomorrow, it's doubtful you'll have a voice for the final competition on Friday."

Overtaxing swollen vocal cords would only lead to additional problems.

"But we might not make it to the final round." Tears bloomed in Megan's eyes.

Ugh. No one ever told me that feeling like the Grinch who stole Christmas was part of a teacher's job description. "I have to put the best performers on the floor tomorrow in order to make sure that we do. Keep resting your voice. By Friday you'll be one of those performers. Okay?"

"Okay." Megan's voice cracked. Yep. By doing my job, I'd officially broken her heart.

More than anything, I wanted to take back my decision. After all, this wasn't brain surgery. No one would die if tomorrow's performance wasn't perfect. But my job wasn't simply to make these kids look good onstage. It was to make sure that those entering the world of performing beyond their high school walls would be prepared for what lay ahead. Megan was going to be a musical theater major. Megan wanted to make a career out of performing. She was ready to study and sweat and do whatever it took to succeed. But hard work was only one of the necessary ingredients in this business. Luck was another.

I gave Megan a hug. Over her shoulder, I spotted Devlyn walking down the hallway toward us. He was the one who taught me that I needed to be more to these kids than their friend. That I needed to teach them that sometimes a performer got lucky and the performance brought the house down.

As Devlyn glanced my way and then turned and walked through the ballroom doors, I though about the other times when—no matter how much you wanted to make something work—the show went on. And how you couldn't help when it went on without you.

Chapter 18

The run-through with Claire standing in for her sister went great—if you didn't take into consideration Megan's depressed face, Devlyn's aloof attitude, and the parents' helpful suggestions that made the rehearsal three times longer than it should have been. But by the time I'd dismissed everyone, I was confident that the students were as prepared as possible. Megan might hate sitting on the sidelines, but it was the right decision. How teachers did this year in and year out was beyond me.

Larry gave the kids a final pep talk and told everyone they had to be in their rooms by ten o'clock. While he spoke, I noticed Christine McCann standing near one of the ballroom entrances. She'd changed out of her work attire. In her light blue denim capris and yellow T-shirt, she blended in with the parents. Except for her eyes. Those were all business as they took in the way the students listened to my aunt discuss the makeup process for the next day.

When the notes had been given and the departure time for tomorrow morning announced, I gave the kids one final warning to get some sleep and called an end to rehearsal. The kids gathered their things and raced out of the ballroom to get in one last swim before bed. I headed in Christine's direction.

"What's she doing here?" Larry grabbed my arm and pointed toward Christine. "Do you think someone else d-d-died?"

Everyone still in the room turned toward us. Oh no. Larry's less than subtle volume had struck again.

"I asked Christine to meet me here to discuss backstage security. The last thing we want is for our costumes to be tampered with. We also don't need parents getting involved in this issue." I sent a deliberate look at Chessie's parents, who had gotten out of their seats and were headed in this direction. "I don't think either of us want our team to get booted before they ever get the chance to compete."

Larry got the hint. He headed off to intercept Chessie's parents while I crossed the ballroom to where Christine McCann waited.

"Your team is impressive." Christine smiled. "I thought they were good when I watched their videos online, but they're better live."

"I'd think most teams are. It's hard to capture the energy of a live show and the mix of the voices on cell phone video."

Christine laughed. "You haven't been in this business long enough to understand how far some directors will go to ensure their team looks like the one to beat. I know several who have spent a great deal of money overdubbing the vocals and touching up the video with enough imperfections to make it look as if it was recorded live."

Wow. If I had that kind of money, I'd find a better use for it than creating a fake version of our team's musical numbers. Who wastes their bank account on that kind of thing?

"Two years ago, a team from the West Coast was invited to this competition based on their moderate competition success and a video that was sent for the selection committee's review. When they got here, it was clear that they weren't in the same league as the rest of the teams. They were eliminated on the first day, but based on their 'success' their coach was offered a position at a private and better-paying school."

Yikes. Although after what I knew about some of the coaches, including the dearly departed Greg Lucas, I guessed I shouldn't have been surprised. I'd thought succeeding in show business was bad. Add academics into the mix, and it brought the stakes to a whole new level.

"Maybe Donna had a similar reason for her actions yesterday." I pulled Chessie's cell phone out of my purse. It took me a few minutes to find the gallery icon, but soon the small screen was filled with Donna's brown-wigged figure coming through a door. "One of my students was playing hooky from her master class and went to our staging room. She heard the sound of ripping cloth coming from nearby and decided to see what was going on."

I slid my finger across the screen and the image of ripped satin appeared, followed by another shot of Donna's back as she headed down the hallway. The photos had been taken in a hurry. I doubted they would hold up in court if it ever came to that. But the widening of Christine's eyes said that she had recognized Donna's face despite the off-kilter photography and all that curly brown hair. The time stamp on the photograph sealed the deal.

"Donna had a family emergency yesterday." Christine's voice lacked the authority she normally had. "She wasn't in the performing arts center."

I flipped back to the first picture. "It looks like Donna was dealing with an emergency closer to home. One that involved Scott Paris."

Christine's head snapped toward me. "Scott? Do you have a photograph of him, too?"

"No, but I'm pretty sure he and Donna are in this together." Quickly, I ran through the things I'd discovered. The perfectly repaired costumes. How Scott warned me off my investigation for Christine. Finally, the look on his face after I accused him of being involved with the sabotage.

Christine shook her head. "There might be a simple explanation for those things. Something that has nothing to do with the damage from yesterday."

There could be, but off the top of my head I couldn't come up with what that might be. Especially not when I factored in Donna's willingness to be blackmailed by a teenager in order to keep her actions confidential. I was going to say that, but Christine was on a roll.

"Donna is such a recognizable face around here." She looked down at the phone in my hand. "It's almost impossible for her to go anywhere without being noticed. She probably didn't have time to deal with the usual fanfare when she came to the theater yesterday. That must be why she chose to wear a wig."

Wow. Christine had earned an A in justification. I almost hated to burst her creative bubble, but there was a lot more at stake than Christine's well-developed fantasy.

"Why don't you call them and see what they have to say?"

Christine's head snapped up. "Do you know what would happen if word got out that I accused a country-western star or one of the most celebrated choir directors of wrongdoing without more proof than this? The sponsors would pull their support for sure. School districts would no longer be interested in sending their students to our program. The competition would be finished. I can't let that happen."

"You also can't risk anything worse happening." I slid Chessie's phone back into my purse and pulled out my own. "What would the press and the sponsors say if another incident occurred tomorrow and they learned you had information that could have stopped it? Unless you want to leave that up to chance, I say we call Donna and Scott now and ask for an explanation."

Christine's eyes narrowed, and I stepped away to give her a chance to think. Christine struck me as the type who hated being backed into a corner. No doubt that feeling was the reason she had forced me to look into yesterday's incidents. I'd done my part, but if she felt like I was being too pushy, she could still make good on her threat to have my kids blackballed.

As Christine mulled over the possibilities, I looked around the ballroom. Larry must have successfully smoothed the feathers of Chessie's parents. They were now gone. The only person remaining was Devlyn. He was seated in one of the chairs, watching me. The anger I'd seen earlier was gone. Now there was curiosity and a hint of wistfulness that, despite my resolve, tugged at my heart.

"You're right." Christine blew a lock of hair off her face. "None of this will get reconciled without talking to Donna and Scott, which I plan for us to do right now."

Christine pulled out her cell phone and started messaging the parties involved. One thing I would say for the woman was that when it came to rapid-fire texting, Christine had skills. I could never manage to get my fingers to hit the right buttons on the first try. Thanks to autocorrect I had a tendency to send messages that meant something completely different from what I'd intended. Christine must not have that problem since moments later her phone dinged. Donna had texted back. She and Scott would be here as soon as they could get across town.

"They'll meet us in the front of the hotel. Is there somewhere more private than this where the four of us can talk?" Christine asked, sending a deliberate look toward Devlyn. "I think we'll have an easier time learning the truth if Donna isn't worried about being recognized."

While I doubted that anything about this conversation was going to be easy, I couldn't deny Christine's point. "We can use my hotel room." If nothing else, I'd have several hands to help stack instrument cases. Multitasking at its finest.

"I have calls I need to make. Let's meet in the lobby in ten minutes."

With those words I was dismissed. Christine put her phone up to her ear, and I headed for the exit farthest from Devlyn's watchful eyes, hoping the hospitality area of the lobby still had coffee brewing. I needed caffeine, and I needed it now.

The coffee urn was still full. The bad news was the coffee machine had been unplugged and the coffee was now cold. Bummer. I'd just have to make do with a soda from the vending machine.

I was debating between a Diet Dr Pepper and a Diet Coke when a voice asked, "Is everything okay?"

Devlyn.

"Everything's fine." Or it would be once I chugged my drink. I unscrewed the top and took a hit before turning toward Devlyn. "There are a few details Christine needs to iron out, but our team will be able to compete fair and square tomorrow."

Devlyn gave me one of his slow, sexy smiles. "That's good to hear. The kids owe a lot to you, even if they don't always know it." His smile faded. "They're not the only ones who owe you something. I owe you an apology. I had a knee-jerk emotional reaction to the news about your audition. It was juvenile and unfair and I'm sorry."

As far as apologies went, Devlyn's was pretty darn good. And he wasn't done.

"Your aunt spoke to me before rehearsal and told me that you scheduled your flights so that you could be here for our team's performances." He shoved his hands into his back pants pockets and sighed. "I should have known you'd never let this audition get in the way of showing your support for these kids. I should've asked you about it, instead of assuming you were abandoning everything we've created together. Can you forgive me?"

Devlyn reached out his hand. Part of me wanted to

meet him halfway. But instead, I looked at my watch and said, "Christine is waiting for me in the lobby. I have to go."

He stepped out of the doorway. As I walked by he said, "You're still mad."

I stopped walking and turned to look at him. His face was just as handsome as the first day we met. I could still remember the way my heart jumped when he gave me a smile. My heart wasn't jumping now.

"I'm not mad." Sad was more accurate. "There's just a lot going on. We need to focus on getting the kids through the competition. Once we're back in Chicago, we'll have time to talk. Okay?"

My phone buzzed in my pocket. I had a text message, but I wasn't concerned about that. All I could think about was the hurt blooming in Devlyn's eyes as the subtext of my words hit home. We could talk when we got back to Chicago, but an in-depth discussion wouldn't change what I knew to be true. The boundaries of Devlyn's life were set. He was looking for someone willing to live within those lines. With a little more time, I could probably fall in love with him. But this week had taught me something important. Devlyn wanted to be supportive of my performing career. He told the truth every time he said he believed in my talent. But I now knew that he also believed the job he was doing was more important than my dream of being onstage. If my career ever took off, I would be forced to choose between him and my dream. It was better to feel sad now than to have my heart broken later.

"Sure." Devlyn's fingers brushed mine. "I'm going to go help Jim play lifeguard. If you need me for anything, just give me a call."

I watched him walk down the hall toward chlorine and chaos and then fished my cell phone out and looked at the screen. Alan had texted. He wanted to know whether I'd decided what I was singing on Friday. If not, I needed to figure it out soon. I tapped back that I would send him my choices tonight, hit "send," and shoved the phone back into my purse. Alan was right. I needed to pick my audition pieces and make sure they were polished and ready to go. And I would. But first things first. I had to meet Christine and company. It was time to learn what Donna and Scott were really up to.

The duo in question was pushing open the glass entryway doors when I arrived in the lobby. Christine was nowhere to be seen. Donna's eyes turned to slits when she spotted me near the concierge desk.

"I should have known you were behind this."

Despite anything negative anyone might say about Donna's songs, which, if memory served, were heavy on heartbreak, the woman knew how to project.

Donna's white, high-heel boots clicked as she stormed across the tile floor. "Who do you think you are, accusing me of trying to ruin this show? Don't you know who I am?"

"We all know who you are, Donna." Christine's voice cracked like a whip from across the room. "And if you aren't careful, everyone at this hotel will recognize you and wonder what you're doing here." Donna opened her mouth to speak, but a strangely subdued Scott squeezed her arm and she closed it with a frown.

Christine nodded. "Now, I suggest we go to Paige's room. She's graciously agreed to let us use the space so we can talk without being overheard."

Taking my cue, I led the three to my door, slid the key card in the slot, and warned, "The room might be a little crowded. Between the broken loading dock door and the damaged belongings, our team has been using this as a staging room."

My team didn't disappoint. Instrument cases were once again piled precariously around the room. With a wide smile, I said, "These all just need to be stacked over there."

Donna's face turned red, but the speed with which Scott picked up several cases and moved them to the other bed ruined whatever angst she was going to unleash. Perhaps it was small and petty of me, but seeing one of country music's darlings be a roadie for my team made me all warm and fuzzy inside. For once, karma had smacked the right person in the ass. And if I was right about Donna's involvement in yesterday's destruction, karma had a whole lot more butt-kicking to do.

When all the instruments were stacked, Donna and Scott took a seat on my bed. I couldn't help noticing the way their legs and arms touched or the tender look in Scott's eyes when he looked at Donna. No wonder Donna was upset when she thought I had a personal interest in Scott. The two of them were definitely a couple and for some reason were keeping that information a secret. Boy, did that sound familiar. I had to wonder whether anyone in this business was capable of a normal relationship. If not, I was doomed to remain single for the rest of my life. Millie would just have to marry Aldo in order to plan the wedding of her dreams.

Christine took a seat on the other bed. "Donna, can you explain what you were doing in the performing arts center yesterday? And before you claim that you were out of town, you should know you were not only seen but photographed."

"That little—"

"Be careful what you say about one of my students, Donna." My voice was quiet, but I could tell by Donna's pursed lips that she'd heard the threat behind the calm. Chessie might be headstrong, exasperating, and a pain in the neck, but she was mine. No one was going to call her names around me. Especially not someone who had done a great deal worse.

Donna took a deep breath and nodded. "I'm sorry. That was uncalled for. I was hoping the young lady in question would keep silent about what she'd seen, that the competition would go on as planned, and that all of this would just go away."

"All of what?" I asked.

Donna looked at Scott. He took her hand in his and answered, "LuAnn Freeman called me three weeks ago. Somehow she had gotten her hands on the list of judges for the competition and had discovered that I had connections to two of them."

Christine sent Scott a sharp look. I wasn't surprised. All coaches were required to sign a waiver that affirmed we had no knowledge of any of the judges in the competition. The judges themselves were given a list of the choirs and asked whether they had personal ties to any of the participants. Since show choir was a tight-knit community, knowledge of or having been introduced to any of the judges was permitted. But a deeper relationship was considered taboo. If a judge did know a coach on the final roster, he or she was supposed to contact Christine immediately so that Christine could secure a more impartial judge. Coaches who learned the identities of any of the judges were also supposed to contact the organization. The system wasn't perfect and relied a lot on the honor system. It was obvious that Scott wasn't all that honorable.

But now wasn't the time to point out the obvious. Christine held off on the much-deserved tongue-lashing and let Scott continue talking.

"LuAnn said if I didn't use my influence with the judges to help her daughter's team get into the finals, she'd report my relationship with them to you and get my team disqualified from the contest." Scott straightened his shoulders. "I told LuAnn that the judges weren't going to cheat for me and that I wasn't about to ask them to do it for her."

And dogs and cats were going to declare a worldwide truce.

"Both judges have since pulled out of working on the contest for personal reasons." Scott looked at Christine in a way that said he believed that should make everything better.

Christine propped her hands on her hips. "How does this explain Donna's actions from yesterday?"

"LuAnn also discovered that Donna and I were seeing each other. She threatened to leak the information to the press."

"I don't understand," I said. "Neither of you are married." Or professed to be gay. "What's the big deal?"

Donna let out a dramatic sigh. "The big deal is that I just landed my own reality dating show. The concept is that as a celebrity it's hard to find true love. The host of the show is the head of a matchmaking website who promises she has what it takes to bring me the man of my dreams. The whole show is going to end with a marriage proposal followed by a blowout wedding to the man of my dreams."

Huh . . . that seemed like a lot for one show to promise. Especially since love had a way of being unpredictable and the people on those shows less than honest about their feelings. Donna was either incredibly brave to promise she'd marry the winning guy or she had stacked the deck in her favor.

"Is Scott going to be on this show, too?"

Scott gave me a sheepish grin. "I planned on putting in my notice to my principal after the competition. Donna and I are already planning to get married. We've been keeping our relationship a secret so that it wouldn't distract our students. When this offer came up, Donna thought it would be a great way of going public and skyrocketing both of our careers."

Donna smiled up at him. "We're going to record an album of duets and release it on our wedding day. Scott has a fantastic tenor voice. Wait until you hear it."

I wondered whether he'd get the chance to record that album or whether the next time he'd use that tenor would be singing gospel songs from jail. The two seemed completely oblivious to the fact that they'd done anything wrong.

"I'm confused," I said. "How does ruining other teams fit into all of this?"

Scott ran a hand through his hair. "LuAnn showed up on Monday with a press release she'd created about our relationship. It alleged the two of us were colluding with judges to make sure our teams were at the top of the podium as well as a bunch of other fairy tales. Donna's seen firsthand that tabloids don't care whether the stories they print are true. If anyone ran with LuAnn's information, Donna would lose the reality show and I wouldn't need to tender my resignation. I'd probably be fired. So when LuAnn asked us to help her damage the competition's costumes, we had no choice. We had to say yes."

"But we tried to find a way to give LuAnn what she wanted without ruining everything for the kids." Donna laced her fingers through Scott's. "It would have worked, too, had it not been for LuAnn's insistence that she help."

Aha. "That's why some of the costumes were ripped in places where they could be easily repaired."

Scott nodded. "All the teams that Donna and I targeted had problems that could be fixed without much effort. Having two teams that hadn't loaded in yet made it easier for us to keep LuAnn out of most of the staging rooms. LuAnn was pissed about Donna's team not loading in. She liked the idea of Donna or me having to destroy the costumes we'd created." Scott looked over at me. "She was pretty angry that your team didn't have costumes and instruments in their staging room, Paige. If she could have blamed me for the broken loading dock door on stage left she would have. I swear the woman looked for reasons to confront people. She was never happier than when she was in the middle of a fight."

It sounded like LuAnn should have gone into law instead of social work. All that aggression would have had a constructive outlet.

"We were just lucky that LuAnn was so happy about the mess she saw in my team's staging room that she never noticed those costumes and most of the others were ripped at the seams. She only noticed the spare ones that I brought, which were already shredded. And she got so freaked by the falling lights and so angry that Paige wasn't booted on her accusation that she never noticed the people I'd hired to fix the costumes hanging around before the theater was closed."

Huh.

Donna sniffled. "We felt really bad about the two teams that LuAnn handled. Their costumes really were trashed, but a costume designer I know in the area has gotten them brand-new outfits, which, according to the directors, were better than the ones they had before. They're practicing with them tonight to make sure the costumes don't hamper the routines."

Okay, the sabotage thing sucked, but I was reluctantly impressed that Scott and Donna had opted to fix what they'd broken. Too bad they'd freaked out a whole lot of kids in the process. Had they been smarter, they would have gone to Christine and had her work on the problem. Of course, now that I thought about it, Christine didn't have the best track record when it came to dealing with LuAnn. As far as I could tell, all three of these people were lucky the cops hadn't dragged them into the station for questioning in LuAnn's death. They all had a motive—or twelve.

"So what happens now?" Scott asked. "Are you going public with what we did?"

"You can't." Donna stood. "All the teams are fine now. LuAnn is gone. Christine, we've done everything possible to make this right. We even found the competition a new sponsor so you wouldn't have to worry about the old ones bailing. There's no reason why anyone needs to know about what we did or why we did it."

"I'm afraid the cops are going to want to talk about it at length," Christine said. "I was late coming to meet you because I had a call from the Nashville police. First thing tomorrow morning they will be at the performing arts center to interview anyone who had contact with LuAnn on the day she died. That means all three of you."

Chapter 19

For a moment, no one said a word as the implications of Christine's declaration sunk in. A thought hit me in the silence. I was standing in a room with three potential murders.

Help.

I took a step toward the door and scanned the room for something I could bash someone over the head with just in case of emergency. But if anyone in the trio was having violent thoughts, I probably didn't need to worry about them being directed at me. For the moment, their focus was squarely on one another.

"This won't affect the competition, will it?"

Wow. That was Scott's first question? Mine would have been "Do they have a suspect or a motive or do they think the killer will strike again?" Call me crazy, but when someone mentioned murder, I tended to think more in terms of life and death than sequins and scores.

Christine shook her head. "The police see no reason to stop the competition, although they will be conducting interviews throughout the day. I've asked that those interviews take place in one of the theater's back rooms and the lead detective agreed. As much as I hate to risk the public learning about the interviews, it's the best way to aid the investigation while allowing the show to go on. Kelly and I will be calling the coaches and asking them to prep their students for what will be happening throughout the day. You'll need to discuss the matter with your students as well."

Donna looked at Scott and then back to Christine. "Do you plan on telling everyone about our part in yesterday's . . . problem? I understand telling the police, but I'd hate for LuAnn's daughter to hear that her mother forced Scott and me to hurt the competition. She's got enough to deal with. Don't you think?"

Oy.

"Yes." Christine's voice was soft, but sharp as a dagger. "I do think LuAnn's daughter has enough to deal with. Which is why I'll be keeping your part in this matter to myself. For now. I also plan on announcing that the Memphis Central High School team will be competing in the finals no matter what their score is tomorrow. I'm sure you'll support my decision."

When Scott and Donna nodded, Christine smiled. "Good. Now, unless the two of you have more to confess, I suggest you get back to your teams and let them know what tomorrow will hold."

Christine didn't have to tell them twice. Scott grabbed Donna's hand, and the two raced by me toward the door.

With a hurried "See you tomorrow," they disappeared out into the hall, leaving Christine and me alone.

"You're really not going to tell the other participants what Donna and Scott said?" I asked. Maybe I was old-fashioned, but I wasn't wild about the idea of them getting away with such a dirty trick. Even if it was prompted by more than a need to see their own teams win.

"I would if I thought it would do any good." Christine rubbed her temples and sat down on the edge of the bed in the spot Scott had just vacated. "Unfortunately, this news would only tarnish the competition's reputation and turn Donna and Scott into the bad guys."

Hello! They *were* the bad guys. "Don't the coaches and students deserve to know?"

"Not according to the lead detective on LuAnn's case. I called him while waiting for Scott and LuAnn to arrive and mentioned the photograph you had acquired. He asked that I keep the news quiet. When the police ask questions tomorrow, they want people to give answers that aren't colored by Scott and Donna's actions. Otherwise, it'll be almost impossible for the police to wade through the supposition and find out what really happened to LuAnn."

Huh. I hadn't thought of that. I guessed that was why I was a singer, not a detective.

"I'd appreciate if you would also keep this information to yourself. I know I haven't given you any reason to want to do me favors." Christine pushed herself off the bed. "But as heavy-handed as my tactics were, I was right to enlist your help. Now I only hope the detectives investigating LuAnn's death have your kind of follow-through.

LuAnn was no longer my friend, but her family should have answers and LuAnn deserves to rest in peace."

Wow. That could quite possibly be the worst apology in history. Then again, when I considered the woman who offered it, I was pretty lucky to receive an apology at all. And now that she'd opened the door to her relationship with LuAnn, I decided it was a good time to walk through it.

"How did you meet LuAnn? You weren't involved with show choir before you started this job, were you?" If so, Google hadn't documented it, which to the students I taught was almost the same as it not happening.

"Hell no." Christine leaned back. "I worked in corporate America for years. My family got tired of the eighty-hour workweeks, so I decided to look for a less stressful job."

"And you thought show choir competitions wouldn't be stressful?"

Christine laughed. "Goes to show what I knew about performers, right? But I made it a point to learn, and Kelly was willing to hold down the fort here at the office and let me. My first year, I traveled to several of the high schools that had been invited to attend the previous year's national competition in order to talk to the coaches and kids about what they were hoping to get out of the program. A lot of them had been friendly with the woman who'd previously held this job. She'd been a high school coach before being offered the position. Many of the coaches were resistant to the idea of someone who hadn't previously been involved in show choir running this competition."

I remembered my first week of work at the end-of-summer show choir camp and empathized with how Christine must have felt. The students had been snarky and the other coaches standoffish. None of them had believed that a trained opera singer had any business working with Music in Motion. Being an outsider wasn't fun. I was impressed that Christine had been proactive in visiting coaches and getting their support, and I said as much.

"It certainly wasn't as easy as I thought it would be," Christine admitted. "Most of them were polite, but more than a few made the suggestion that I hire a real show choir person to handle the creative side. That would leave me free to do what I was good at—monitoring the finances."

Ouch.

"LuAnn was helping out at one of the rehearsals I attended. Her son was in the choir then. When rehearsal ended, she came over and introduced herself. She said she knew what it was like to be an outsider in the close-knit show choir world and wanted to let me know that my ideas to broaden the competition experience had her full support. You have no idea how good it felt finally to have some appreciation of the work I was doing and from someone who understood how frustrating it was to be doubted because I hadn't been involved in this business for years."

Oh yes, I did. Too bad in both our cases, one of our biggest supporters had turned out to be full-out wacko. At least Christine didn't have her first show choir friend turn a gun on her. I'd been in that position. Trust me, it sucked.

"When did LuAnn stop being so nice?"

"I'd heard stories about LuAnn's conflicts with other people, but I never experienced it personally until this year. The coach of Central Memphis High School denied

LuAnn's application for the assistant coach position, claiming that it was a conflict of interest for the coaches to be related to students who were trying out for the team."

"Makes sense to me."

"To me, too, but LuAnn was furious. She insisted they hold the position open until her daughter graduated. Not surprisingly, the head of the music department refused. That's when LuAnn asked me to deny the school a place in the competition that year. I was shocked since her daughter was on the team, but LuAnn was determined to do whatever it took to make her point. She said her daughter would have other opportunities in the future."

My phone buzzed. I ignored the text. "You didn't do what she asked."

Christine frowned. "I couldn't in good conscience withhold extending the invitation. Their team was too strong. Not including them would have caused people to speculate on the reason behind the snub. Competitions like ours only succeed if the public views our integrity as above reproach."

Christine hadn't been too concerned about that integrity when she threatened to blackball my team, but I figured now wasn't the time to point that out.

"I take it LuAnn wasn't happy?"

Christine laughed. "That's an understatement. LuAnn went crazy. She called at least a dozen times a day, threatening to have the sponsors pull their support. I grew tired of placating her and finally asked Kelly to field LuAnn's calls."

"You weren't worried she'd go through with her threats?"

Christine smiled. "I might not know a lot about singing

and dancing, but I know how to write a contract. The only way the sponsors could extricate themselves from the agreement was if the competition disbanded or did something that could negatively impact the sponsors' image due to their association with our organization."

"Which was why LuAnn wanted to sabotage the costumes."

Poor sportsmanship combined with the information LuAnn learned about Scott's connection to the judges that mysteriously resigned would be enough to give the contest a lot of bad press and the sponsors a reason to use their escape clause. LuAnn could take out a bunch of birds with one stone. Only someone had plucked her first.

"I should have known LuAnn had something planned when she called and asked if she could volunteer with check-in." Christine shrugged. "I thought she was trying to make amends for her poor behavior, so I agreed. Still, I made sure to keep my eye on her at first. But she was so professional, coming in on Sunday—a day earlier than required—to help organize things and handling the loading dock issue, that I believed the worst was over."

Wait a minute. "LuAnn was working on fixing the loading dock?"

"She discovered the problem. First thing Monday morning, she checked to make sure both loading docks were ready for the teams to arrive. When the stage-left loading dock didn't work, she locked the door to the room that leads to that area and posted a sign on both the inside and outside doors to make sure arriving schools knew to use the other entrance. She then called for a technician to fix the problem. Unfortunately, we couldn't get on the schedule until today."

"So the loading dock door is fixed?"

"It was by the time I left the theater tonight. As it turns out there was a small metal piece jammed into one of the gears. Had I known that, I would have gotten a pair of pliers and removed the thing myself. It would have saved everyone a lot of trouble. But to make sure it doesn't happen again, the technician promised to drop by tomorrow to verify that the door's working the way it should."

"Have you told the police about the loading dock malfunction and LuAnn's involvement with it?" The whole thing seemed strange to me.

"I can't imagine that they'd be interested in a door having a mechanical issue, but I can mention it when I speak to them tomorrow morning." Christine stood. "I have a lot of phone calls to make between then and now. If I don't see you before your team takes the stage, good luck."

Once Christine was gone, I looked at my phone. Alan had sent another message with a list of songs he thought would make a great impression during my audition. A not-so-subtle reminder that I had not yet informed him of my choices. Grabbing my music binder, I took a seat at the desk and flipped through the pages. Now that the threat of an undeserved early exit from the competition was no longer hanging over my team, I was able to focus on picking music for me to sing on Friday.

Alan wanted me to sing "Dove Sono" from *Le Nozze di Figaro*. The song was beautiful and was filled with longing and sorrow. I'd be able to demonstrate a strong dynamic range and legato singing, but the piece wouldn't showcase my acting skills. Acting was one of my strengths, especially in the opera world. Opera performers excelled at infusing their singing with a wide variety of feelings, but they weren't always comfortable physically expressing those emotions. If I wanted to convince a big-name artistic director to take a chance on me, I had to prove I had more in my bag of tricks than pretty singing. Which was harder to do than one might think. As a lyric soprano, I found a great number of the age-appropriate songs available to me were about falling in love or being tortured by love, with the occasional prayer to God thrown in for good measure. Great music, but not exactly what I was going for.

After an hour of humming through music, I settled on two pieces that I thought were my best chance of making a strong impression. "Quando me'n vo" from *La Bohème* and Elsie's "Tis Done! I Am a Bride" from *Yeomen of the Guard*. The second was technically operetta, but the music was challenging and the song gave me a chance to flex my actress muscles. As a backup, I chose Rosalida's second-act aria from *Die Fledermaus*. It never hurt to have a German song ready to go.

That decided, I sent a message to Alan, changed into my T-shirt and ratty sweatpants, and made a beeline for the bed. I had just settled in when someone tapped on my door. There was only one person I could think of who would be outside waiting to see whether I'd let them in. Well, if Devlyn thought we were going to kiss and make up, he was going to be disappointed.

I flopped onto my pillow and closed my eyes. More tapping. I wasn't going to answer. Right?

Wrong.

After flipping aside the covers, I padded across the carpet, unlatched the door, and opened it to reveal . . .

"Aldo?"

He waved his wrinkled hand at me and took a step backward. "You were asleep. I should not have-a come."

When he turned to leave, I realized he was wearing the maroon robe and slippers that my aunt had given him for Christmas. The attire wasn't an unusual sight considering the two of us lived under the same roof. But seeing Aldo wear them in the middle of a hotel hallway was.

"I wasn't asleep. Please, come in." I reached out and pulled him inside before he could shuffle away. Hitting the lights, I asked, "What's wrong?"

"Nothing." Aldo sighed. "Well, maybe a little something. For months your aunt has refused to speak of marriage. She would not stay in the same hotel room with me because we do not set a good example by not being married. But tonight she comes to my room and says we should . . ." His face turned the color of his robe. "Well . . . she a . . . you know."

I did know, and I was pretending that I was perfectly comfortable hearing that my aunt jumped Aldo tonight. And that I wasn't a little wigged out with Aldo calmly waiting for me to comment on that event.

"Is Millie still in your room?" I asked, not sure why Aldo was here instead of there.

Aldo's mostly bald head bobbed up and down. "Your aunt's a-sleeping. She always sleeps soundly after . . ."

This discussion was getting more uncomfortable by the minute. I searched for the safest thing to say and asked, "Why are you here?"

"I'm confused."

That made two of us.

Aldo paced the length of my room while his bathrobe flapped in the breeze. "Millie has been clear about what she does no' want. But tonight she acts different. And now I do not know what to do."

Ah. Now I understood. Millie must have thought about what she and I had discussed and was now looking to broach the marriage conversation. No wonder Aldo was baffled.

Smiling, I put my hand on Aldo's arm to stop him from traveling the length of the room for the fourth time. "Aunt Millie likes to believe she always knows what's right. When she's not, it takes her a while to admit it. I think tonight she was trying to demonstrate that she's had a change of heart."

"You think?" Hope shined bright in Aldo's eyes. "You believe your aunt will consider marrying me?"

"It couldn't hurt to ask her."

"You're right." Aldo marched over to the door. Turning, he said, "You are a good girl. Now get some sleep. You have a big day tomorrow."

Aldo was right. Tomorrow the team would learn whether they had a place in the finals. I'd catch a plane for the biggest audition of my life. And the police might decide that LuAnn's death was a murder after all. As far as days went, tomorrow was almost as big as they got.

Chapter 20

Most of the kids barely spoke during breakfast. Their expressions were tense as they picked at their breakfasts. Not even Killer's pathetic pleas for bacon or his energetically wagging tail could get the most nervous of them to laugh. A few well-meaning parents tried to soothe their kids' anxiety by saying things like "Music in Motion has competed over a half dozen times in the last few months." And "You have nothing to worry about."

While both were true, I understood why many of the team members were leaving the food on their plates untouched. This was it. The final leg in the journey we had all taken together this year. Hundreds of hours of work had gone into learning and polishing these routines. If they didn't do well today, many would feel that time had been wasted. They'd be wrong. The work we'd done was bigger than one ten-minute set on this Nashville stage or the opinions of eight judges who may or may not appreciate the choreography. But telling a group of fifteen- to eighteen-year-olds that the journey was more important than the outcome wasn't going to help. That was a lesson only time could teach. And even then it was a hard lesson to remember.

"Ms. Marshall."

Learning to accept that you had to sometimes step to the side was another hard lesson. Looking up from my mostly full plate of eggs and fruit, I asked, "How are you feeling today, Megan?"

Her answering smile was big and bright. "That's what I wanted to talk to you about. I warmed up in the shower this morning and my voice is a lot better. Nothing hurts or feels swollen. So, I was hoping you'd change your mind and let me perform today. I talked to Mr. DeWeese about it, but he said you had to be the one to make the call."

Good for Larry. His tendency to look and sound distracted gave the students the false illusion that he wasn't all that bright. They were wrong. Larry knew the only reason Megan would come to him asking to be put into the number was because she knew what my answer would be.

"I'm glad you're feeling better." Megan's smile grew bigger but faded as I added, "That means your voice will be even stronger tomorrow for the finals. Until then I want you to continue to stay hydrated, keep quiet as much as possible, and take more zinc."

Megan's shoulders slumped.

"Look," I said gently. "I know you're disappointed. But I need you to answer a question. Do you think this team is good?"

"Yeah."

"Good enough to win this competition?"

"Of course."

"Then you'll be on that stage tomorrow. Just make sure you don't scream or do anything between now and then to change that." I pushed back my chair and stood. "That goes for all of you today. We're scheduled to perform second. Once we're done and you've changed out of your costumes, I expect you to sit in the audience and support the other teams as they perform. But no yelling or doing anything that might affect your voice. Today is just the first step. You'll need to be even better tomorrow. Got it?"

They cheered.

"I said no yelling."

The laughter that followed my exaggerated eye roll eased the tension. The kids went back to eating, but this time friendly teasing accompanied the other mealtime sounds. By the time breakfast was over and everyone was carrying their costumes onto the bus, the group's attitude was one of eager anticipation. They'd worked hard and were ready for this step. As a matter of fact, I thought, sliding into the seat across from Larry, so was I.

Or maybe I wasn't.

My pulse spiked as the kids hurried off the bus at the performing arts center. I couldn't say how much of my nerves were due to the upcoming performance or related to the three police squad cars parked near the entrance. Despite the text Larry had received saying that the left-stage loading dock was now operational and that the police were allowing people to use that entrance, we opted to have the bus park in front. The day was going to be stressful enough without the kids seeing the exact spot where LuAnn Freeman had been mowed down.

A slightly stuttering Larry, an enthusiastic Jim, and

an overly polite Devlyn helped the kids get their costumes and instruments off the bus and into our staging room. Meanwhile, I helped Millie with her makeup kit.

"Kit" implied something small and contained. So that might have been a misnomer for the arsenal that Millie had hauled all the way from Chicago. Lit mirrors. Six sets of curlers and four curling irons. Two blow-dryers. Dozens of large powder puffs, eyelash curlers, bottles of cold cream, and application sponges. Not to mention box after box of foundation, eye shadow of every hue, mascara, lipstick, and blush. Hurray for Mary Kay!

Between the instrument cases (which I noticed were stacked far more neatly by the students than ever before), racks of costumes, and Millie's hair and makeup emporium, the staging room was uncomfortably full. When you added fourteen students, the ten band members, four directors, Millie, Aldo, and Killer to the mix, it was a recipe for bedlam. Killer had been scheduled to stay at the hotel, but apparently his time alone yesterday had been spent eating the hotel's extra-fluffy pillows. Which meant he was up a lot of the night, throwing up those extra-fluffy pillows. To prevent an exorbitant hotel bill and a trip to the vet, Killer was now curled in the corner watching the madness. Lucky us.

The boys got dressed in their black pants, white shirts, and satin vests while the girls had their hair set, brushed, styled, and squirted with enough hair spray to eat a hole through the ozone layer. The environment might suffer, but the girls' hair wasn't going to lose its curls. We had that going for us.

When Millie cracked open a second can of hair spray, I used the excuse that Killer needed a walk, grabbed his leash, and bolted for the door in search of fresh air. Kids raced up and down the hall. Some were in jeans. Others were already decked out in their competition attire. The preliminary performances would begin in an hour, and the energy level was high. Killer barked as the kids raced past. To make sure the dog didn't mistake any of their shiny costumes for the fancy stuffed chew toys Millie liked to buy, I tugged on his leash and led him down the hall toward the loading dock so we could both get some air. At least, that was the story I was going to tell anyone who asked what I was doing.

I knew the cops were looking into LuAnn's death, which meant I should pay attention to the competition and leave the investigating to them. But I couldn't get Christine's words about LuAnn's involvement with the malfunctioning loading dock door out of my head. I probably wouldn't learn anything, but it couldn't hurt to take another look, right?

With the competition still more than an hour away, the backstage area was quiet. It felt dim and soothing after being in the middle of pre-show preparations. Killer growled at me and then walked back toward the door leading to the staging rooms. Killer liked chaos.

When I refused to give in to Killer's scare tactics, he whined and followed me into the empty space on the stage side of the loading dock entrance. I walked toward the large metal door. Huh. I studied the exposed mechanism that caused the malfunction. Yeah—it wouldn't be hard to jam something into the door to make it stop working. Of course, it was hard to imagine a reason why anyone would want to do that. Knowing that LuAnn was the one who discovered the malfunction made me wonder whether she didn't have something to do with it. She was, after all, the one who masterminded the costume issues. But without LuAnn around to ask, it was impossible to know whether she was behind this problem, too.

I took one last look at the door and then looked at my watch. The first performers would take the stage in forty-five minutes. It was time to go back and make sure my kids were ready.

"Come on, Killer."

I tugged the leash, but the dog wouldn't budge. Something on the floor near the door had caught his attention and he wasn't ready to stop sniffing. I tugged again. Killer turned and bared his teeth. Great. High-strung teens and a dog that was ready to bite my hand off if I pulled him away from a stupid piece of paper on the ground. Could my day possibly get any better?

Wait a minute.

I gave Killer's leash a hard yank. His head came up, and I made a grab for the piece of paper. Eureka. Killer growled. I grinned and stuck my tongue out. Juvenile? Absolutely. But I couldn't help it. It wasn't often I managed to outmaneuver Aunt Millie's prized poodle. I had to take my victories where I could get them.

Killer made unhappy noises and leapt up to snatch the paper out of my hand, but I was quicker. I held the rectangular piece of paper up over my head, out of his very agile jumping reach, and tried to ignore his subsequent leaps as I struggled to read what was written on it.

CMHS Showstoppers

Ignoring the way Killer flopped his pompon butt onto the ground and began to howl, I turned the paper over.

The back side was covered in dust and what looked like small bits of cardboard. This wasn't paper. It was a label that must have come off of the boxes that the mechanic had pointed out to me yesterday. Boxes that, according to this label, belonged to the CMHS Showstoppers. I didn't have to look at the program to know the acronym stood for Central Memphis High School.

Killer let out another howl. This one made the hair on my neck stand on end. Aunt Millie could make a fortune renting him out to haunted houses at Halloween. His werewolf imitation was dead-on and sure to draw attention. Something I wasn't sure I wanted. Sliding the label into my pocket, I gave the leash another tug, hoping that the disappearance of the object of his desire would silence him.

No such luck.

Well, I couldn't take a dog back to the staging room. And I couldn't stay here. Not while he was making these sounds. I'd get accused of animal abuse or worse.

Sighing, I pushed the loading dock door button, watched it go up, and then stepped outside, dragging a still-yelping Killer behind me.

"I guess you just saved me the trouble of testing to see if the door works."

I squinted into the sunlight and spotted the mechanic from yesterday standing next to a pickup truck parked in the loading zone. He was situated below the raised dock area where Killer and I were standing. I'd been so intent on the howling animal I was dragging behind me that I hadn't noticed him standing there.

"Hey, boy," the guy said, pulling his hand out of his pocket and holding it out to the dog.

I was about to shout for him to be careful of Killer's

professionally whitened teeth when I noticed the piece of beef jerky extending from the man's fingers. The were-wolf imitation stopped as Killer nipped the dried meat out of the mechanic's hands and happily chowed down.

Note to self: Carry meat products at all times.

"Thanks." I gave the man a smile and looked down at the pocket of his shirt. The stitching said his name was Marshall. "Killer here was starting to get a little restless so I brought him outside." Was I the master of understate-ment or what?

Marshall smiled back. "Not a problem, ma'am. I have a couple of dogs of my own. I don't typically take them to the theater, though."

"Oh, he's not mine." Killer looked up at me. If I didn't know better, I would have thought he was injured at my disavowal of ownership. "My aunt decided to bring him here. He had some minor issues yesterday while being alone at the hotel."

Killer, 4. Foam pillows, 0.

"So, Marshall, you're the one we have to thank for fixing the loading dock door?"

He tipped his ball cap, climbed up the stairs, and joined Killer and me on the dock. "I can't say I did much."

"Well, all of us who have been waiting since Monday to have this door work thank you."

Marshall's left eyebrow rose. "You say the door hasn't been working since Monday?"

"Well, it might have been malfunctioning longer. But our team got a message Monday morning from the theater telling us this loading dock wasn't operational."

"I wonder why they didn't call to have it looked at sooner."

"They did," I said. At least, Christine thought LuAnn had called for assistance. "Whoever they talked to at your company said the earliest you could come out to look at the problem was yesterday."

He frowned. "I took the call myself on Tuesday night. I offered to come out first thing the next morning, but she insisted that someone was using the space to store some boxes and they wouldn't be out of there until Wednesday afternoon. She asked for me to come by then. Only the boxes were still there when I arrived and I had to move them out of the way. The man who picked up the boxes was apologetic for running late and making me go to the trouble."

Killer sniffed at Marshall's hand. Absently, Marshall reached into his pants pocket and pulled out another piece of jerky. Meanwhile, I considered the importance of his words.

"Did you catch the man's name?"

"If I did, I can't recall."

Before Marshall could wonder why I was so interested, I asked, "Would you mind telling me what he looked like?"

"Dark skin. Short hair. I'd guess he was around my grandson's age. Or maybe I just thought he was in his early twenties because he was wearing a University of Tennessee sweatshirt." He smiled again. "My grandson wears his all the time. The two don't look anything alike, but the boy was polite, just like my Jimmy. And he seemed so upset that he was late and I had to move boxes that I offered him a hand carrying the boxes to his car. The boxes weren't very big, but they were sure heavy."

"Did you happen to look in the boxes?" He stiffened

and I hurried to add, "I know when I move boxes at our school, they aren't always sealed well. The flaps have a tendency to come up, which gives me a peek inside. If the boxes weren't sealed, I figured you might have gotten a glimpse of whatever was packed in them."

Marshall didn't look convinced with my improv skills. "Why would that be important to you? If you don't mind my asking."

Good question. Lucky for me I had a good answer. "I was wondering if maybe you should talk to the police. You see, the woman who called you also packed those boxes. She was killed not too far from where your car is parked. The cops are inside right now, interviewing people to determine whether her death was an accident or something more."

"Holy crap." He blushed and tipped his cap again. "Pardon my language, ma'am. I was surprised. And I guess maybe I should talk to the police. The jars in those boxes weren't marked. At first I thought they were empty, but the minute I picked up one of the boxes I realized they were filled with clear liquid. Probably some kind of fancy water. People are always paying lots of money for fancy water from mountain glaciers or some kind of special pond even though they could use the stuff from the tap for free. I guess it takes all kinds."

It did indeed.

I gave Marshall the name of the lead detective on LuAnn's case and suggested he enter the building from the lobby instead of back here. Unless, of course, he wanted to have an epileptic seizure from looking at all the sequins and rhinestones that would be glistening in the halls. Marshall gave Killer one last piece of beef jerky before walking to his car. I watched him drive off and then went back inside the theater.

Hitting the button to the loading dock, I watched the door come down and thought about the boxes that had been stashed here earlier this week—presumably by LuAnn. The same person who discovered the loading dock door on this side of the stage wasn't working. Coincidence? I doubted it, especially after knowing she was the mastermind behind the costume destruction. She was the one who'd discovered the ruined clothing. Her outrage and very loud accusations automatically shifted focus away from anyone considering the possibility she might be involved.

Smart. Something told me she had been equally smart when it came to sabotaging the loading dock. Christine said LuAnn volunteered to check the doors to make sure they were in working order. Suddenly, one door wasn't working. Yeah, I wasn't buying the coincidence.

But why prevent this door from opening? What good would it serve? Yes, it inconvenienced those of us with staging rooms on this side of the building, but we were still able to get our costumes and instruments loaded into the theater through one of the other doors. Did she hope the frustration of the extra work would distract some of the teams enough that mistakes would be made? That seemed far-fetched.

So what was special about this place?

I studied the large loading dock area again. Cement floor. Metal door. Lots of empty space between here and the large retractable door that led to the stage. When touring companies arrived, they used that enormous door to bring in their set pieces. Those doors weren't opened for our groups. Instead, we used the normal-sized door that led to the staging room hallway. There was no reason for anyone to come into this area unless to load or unload something into the staging rooms or the theater. With the door not working, people automatically went to the other loading dock. Especially since there had been signs posted all over the place to serve as reminders that this door was out of order.

If I wanted to store something in this building that wouldn't be in anyone's way, the off-limits loading dock would be the place to do it. So, what had LuAnn wanted kept out of sight? The boxes were marked with CMHS stickers, but the Showstoppers team had a room to store their belongings. And I couldn't imagine LuAnn or anyone on the team would want to leave some of their things where other teams could potentially damage them. And face it: If Marshall was right and the jars were filled with fancy water, the singers would want to keep those nearby. What good was having several cases of special water in tow if it wasn't close enough for use?

My gut told me water wasn't the clear liquid inside those jars. Otherwise LuAnn wouldn't have hidden them back here or disabled the loading dock until she arranged for someone to pick the boxes up.

But I was still no closer to understanding why.

Unless LuAnn's ghost was haunting this area and decided to give me guidance, I wasn't going to learn anything standing here. Besides, the show would start in half an hour. The police would just have to find the answer to that question on their own. I had a choir to coach and a competition to win.

Chapter 21

The team had never looked better. The girls' silver, blue, and white dresses accented with rhinestones looked fabulous. The boys in their black pants, silver and blue cummerbunds, vests, and bow ties looked dashing. Thanks to Aunt Millie's practiced hand, the makeup and hairstyles looked as if they'd come right off the glossy pages of a fashion magazine. Even the band members with their new accessories looked as if they belonged stepping onto a Broadway stage. Well, this stage wasn't as well-known as the ones lining Times Square, but in terms of importance to these kids, it couldn't be any bigger.

Larry held up his hand to quiet the team. The clock on the wall above him said the first team would take the stage in less than five minutes. Once they were done, we'd have ten minutes to set the risers, get the band in place, and put the pieces needed for the planned costume changes in the wings. Then it would be our turn to impress.

"I just want to tell you how proud I am to be standing here with you today." Larry beamed. "No matter what the scores say, I think you're all winners."

The clichéd speech made a couple of the boys roll their eyes. But while the words might be unoriginal, the joy on Larry's face was undeniable. He had wanted this moment for these kids badly enough that he'd swallowed his pride, admitted his skills weren't strong enough to help this team win, and gone out in search of someone who could. He went looking for a teacher who wouldn't accept less than the best. It was still hard to believe that he had hired me. This was a job I'd never wanted and had thought I was ill-suited for. Yet, here I was, taking my turn standing in front of this team who had worked so hard and come so far.

Would this group impress the judges enough to make it to the final round? It was time to find out.

"Don't forget: I want you to have good diction, lots of emotion, and, most important, you need to have fun. If you're having fun . . ." I let my voice trail off and smiled as the kids said in unison, "The judges will have fun, too."

A year ago, I would have laughed if someone had said I would be standing here enjoying this moment. Just goes to show how far I had come.

"Okay," I said, lifting my eyes to the clock. "Then let's put on a show they'll never forget."

Claire stumbled on a turn. Eric almost missed a step walking down the riser and had to check his balance. And the costume change into the third number left Jeffrey without a bow tie. Minor mistakes. All things that had happened in past competitions. We'd taken first in every one of them. But this was the best of the best. I could only hope that the strong singing, complicated lifts, and high-energy dancing eclipsed the missteps enough to see us through to the next round.

When the kids had changed out of their costumes and had hung them back on the racks, they headed for the theater to watch the rest of the teams perform. I was about to go, too, when Devlyn touched my arm.

"They did good."

I nodded. "It wasn't perfect."

"The judges won't notice. Remember, the closer you are to something, the easier it can be to see the flaws." His expression turned serious. "What time's your flight?"

The reminder of my own upcoming performance made my stomach roil. "Five thirty. The scores should be posted before I leave for the airport."

"If not, I'll make sure you learn the results." He looked as if he wanted to say something more but shook his head.

The silence stretched for several uncomfortable seconds. Finally, I broke it. "I guess we should go see what our competition is doing."

"Yeah. We should do that."

The lobby was devoid of all but a few stragglers getting tickets at Will Call. As I pulled open the door to the theater, Devlyn put his hand on my shoulder before I could head inside.

"Paige, in case I don't get another chance to tell you—good luck tomorrow." He gave me a sad smile. "I hope you get everything you want. You deserve it."

He went to take his seat. I did the same, understanding the words for what they were. Not just a wish of luck, but a way of saying good-bye. As I slid into one of the spots in the back, I realized I wasn't upset. Breaking up with

Devlyn was sad, but my heart wasn't broken, which said louder than words what I should have known all along. The two of us didn't belong together. We needed to move on.

The competition flew by as the teams danced, twirled, and sparkled onstage. Central Memphis High School made the most noticeable mistakes. Missed steps and tentative singing were in evidence. But the minute they were done, everyone in the audience got to their feet. The team's performance was flawed, but they went onstage after being dealt a huge blow. They had earned everyone's admiration.

Before I knew it, all twelve teams had performed and the lunch break had begun. After lunch, the women's division would take the stage. Sometime between lunch and the end of the day the list of teams who made the mixed-division finals would be posted. If the judges spotted the flaws in the other routines that I did, Music in Motion would be back on this stage tomorrow. Unfortunately, when it came to judging, there was no guarantee. All we could do was wait.

The kids were in high spirits when we reassembled in our staging room and then tromped around the corner to get lunch. They professed to be famished. Clearly, they dealt with nerves better than I did because the thought of food made my stomach heave. Still, I ordered a soda and fries so I could enjoy the moment with them. Regardless of whether or not I came back to coach Music in Motion next year, this would be one of my last opportunities to work with this group of kids. Graduation was just weeks away. Soon they'd be off to college—off to live their dreams. I hoped Chessie was right and they would understand my need to live mine.

Once lunch was over, the attitude was a little more

subdued as we went back to the theater in search of the list of finalists. Drat. It hadn't been posted yet. Everyone started to head out the door to the theater, but stopped when I said, "Could you guys wait a minute?"

All eyes turned toward me.

I took a deep breath. "Earlier this week, I received a phone call offering me an audition at the Lyric Opera. The timing isn't convenient, but this was an audition I couldn't turn down. I'll be catching a plane back to Chicago tonight. I hope to still be here when the list is posted. If not, Mr. DeWeese and Mr. O'Shea will let me know the minute the results are announced. If everything goes as planned, I'll sing my audition tomorrow morning and be back here in time for you to take the stage tomorrow night."

The team started talking all at once. A few yelled reminders for me to have fun while auditioning. A couple others reminded me to watch my diction. Not a single member of Music in Motion looked angry or betrayed by my defection. Score one for Chessie.

Laughing, I told them that I wouldn't forget their advice and shooed them off to the theater to watch the next round of the preliminaries. Larry gave me an awkward fist bump before following the kids. The minute I was alone, I shoved my hands in my pockets and let out a relieved sigh. My fingers brushed against the sticker from the loading dock, and I looked up at the clock. I had two hours until I had to go to the airport. Time enough to see whether the police had learned anything new about LuAnn's death or the mysterious boxes from the loading dock. If nothing else, it would give me something to focus on besides worrying about the judges' scores.

I dodged a couple of boys still wearing their tux shirts

and sparkly bow ties and headed to the lobby in search of the Nashville boys in blue. Or girls in blue, as the case may be. Unfortunately, I don't think Officer Durbin was any happier to see me than I was to see her. However, since she was the only law enforcement official in sight, I decided to give talking to her a whirl.

"Officer Durbin," I said with a big smile. She didn't smile back. Great. "I didn't expect to see you again. Are you helping conduct the interviews? The head of the competition told me the police would be talking to everyone who dealt with LuAnn on the day she died."

"The Nashville Police Department is giving this matter the utmost attention. Did you have something you felt you needed to add to your statement? If so, I'd be happy to take a report."

If that was her version of happy, I'd hate to think what sad looked like. Pretending not to notice her lack of enthusiasm, I said, "LuAnn Freeman called a mechanic to fix the loading dock doors. I ran into him earlier and thought there was a chance he saw something important. I'm hoping he took my advice about speaking to one of the detectives and came this way."

"He was here. I'm sure the detective fully appreciates his cooperation as well as yours. Now, if you'll excuse me—"

"I know you're really busy, but I was hoping you might be able to tell me if they've gotten any closer to finding the driver that hit LuAnn? I'm going to be going out of town in a couple of hours, but my team is still going to be here." I gave Officer Durbin my best vulnerable and worried look. "I'd feel a lot less nervous about leaving them behind if I thought this matter was settled."

Officer Durbin studied me and then smiled. I felt a surge of triumph as she said, "I can understand how you'd be worried about your students. But my job is to help close cases, not ease your mind. If you don't mind, I'll get back to it." With that, Officer Durbin stalked off, leaving me standing alone.

Well, crap. If this had happened back home, I could have asked Mike to poke around and see what he could learn. As it stood now, I would just have to wait like everyone else and hope to hear news of an arrest soon.

"There you are."

I turned to see Aunt Millie barreling toward me. "Is the list up?" I asked as my heart plummeted to my feet.

"No." Millie looked over her shoulder at the easel standing outside the theater doors where the finalists would be posted. "I swear, trained monkeys could add up scores faster than these people. Eight scores. Twelve teams. The highest six scores move on. How hard could that possibly be?"

Since almost every competition took hours to do what most first graders with a calculator could handle in less than ten minutes, I had to guess there was more involved than we thought. Either that or the people in charge of posting the scores got their kicks knowing everyone was waiting for them.

"If the list isn't up, why were you looking for me? Did another team try to enlist you for their hair and makeup?" That had happened at two of the regional competitions. Both times, Millie happily sketched makeup designs that complemented the team's costumes and included a list of the Mary Kay products that would be necessary to make the look a reality. No moss growing under Millie's feet.

"Not yet," my aunt said. "But whoever was in charge of the makeup for the Minnesota team should. The lipstick color was all wrong. Under no circumstances does a self-respecting designer pair magenta and orange together."

She sniffed.

I smiled. "Then why were you looking for me?"

"Oh, I wanted to let you know that Aldo will be waiting in the car outside the theater at three thirty to take you to the airport. I'd drive you myself, but I thought you'd rather have me and Killer stay here and look after things for you."

"I'm happy to drive with Aldo." Delighted, actually. Millie's driving always left me worried about whether I'd arrive at my destination in one piece. The only trouble Aldo ever had with a car involved a bomb. The chances of that happening again were slim to none. The odds of Millie getting ticketed for a moving violation were ones every gambler in Vegas would bet on. "We'll just have to make a stop at the hotel so I can get my bag before we go."

"Why don't you give me the key so Aldo can do that for you? That way you have more time to spend looking into that poor lady's death. From what I've heard, the investigators aren't any closer to coming up with a suspect than they were yesterday."

"Who told you that?"

"The director of Central Memphis High School." Millie pointed across the lobby to where Nikki was talking on her cell phone. From the angry look on her face, I was guessing the call wasn't going well.

"Why were you talking to Nikki?" I asked. If the woman didn't want LuAnn helping out with her team, I seriously doubted she would take cosmetics advice from my aunt.

"I overheard her talking to one of her students when I came out of the bathroom. They were standing in that little alcove. The boy kept talking about things ending because of LuAnn's death. He sounded angry and scared, which is understandable considering what's happened this week. I was impressed at the way Nikki kept her voice low and soothing as she told him that endings meant new beginnings and while that was scary she was willing to help him put his life on the right track. You have to admire that."

Yeah. You did.

"Once the kid walked outside to get some fresh air, I walked over, introduced myself, and offered my condolences." Millie looked at Nikki, who was looking satisfied with whatever turn her conversation had taken. "When Nikki realized who I was, she thanked me for trying to help LuAnn and asked if there was anything I'd seen that could help identify the person who ran her down. She was disappointed when I said I didn't get a good look at the car or the driver. That's when she mentioned that she felt the police were just going through the motions on the investigation and that they were wasting their time with talking to people who had never even met LuAnn face-to-face."

"Did she say who?"

Millie shrugged. "There were a bunch of them. A couple of parents who didn't get into town until yesterday, the FedEx delivery guy, and I think there was even a mechanic who fixed one of the theater doors."

"I met the mechanic." I glanced around to see whether

Officer Durbin could hear me. Nope—she was busy talking to Kelly. Neither woman looked all that thrilled about it. "He fixed the loading dock. While he was there, he saw a college kid take some boxes LuAnn left there."

"You think those boxes were the reason LuAnn was killed?"

I shrugged. "I'm not sure how sealed glass jars would prompt anyone to get run over, but stranger things have been known to happen."

"Nikki should be able to shed some light on the boxes since they must have traveled here with her team. Regardless, I hope the police figure it out soon. These kids deserve to end this week without having to worry about something else bad happening."

A couple of the teens she was worrying about came out of the theater and made a beeline for the easel. Still no list. Millie snickered as one of the kids colorfully commented on the competition head's lack of math skills.

"You know," she said with a grin, "I'm glad you had a chance to teach this year. This wasn't the job you wanted, but I think you've become a better performer as a result. And I've had a hell of a good time getting a chance to get to know these kids. It's brought back memories of when I was in high school. They're way better behaved than I was at their age. I would have snuck out of the motel and been in a field somewhere, drinking homemade wine my best friend's father made in his basement. The stuff tasted like lighter fluid, but we felt so grown-up drinking it. Annie still sends me a bottle of homemade brew every year on my birthday as a joke. The joke's on her because I've consumed every single bottle. Still burns my stomach, but it makes me feel like I'm sixteen again. Kind of like being around these kids does." Millie's smile faded. "Look."

I glanced to where Millie pointed and my heart lurched. Christine McCann was standing next to the easel with tape in one hand and a pink piece of paper in the other. The list of finalists for mixed company was going up.

The lobby went dead quiet. All eyes around the expansive space watched Christine tape the paper to the easel and walk away. For a minute no one moved. It was as if people were waiting for someone to be the first to break the tension. So, I did.

That step acted like a starting gun. The dozen or so kids ran across the carpet toward the list. The adults didn't run, but we broke records for speed walking as we hurried toward our goal.

Drat. There were too many people huddled in front of the list. I couldn't see. But shouts of joy and tears of sorrow gave me an idea of some of the results. Several kids from Scott's team were exchanging high fives. Girls from Donna's group were in tears. I shifted to the left and ducked so I could sneak a peek in between the half dozen girls who were currently squealing.

Yes! Six teams were on the list and Music in Motion was at the very top. My kids would get one more performance, and this time it would be winner take all.

———

"When you get back to the hotel, don't forget you need to run the numbers with Megan," I told Larry as I stood next to Aunt Millie's car. My bag was in the backseat.

Aldo was sitting behind the wheel, listening to Killer bark and Millie tell him to be careful. Larry had verified and both he and Jim still had a key to my hotel room to store the instruments and costumes. It was time to go. "Don't let Megan sing, though, no matter what she tells you. She still needs one more day of vocal rest. And try to fix the spacing at the end of the last song. Eric and Chessie weren't in their window."

"I have everything under control, Paige." Larry beamed. He'd been wearing the same deranged grin ever since I'd found him in the back of theater and given him the results. "Devlyn and I will hold down the fort until you get back. Just make sure you text me as soon as the audition is over. The kids are going to be going crazy waiting to hear how it went." His cheeks flushed. "Well, maybe not just the kids. I'm going to be wondering, too. Break a leg."

"Thanks," I said, looking over his shoulder. Devlyn hadn't come to say good-bye or wish me luck. Climbing into the pink car, I yelled, "See you tomorrow." And off to the airport we went.

"You should be so proud," Aldo said, keeping his eyes firmly on the road in front of him. "The team did good. Tomorrow will be even better. And Millie says the police are getting closer to catching the person behind that poor woman's death. If there is anything to worry about with the police, my Millie will take care of it. You have only to worry about looking *bellissima* and singing. Yes?"

"I'll try to do both," I promised. Then, since I couldn't help being curious, I asked, "Was Millie awake when you got back to the room last night? Did you get a chance to talk?"

Aldo gave me a toothy smile. "She was awake, but we no have time to talk much. Your aunt was interested in a more . . . How do you say? Nonverbal communication?"

Eek. That was what I got for being nosy. Next time I'd just wait to find out what happened.

"But," Aldo said, flipping on the turn signal, "at breakfast, I say to your aunt that I am thinking about exchanging the ring for a pair of earrings. That way it no go to waste, but she tells me not to. Then she gives me a wink. That is good, no?"

A definitive yes to Aldo's marriage proposal would be better, but, hey, this was superior to Millie packing Aldo's underwear and putting it on the front stoop without sealing the box. Although, the memory of watching a squirrel build a nest from Aldo's tighty whities was going to make me laugh for years to come.

"Oh." Aldo snapped his fingers as he steered us under the sign that directed us to my terminal. "Before I forget. Your aunt arranged for someone to pick you up at the airport. You just have to wait outside the baggage claim. *Capisci*?"

"*Capiche*. Who's picking me up?"

"She did not say, but I am guessing you will know them when you see them." Aldo pulled up to the curb and wished me luck. I kissed him on the cheek and climbed out.

Chicago, here I come.

Chapter 22

The woman seated next to me on the plane snored all the way from Nashville to Chicago, so I was thankful the flight wasn't that long. It was still light when the plane touched down and I turned my cell phone back on. Every time I flew, I was tempted to leave it active just to prove that the device wasn't dangerous. But at the last minute I always wimped out. I was 99.9 percent sure my phone was incapable of making the plane crash, but that .1 percent got me every time.

As soon as my phone powered up, I heard several dings. I had text messages. Lots of them. Two were from my manager, Alan, confirming the audition time and asking me to meet him at the Wacker Drive entrance of the Lyric thirty minutes before my audition time. The message made my nerves jangle. Managers set up auditions. They didn't attend them. Knowing that Alan felt it necessary to be present in body as well as spirit made me more than a little nervous.

The plane came to a stop, and I rolled my eyes as everyone stood and jockeyed for position in the aisles even though the plane doors were still locked up tight. Those who didn't get into the aisle soon enough stood with their necks crooked at a forty-five-degree angle to avoid bashing their heads into the bins above. I'd learned long ago to just sit and wait until it was my turn to leave. Disembarking two minutes earlier wasn't worth the frustration or the kink in my neck.

While waiting for my turn, I sent a quick message back, confirming that I was in the city and would meet him at the appointed time. I followed that up with a teasing question, asking whether he was coming because he didn't trust me not to get lost inside the building if left on my own.

As I waited for Alan to respond, I checked my other texts. One from Larry reporting a successful rehearsal. Another from Millie reminding me that she'd arranged for someone to pick me up from the airport and to wait until they arrived. And ten messages from assorted members of my team wishing me luck on my audition. By the time I'd read half of them, I had started to sniffle. After reading the final message, my eyes were filled with tears.

I swiped at my runny nose as the doors opened and people began filing out. The guy in the row across from me must have decided my tears meant I was on the verge of a nervous breakdown, because he insisted I go in front of him. Who said chivalry was dead?

Even though the flight hadn't been very long, it felt wonderful to stretch my legs, so I didn't mind the walk to baggage claim. A gust of cool air hit me as I went outside to search for my mysterious chauffeur. Aldo had said I'd know the person when I saw them, which sounded reasonable. Of course, now that I was here at O'Hare, it occurred to me that cars weren't allowed to park and wait for arriving friends and family. Police officers standing outside each terminal made sure of that. Unless I recognized the car the person drove, I wasn't going to have a clue whether the car driving past was supposed to be stopping for me. This was a problem.

Or not.

My heart did a funny little skip as I noticed the black Mustang parked at the curb and the dark-haired man standing next to it. The man was wearing a beat-up gray sports coat while chatting up the policewoman who was currently shooing cars away from the curb. Well, all cars but his. Because he was a fellow cop. My mystery driver was none other than Prospect Glen's own answer to *Law & Order*—Detective Michael Kaiser.

His curly hair blew in the breeze as he scanned the area with those dark eyes that more often than not looked at me with a mixture of annoyance and desire. But when those eyes landed on me, I saw only a mild pleasure. Pushing aside the irrational disappointment swelling inside, I headed over with a wave.

"You look surprised to see me," he said, sliding my bag off my shoulder and stowing it in the trunk.

Buckling in, I admitted, "Aunt Millie didn't tell me you were the one picking me up."

"That's my fault." He waved to the policewoman and pulled away from the curb. "When she asked if I'd be willing to give you a lift to your house, the audition, and back to the airport, I warned her you might not be excited about the idea, since . . ." He shrugged. "Well, you know."

"Since you told me you thought you were in love with me and stopped returning my calls."

Mike laughed and flashed a boyish grin. "I've missed the way you're never afraid to pin me to the wall." His eyes turned serious as he watched me in the rearview mirror. "I've missed you."

The simple sincerity with which those words were said made me bite back the snarky comment that immediately sprang to mind. Calmly, I said, "I've been here. You were the one who stepped away."

"Guilty as charged." Mike glanced over at me and then back at the road. "I'm sorry about that. There were some things that I needed to think through."

"And you couldn't think if you answered my phone calls?" The hurt I'd buried had bubbled up.

"I told myself I couldn't." He changed lanes and hit the gas. "That was probably a lie, but it was easier to believe than the truth."

"What truth?"

Mike sighed. "This wasn't the way I pictured having this conversation. I was going to take you out to dinner and explain what happened."

He changed lanes again. His eyes were focused straight ahead, but I could tell by the way they narrowed that he was thinking through the situation. Calculating what to say and how to say it to get the reaction he was looking for. Two things that as a homicide detective he was trained to do.

After what seemed like an hour but the clock on the dash claimed was only two minutes, he blew out a breath and said, "I was scared."

I blinked. "Scared? Of what?" Killer? If that was the

case, I could understand Mike's fear. Having to come to a house where the dog pretended to be Cujo was bound to freak out most sane people.

Mike smirked. "For a smart lady you can be awfully dense. You, Paige. I was scared of you."

"Me? Why?"

He zipped the Mustang onto the exit ramp, hung a left, and steered the car into the McDonald's parking lot. Putting the car in park, he shifted so those dark eyes were now focused squarely on me. "I've dated a lot of women. Most of them liked the idea of being with a cop. I guess there's something exciting about dating a guy with a gun."

I'd never thought that, but hey—it took all types.

"I always figured I'd get married someday in the future when I found the right woman. Then I met you and realized the joke was on me. For the first time a woman had gotten under my skin and made me think about settling down, only she wasn't interested in settling."

Mike looked as if he expected me to comment. Too bad I was totally lost. Since honesty was the best policy, I said, "I don't understand."

"Why did I know you were going to say that?" He rubbed the back of his neck. "I knew you were a singer. The background information I'd dug up on you after we first met told me you were good at it."

"You ran a background check on me?" Yikes.

"You were a primary witness on a murder case and a potential suspect. Of course I ran a background check."

Well, when he put it that way. Still, I couldn't help feeling a little wigged out. The man probably knew everything about me down to my credit score and underwear size. All I knew about him was that he drove a muscle car and didn't arrest me for my forays into snooping no matter how angry I made him.

"My point is that I thought I understood what you did for a living and what that meant. Then I heard you sing."

Um . . . "What's wrong with my singing?" With the biggest audition of my life tomorrow, I wasn't sure I could handle a no-holds-barred critique, but I'd opened the door and now Mike was walking through it.

"I don't know jack about classical music. No one dresses in fancy clothes for the concerts I go to. Give me Bruce Springsteen over a bunch of snooty songs any day. But when I heard you practicing at your aunt's house . . ." Mike took my hand in his and held it when I tried to pull away. "I can still hear that song and feel what I felt. Your aunt used to sing your praises and tell me how wonderful you were. I figured she was exaggerating. But she wasn't. You're better than she described. And you were better still the night I watched you on that stage. That's when I knew."

"Knew what?"

"That you were out of my league. And that someday soon you were going to get your big break and you'd leave Chicago and me behind. Which is why I left first. Dealing with emotional issues has never been my strong suit."

No kidding.

"So what do you think?"

I had no idea what to think. A half hour ago I'd never thought I'd see Mike again. Now here he was telling me that he not only believed that I would make it as a singer, but that he wasn't good enough for me. The change of direction had given me whiplash.

"I'm not sure what to say." Which was perhaps the

understatement of the year. "I thought you'd lost interest and didn't want to tell me. I moved on."

"I know." Mike's fingers tightened on mine. The vein in his left temple began to twitch. "When your aunt called to ask if I'd meet you at the airport, she mentioned that you and Devlyn have gotten serious. She's expecting you to announce your engagement any day."

"My engagement?" I shook my head. "But—"

"I figure I'd missed my chance, but I wanted you to know how I feel before you decide to walk down the aisle." He pulled his hand away and reached for the gear-shift. The set of his jaw told me he considered this case closed even though to me it had just opened. Now I had to decide what the verdict would be.

It took until Mike steered into Millie's neighborhood with its sprawling, meticulously cared-for lawns for me to sort through my feelings. Joy that Mike thought I was talented. Resentment that he made the decision to walk away without ever asking me what I wanted from my future. Anger that it took Aunt Millie's fictionalized account of my relationship status to get him to speak up. And nerves. Because the fluttering in my chest and the hopeful yearning I felt told me that Mike and I had a whole lot more to talk about.

Mike parked the car in Millie's driveway, got out, and grabbed my bag out of the back. When I slipped the key in the lock and turned the handle, he handed me my duf-fel. "Your aunt said your audition was at nine o'clock but that you'd like to arrive early. I figure if I'm here by seven fifteen, I should be able to get you downtown in plenty of time. But if you want to leave earlier, let me know."

When he started to walk away, I asked, "What about dinner?"

Mike stopped and turned. "What about it?"

The annoyed confusion on his face made me smile. "You said you planned on talking to me over dinner."

He jammed his hands in his pockets and gave a half-hearted shrug. "You need to focus on your audition. I know how important it is."

Mike was right. I needed to focus. The audition was important. But so was this. "Well, then, I expect a rain check because we still have a lot to talk about."

"Like what?"

"Like this." I stepped forward, stood on my tiptoes, and brushed my lips against his. Taking a step back, I almost laughed at Mike's stunned expression.

"I don't understand."

Now I did laugh. "My aunt might have exaggerated my relationship status a bit."

Mike's eyes locked onto mine. "By how much?"

"Are we measuring in miles or kilometers?"

Mike moved fast. Before I had finished speaking he had closed the distance. His lips touched mine with a fierceness that made my head spin and my body hum. The kiss lasted only a couple of seconds, and when Mike moved away I put my hand on the door to steady myself.

For a moment we just looked at each other. Finally, he flashed me a smile. "Get some rest," he said as he headed for his car and slid behind the wheel. "Tomorrow's a big day."

He couldn't be more right. Once I shut the front door, I made a beeline for the living room to sing through the pieces I'd selected. If I wanted to make a change, now was the time to decide.

I propped my repertoire book on Aldo's shiny grand piano and sang a couple of scales to warm up. Then I plunked out the opening chord to Musetta's aria and started to sing. Since I always performed better with an audience, I directed my attention to the four glassy-eyed dogs reclining near the French doors.

Like Killer, they had all been champions on the dog show circuit. Unlike Killer, their teeth could no longer do damage since the animals in question had passed to the great beyond some time ago. Determined to keep their spirits, if not their bodies, alive, Millie had had the dogs taxidermied. Millie thought the dead dogs were adorable. Killer thought they were creepy. On this point, Killer and I were in complete accord. Still, the dogs made a respectful audience as I hit the high B-flat, portamentoed down to the final note, and flipped to the next song.

By the time I went to bed, I had sung my pieces twice, eaten the leftover manicotti Aldo had made for Sunday dinner, and picked out my audition attire. I had also talked to Millie, who swore the kids were all tucked in their rooms despite the earlier excitement.

"Excitement?" I asked. "What kind of excitement?"

"I probably shouldn't have mentioned anything. I don't want you to worry." Uh-oh. "The hotel staff interrupted the very end of rehearsal because housekeeping found the door to your room unlocked and the room trashed."

"Someone trashed my hotel room?"

"Well, technically nothing was destroyed. Just thrown around a bit."

Oh. That's all.

"Larry and Jim think the kids in the band had something to do with it since they were the last ones to have your extra key. They swear they left it in on the drum case in our staging room, but when Larry and I drove over there to check, we couldn't find it."

"You're not convinced that the kids were behind this."

Millie paused. I could tell she was weighing her need to gossip with my need to focus on tomorrow's audition. Gossip won out every time. "Let's just say I think lots of people stopped by the staging room before we came back to the hotel."

"But why would they take a hotel room key out of the room and how would they even know which room it went to?" The hotel key cards were all identical.

"Larry and Jim spent a long time debating whether the instruments should be stored in the staging room or go back to your room at the hotel. Someone could have overheard them."

If Larry and Jim used their normal decibel level to discuss the matter, I'm certain everyone within twenty square blocks heard them.

"Do you remember who you saw around while that was going on?" I had no idea what would cause anyone to toss my hotel room. It was easier to think a bunch of rowdy high school boys had done it as a prank, but just because I wanted to believe something didn't make it true.

"The handsome coach with the tan face stopped by with Donna Hilty. I was going to ask for Donna's auto-graph, but she didn't look like she was in the mood. Although she looked pretty happy when she heard you'd left town."

I wasn't surprised. Scott and Donna would probably be happy never to see me again.

"Who else?"

"Nikki dropped by with another director whose team made it to the finals. Larry and Devlyn also talked to a couple of people who are involved in running the competition. The head honcho looked annoyed to hear you'd gone back to Chicago. If I had to put money down, I'd say she was the one who broke into your room."

Christine? "Why?"

"She asked a whole lot of questions about where you were going, when you'd be back, and what you took with you when you left. She was intense, and the questions felt a little strange. From the look on her face, I'd say the other competition official she was with thought so, too. I bet if I talked to her, she'd give me the scoop on her boss."

"That's not necessary," I said.

"I know, but I can't help being curious."

"Well, keep your curiosity in check until the competition is over," I warned. "Christine McCann has already threatened to have the team blackballed once. I'd rather not give her reason to do it again."

"Don't worry. Nothing is going to happen. Trust me. I won't give Christine McCann a reason to penalize these kids. Now, get off this phone and get some rest so you can knock the Lyric Opera's artistic director off his feet."

Despite the travel and show fatigue, sleep was slow to come. My mind was too revved from my encounter with Mike and the mystery of the glass jar boxes to settle down. Why would LuAnn bring boxes marked as belonging to her team's high school to this competition and store them in the loading dock only to have them picked up and taken away?

Huh. Maybe it wasn't just this competition she brought boxes to. I hit the lights and walked over to the ornate desk where my laptop was sitting to call up the same search I'd done on LuAnn down in Nashville.

From what Nikki said, despite Nikki's assurances that the team did not need the help, LuAnn had traveled to all six regional competitions this year. Two were located in Tennessee. The others took place in Kentucky, Ohio, North Carolina, and Texas. Feeling like I was on to something, I did a search for the other activities with which LuAnn's children had been associated. All the sporting teams and social organizations her kids participated in required a high amount of in-state and out-of-state travel. And from the lists I found on various websites, LuAnn always appeared to volunteer as chaperone. Either she was parent of the year or she had an ulterior motive. I knew which one I was betting on.

If I had to wager a guess, I'd say LuAnn had a side business. One that required her to transport boxes like the ones Marshall saw from Memphis to various places around the country. Normal people used FedEx. Unless, of course, the shipment contained something illegal that the shipper didn't want being searched. Then it would make sense to transport the items yourself. And what better cover for lugging boxes around the country than traveling with a show choir or sporting team. If my speculation was correct, it would explain why LuAnn was desperate to snag the Central Memphis High School assistant coaching gig. Her daughter would be graduating, taking with her the excuse for the travel. Being a coach was the only way to continue with business as usual.

My brain told me this explanation was far-fetched, but deep in my gut I thought I was right. If so, the next question was what was the clear liquid in the jars? Millie used to drink homemade wine out of those kinds of containers, but homemade wine wasn't illegal. However, a quick Google search told me that while brewing homemade alcohol wasn't necessarily illegal, selling it without the proper federal and state permits was. Doing so could result in hefty fines and jail time. Transporting it across state lines could raise the penalties a whole lot higher. LuAnn could be using the show choir and her kids' other travel teams to do both. If so, she must be doing pretty well at it considering she was able to quit her social work job and still afford her impressive home.

Assuming I was correct, I had to ask myself whether someone could have learned about LuAnn's illegal transport and sale of the alcohol and killed her to put a stop to it. Or could she have been run down by one of her alcohol operation associates? Nikki's conversation with the young man who knew LuAnn seemed to suggest that she might know about the business and that she might even want a cut of the action. But Nikki had been onstage when the light bar dropped. Could someone else be behind the falling beam? And what did any of this have to do with LuAnn blackmailing Donna and Scott or my hotel room getting ransacked? Sadly, I didn't have any of the answers, but I was determined that after I finished my audition tomorrow and got back to Nashville, I would help the police find them before a murderer had the chance to strike again.

Chapter 23

Somehow I managed to get enough sleep. Either that or I was so caffeinated and filled with nervous energy that I wasn't feeling fatigued as I hopped into the shower to wash my hair and do my vocal warm-ups. The old saying that everyone sounded good when they sang in the shower was true. With all the tile and glass, bathrooms were acoustically ideal for singing. Where carpet soaked in sound, tile and other hard surfaces reflected it, making every note sound rich and full and fabulous. Bathroom singing was the ultimate confidence builder. I just had to hold on to that confidence until I finished singing for Sir Andrew David and I'd be set.

Mike rang the door at seven fifteen on the dot. The appreciative look he gave me when I walked out wearing an electric blue dress with a cinched waist, cap sleeves, and a slightly flared skirt made my confidence level rise again. Classical singers often wore black or other subdued colors for auditions. I'd originally chosen a dress in a deep gray for that reason, but changed my mind at the last minute. Maybe all those sparkly show choir outfits had rubbed off on me. For years I'd gone to auditions looking like everyone else. This time, if I was going down in flames, I was doing it my way.

Mike scored more points by having an extra-large vanilla latte and a cinnamon bagel waiting for me in the car. I tried to stay calm as his Mustang ate up the miles between Millie's house and downtown Chicago. For a while it was working as Mike regaled me with funny details of the most recent case he'd closed. But that changed when the skyline rose into view. I clutched my black repertoire binder to my chest as the buildings grew larger with every passing mile. Mike kept talking. I made sounds like I was listening, but Mike could have been reciting the Gettysburg Address and I wouldn't have known it. Yep. It was official. I was starting to panic.

Strike that. I was way beyond panicked as Mike came to a stop in front of the Lyric's main entrance. Near the door, tapping buttons in his phone, was my manager, Alan Held. This was it. I was going to be ill.

"I'm going to find a place to park. Text me when you're done and I'll come back to get you. Okay?"

I saw Alan squint at the car and smile as he spotted me inside. "What?" I asked, feeling my mind go in and out of focus. "Oh. Yeah. That sounds great." Witty was my middle name.

"Hey." Mike flipped on his cop lights to stop the honking from the car behind us and turned toward me. "This guy you're auditioning for is supposed to be good, right?"

"The best."

Mike gave me a crooked smile and reached out to brush my cheek with the back of his knuckles. "Then you don't have anything to worry about. He's going to know how special you are the minute you sing the first note." Leaning in, he brushed his lips against mine and said, "That was for luck. Not that you need any. Now go show the Lyric Opera what you're made of."

He unlatched my seat belt, and I did the only thing I could. I got out, straightened my shoulders, and smiled up at my manager, who had walked to the curb to meet me.

"You made it." Alan leaned down, gave me a peck on the cheek, and watched Mike's Mustang as it pulled away.

I shivered in the cool spring breeze. "I'd have to be crazy to miss this opportunity."

"Yes, you would." A lock of ash blond hair fell over Alan's forehead as he put his hand on my back and ushered me toward the door. "Sir Andrew is waiting for us upstairs. He'd like you to run through the pieces you prepared. Once you're finished, he'll probably have you sing your selections again with different acting choices. Sir Andrew likes performers who are willing to take risks. Since you're not afraid to take on a murderer or two, you should be exactly what he is looking for."

My heels clicked against the tile as Alan led me across the enormous lobby. The chandeliers overhead glistened. This building never failed to inspire amazement and hope. "Did you fly into Chicago just to tell me that?" If so, the man really went above and beyond the call of duty.

"No. That's just a bonus." He stopped walking. "I want Sir Andrew to see me here with you. He'll understand what that means."

"What does that mean?" That Alan didn't trust me to meet Sir Andrew on my own?

"That you aren't just another client. You're the real deal. I'm here to make sure he doesn't assume any different. Got it?" His deep blue eyes twinkled, and my heart soared.

"Got it."

"Good. Now get in there and show him that you're the next Lyric star."

I sang. I strutted. I sneered. I sighed. Then Sir Andrew asked in his fabulous British accent for me to do it all over again.

He was just as debonair and dashing up close as he appeared when he was at the conductor's podium. I tried not to let my awe of his standing in the music community overwhelm me as I turned tragic songs into parodies and pretended to seduce my accompanist. When it was over, Sir Andrew complimented me on my singing, thanked me for my time, and escorted me to the door. That was that. An actress dreamed of the moment when a director would point to her during an audition and tell her the part was hers. Maybe that had happened in real life, but never to me. Today was the same. The proverbial "don't call us; we'll call you."

Alan wasn't concerned by the lack of conversation after the audition. He gave me the typical lines. Sir Andrew had a flight to catch. He'd heard everything he needed to. I had performed flawlessly, and no matter what came of this audition, he was certain Sir Andrew would keep me on the radar for future roles.

I smiled like a pro, sent a text to Mike that I was ready to leave, and assured Alan I wasn't disappointed by the lack of star treatment. After all, I wasn't a star. I was Paige Marshall, show choir director. Still, as much as I had grown calluses over the rejections that had piled up over the years, I felt the ache that came with wondering whether I was good enough for Sir Andrew. Self-doubt was just as much a part of the business as the applause. Sometimes more.

"My ride's here," I said as Mike's Mustang roared to the curb.

Alan nodded. "Have a safe trip. I'm going to go back inside and see if Sir Andrew is willing to share his limo to the airport. That'll give me a chance to talk to him about the roles you're appropriate for not only now but in future productions." He kissed my cheek again as Mike got out of the car and waved. "I'll call you later to give you the news and find out how your choir performed in the finals."

This time my smile was real. "How do you know my team made the finals?"

"A good manager knows all." With that he disappeared behind the large gold and glass Lyric Opera House doors. Taking a deep breath, I walked to Mike's car and climbed in.

To his credit, Mike didn't ask any questions. He just drove. Which was good because I wasn't sure what to tell him. If Devlyn had been sitting beside me, the two of us could have talked about the agony that came with waiting for news after an audition. We could grab a drink and compare war stories and I'd know I was talking to someone who understood exactly how I felt.

I wasn't sure how to explain the emotions that I felt after an audition. Pride. Despair. Hope. Angst. Just because the audition went well didn't mean I'd get a contract. It was impossible to know what a director was looking for when casting a part. Once a decision was made, Alan would be able to get some feedback about why I was or wasn't chosen. Until then, I would do my best to forget that I'd even had an audition or that I'd wanted this opportunity more than anything I'd wanted before in my life.

We were halfway to O'Hare when I finally said, "Thanks for giving me time to decompress."

Mike glanced at me. "I figured you needed to go over the audition piece by piece in your mind. That's what I do after I visit a crime scene. I sit and mentally walk through everything I saw and every word I heard spoken, making sure I covered all the angles. No matter how hard I try to be perfect, I always wonder if I used the right tone to make a witness feel comfortable or nervous enough to share what they know or if I could have looked harder to find more evidence."

Weird. I'd never thought of Mike as the questioning-himself-or-his-abilities type. "The only difference about the self-doubt is that your job deals with life and death. In the grand scheme of things, singing and dancing are trivial."

Mike shook his head. "It's your work. There's nothing trivial about that. And I'm betting everyone in the audience of *The Messiah* still remembers how you made them feel. You provide inspiration and an escape from everyday worries. If that isn't important, I don't know what is."

If Mike was looking to score points, he did. Big-time. My heart turned over as he took one hand off the wheel and held it out for mine.

How strange, I thought, looking at the way our hands fit together. Devlyn seemed so perfect for me on paper.

Theater background. Check.

Love of music and dance. Check.

Attractive and intelligent. Check. Check.

Yet, here I was with Mike, contemplating the possibility of a real future together. It just went to show that you never knew how life was going to turn out. That shouldn't have surprised me. Nothing about this week had gone as I'd suspected. I mean, who would have thought there would be a potential alcohol-smuggling ring and murder at the performing arts center?

Since I wasn't interested in regaling Mike with more of my audition neurosis, I opted to use the last leg of our journey to the airport to tell him about the past couple of days. Mike rolled his eyes when I told him about Millie bringing Killer to the hotel. He frowned when I talked about the damaged costumes and fallen light bar, and almost growled when I described my attempt and failure to save LuAnn's life.

"Whatever possessed you to go to a meeting at night with a person whose identity you didn't know?"

Out of everything, that was what he'd chosen to focus on? "I wasn't—"

"And why were you examining the loading dock and questioning a potential witness when the police were already investigating the crime?" Mike's cheeks turned red and shiny. It had been months since I'd last seen the expression on his face, but I recognized it immediately. Mike was ready to blow.

Well, he wasn't the only one. Part of me had forgotten the reason why Mike and I clashed so frequently during our encounters. I remembered now. Pulling my hand away, I said, "I'll have you know that if I hadn't, the witness would never have known to talk to the police or told me about the boxes."

"The boxes you *think* were filled with an unknown type of illegal alcohol that the victim was selling to some guy who might or might not have been a college kid."

When he put it that way, my deductive reasoning didn't sound so fabulous.

"Tell me this, Ms. Marple." Mike's sarcasm made me ball my hands into fists. "How would your Memphis stage mom have the kind of connections to run an illegal liquor ring? From what it sounds like, she was the white-picket-fence and bake-sale type. Most people like that don't run around with criminals, and it isn't like they're posting for black market partners on craigslist."

"I don't know," I admitted. But when Mike gave me a smug grin, I came up with something. "The victim used to be a social worker for the city of Memphis. Most likely, she met a number of people who were used to breaking the law. It doesn't take a huge leap of logic to believe she was enlisted by one of them to help with their enterprise."

"It's a good thing you aren't a cop." Mike rolled his eyes. "Your would've's and could-bes would make the courts toss you on your ass. Cops need pesky things like evidence and facts and the chance to investigate without well-meaning but misguided women with an unhealthy curiosity level poking their attractive but unnecessary noses in their cases."

"I wasn't—" The sound of my phone made me stop talking. Thank God, I thought, fishing my cell out of my purse. This argument was good for taking my mind off waiting for my manager to contact me, but it was making me seriously rethink the possibility of a future with Mike. I looked down at the screen. Aunt Millie was calling to get an update on my audition.

"Hi, Aunt Millie." I glared at Mike. "I'm sorry I didn't call earlier. The audition went well and—"

"*Scusa*, Paige."

I blinked at the Italian voice. "Aldo? Sorry; I thought you were my aunt. Are my students okay?"

"*Si*. The students are fine. Your aunt is why I am calling. She asked me to drive with her and Killer to the theater building so she could talk to the lady who is the head of the competition."

Oh no. I'd told her not to talk to Christine. "What happened?" I braced for the worst.

"Well, your aunt and Killer went inside the building. When they no come out after thirty minutes I go in. Killer was in the lobby with the woman your aunt went to meet."

"Where was Millie?"

"Well, that is the problem. You see, no one has seen your aunt." Aldo's breath caught. "She is a-missing."

Chapter 24

Something had happened to Aunt Millie.

Fear punched into my heart, stealing my breath. "Are you sure?" I whispered.

Mike took his eyes off the road and gave me a hard look.

"The lady in charge had the entire building searched. I even took Killer to see if he could find her. But she is nowhere."

In the background I heard Killer let out a howl that turned into a heartbreaking whimper. It was that sound that made this real. My hands shook. My throat tightened, and tears built behind my eyes. When the first one fell, Mike pulled to the side of the road and took the phone out of my hands.

"Aldo?" he asked, putting the car in park. "It's Mike Kaiser. What's going on?"

Mike asked dozens of questions. When he finally hung

up, he took my cold hand in his, promised me that everything would be okay, and punched the button that made the cop lights flare to life. Up until that moment, I'd thought the scariest driver on the planet was my aunt. Mike proved me wrong. The car zipped forward and around traffic as Mike pulled his own cell out of his pocket and started dialing. Mike looked and sounded calm and cool as he drove his car into short-term parking while at the same time ordering someone on the other end of the line to call the Nashville PD.

By the time he'd parked the car, I had a newfound respect for NASCAR drivers and their ability to deal with high speeds. I also had a new appreciation for Mike's ability to drop any signs of frustration from our earlier conversation and focus on the problem at hand. And part of the problem was me, because I was having a hard time pulling it together. Millie and Aldo needed me to be strong, smart, and resourceful. But no matter how hard I tried, I couldn't get the tears to stop falling. Aunt Millie was my support system. She believed in me like no one else. I wasn't sure what I would do if it turned out she wasn't found. Or worse, if she was found . . .

"Hey." Mike put down his phone and wiped a tear from my cheek. "Your aunt is going to be okay. I just talked to the Nashville Police Department. The head detective on the hit-and-run case is going to give me a call and let me know what's going on. He was already on scene when your aunt vanished. Technically, the police can't officially rule that she's a missing person until twenty-four hours have passed, but with everything else going on, they're treating her as a person of interest and using that technicality to start a search. In the meantime, the two of us are going to go over every detail you can remember from this week. If the cops haven't found Millie by the time we land, we'll have come up with a few thoughts about where else to look."

"We?" I asked as he grabbed my bag out of the trunk.

For the first time since Mike had talked to Aldo, he smiled. "Yeah. We. Because there's no way in hell I'd ever let you go through this alone. Come on."

Somehow Mike not only managed to get me moved to an earlier flight; he also got himself the seat right next to me. Flashing a badge had its advantages. Forty-five minutes after entering the airport, we were taxiing on the runway and headed for Nashville. En route, Mike kept me calm by writing down a step-by-step account of the week's events. I relived everything from the drive on the bus, the request to teach a master class, to the conversation I'd had with Millie last night. When I was done with the timeline, I let out a sigh of relief. But Mike wasn't finished. The questions he asked were baffling. Frustrating, even. What did it matter what LuAnn was wearing when she accused me of destroying the costumes? But I answered every question because Mike was the expert and Millie's life could be on the line. Nothing was more important than that.

The pilot announced our descent, and Mike stopped asking questions. He just studied the list. Occasionally, he made a note to himself. Every time he frowned, I stiffened as I waited for him to make some amazing revelation or reveal something terrible. By the fifth time, I turned and stared out the window at the ground far below. Millie was down there somewhere. I wanted to believe that Mike could help find her, but I couldn't see how. Yes, he was a cop, but he wasn't from Nashville. He didn't know the parties involved in this case. All he knew was that LuAnn was wearing a pink shirt when she accused me of the mad-seamstress routine and a red one that matched her boots when she was killed later that night.

I blinked. LuAnn had changed her shirt. Now that I thought about it, LuAnn wasn't only wearing a different shirt. Her makeup had been different, and she'd changed her pants. She'd been wearing slacks instead of blue jeans. From what I remembered, the look wasn't sexy. It was professional. Well, as much as a person could look professional after being run over by a car. None of the parents who came on trips with Music in Motion bothered to spruce up after the day of rehearsals was over. They were too tired after refereeing teenagers to care what they were wearing. I know that was how I always felt.

But after a day of volunteering at registration, playing with scissors, helping with rehearsal, and almost being beaned with a light bar, LuAnn had altered her look and come back to the theater. The lack of a plunging neckline and sexy heels made me believe it wasn't a man she was meeting. At least not one she was interested in. LuAnn was at the theater to conduct business, and the wardrobe was chosen to make sure she was taken seriously.

Who had she been meeting? Obviously not the guy coming to get the boxes. A college-age kid in a hoodie sweatshirt wasn't someone LuAnn would bother to dress up for. Me? Yeah, right. Even if she was my mystery caller, intent on threatening or harassing me, I doubted LuAnn was impressed with me enough to undergo a transformation. No, the person she was looking to impress had to be the one behind the wheel of the car.

The car.

I'd been so focused on the missing purse detail and the boxes filled with mason jars that I'd overlooked the car. Mike had asked a dozen questions about it. The size. The make. The model. The color. I couldn't be very specific about any of it. But that wasn't the point. The point was that LuAnn was mowed down by a car. That meant the person driving it was most likely local or one of the volunteers who came to Nashville early, because most coaches and students came in vans or buses to these events.

Of the people I'd talked to about LuAnn, the ones who were from Nashville were Christine, Donna, and Kelly. Christine might have had cause to bash LuAnn with her bumper, but I couldn't see her cast in that role. Not unless she'd missed her calling as a world-class actress. Her surprise over LuAnn's death and the cause of it had felt too real.

Donna? The woman might have been willing to do whatever it took to keep her reality dating show, but she had an alibi. She and Scott claimed to have been together, schmoozing a new potential sponsor for the contest, during that time. Would they lie for each other? You betcha. But I was betting they were telling the truth since there was a third party who, if questioned, would have to verify their story. While they might lie to keep each other out of jail, I didn't think the money guy would be interested in risking his current address and wardrobe for orange jumpsuits and a room with a view encased by bars.

That left Kelly and her sparkly jewelry. Kelly who had listened at our staging room door. Who worked year-round on this competition and would have known about

LuAnn's threats to have the sponsors pull their cash. If that had happened, Kelly would not only have been saddened to see the students lose this creative outlet that she and her husband had helped create; she would also lose her job.

Huh. Her job. Why did Kelly have a midlevel job for an organization that her husband and she helped create? If I remembered the bio from the competition website correctly, Kelly had only been working as a member of the office staff for a few years. Could that have been just after her husband, daughter, and granddaughter were killed in the car crash? I was pretty sure that it was. The sparkles on Kelly's fingers suggested money wasn't the reason behind her employment. The need to stay busy and connected to her family was. And LuAnn put that connection at risk. LuAnn threatened not only the financial future but the reputation of the organization that Kelly's husband and she had together helped create. The organization that was one of the few things she had left of her family. Did I think Kelly was the type to sit back and take that threat lightly? No. No, I really didn't. And if Millie went to talk to Christine about my ransacked room and ran into Kelly instead . . .

As the plane wheels hit the tarmac, I said, "I think I know who killed LuAnn Freeman and who kidnapped Aunt Millie."

I had to run to keep up with Mike as he barreled through the terminal, toward the exit. All while we walked, Mike talked to the lead detective on the case and I read my texts, which told me that, though Devlyn and Larry had been informed about my aunt's disappearance, my students were in the dark. Good. I didn't want them to be upset. Between the dozens of texts from Devlyn, Larry, Chessie, and the rest of the team, I almost missed the one sent by a vaguely familiar number.

I stopped walking as I realized why I knew that number. It was the same one that called and told me to meet at the theater on Tuesday night. Ignoring the people swearing as they walked around me, I tapped the screen to display the message sent an hour ago.

> Let's trade. Your aunt for the bag. 3:00 at
> Parthenon. Don't be late.

The bag? What bag? Aside from what was in my hotel room, the only bag I had was currently on my shoulder. Kelly wasn't going to be interested in my toothbrush, driver's license, and sheet music. She wanted something specific. Something, if I had to guess, that would incriminate her in LuAnn's death. A bag she must have been looking for when she stole the band boys' key and ransacked my room.

Suddenly, I knew exactly what Kelly was looking for. LuAnn's missing purple purse. The purse that LuAnn never let out of her sight. The purse I told the police was missing after she was run down. I'd assumed the person in the car must have taken it before they raced away. According to this text, I was mistaken. Unfortunately, I didn't have the purse. So who did? And how was I going to keep Millie safe without it?

"I'll be there," I typed back. I wasn't sure what I would do when I got there, but I'd just have to jump off that bridge when I came to it.

A new message appeared. "Come alone or else."

Clearly, Kelly was getting her cues from bad action flicks. The cliché made me want to roll my eyes even as it made my worry level spike.

"What's going on?" Mike asked. "I turned around and you weren't behind me."

I showed him the message. His fist clenched, either from Kelly's words or my response, and he said, "First things first, we get a rental car and figure out where this place is. We'll call the Nashville police on the way."

"But she said to come alone."

"Don't worry. If we do this right, she'll think you're flying solo. Unless, of course, you want to face a killer alone."

Been there. Done that. "No."

"Then what are we fighting about? Let's move."

The Parthenon was exactly what it sounded like. A replica of the building in Greece, complete with columns and fancy stonework. As my phone's GPS directed us through the city streets, Mike called the lead detective and ran him through recent events while I called Aldo and let him know where we were headed. I watched the dashboard clock. We had thirty minutes to meet Kelly or the "or else" part of her message might click in.

The Parthenon was located smack in the middle of Nashville's Centennial Park, which meant it should be easier for Mike and the police officers who were on their way to blend in. Right? Kelly couldn't expect a public park to be empty of people. She was crazy, but I didn't think she was completely nuts.

Mike parked the car a block east of our destination. The sky was dark. Rain threatened. The clock read 2:35. Twenty-five minutes until I needed to meet Kelly.

"Stay here. The Nashville police gave me a description of the suspect's car. I'm going to take a quick look around and see if I can spot where she parked. If she does plan on making a swap, your aunt will most likely be waiting in the vehicle. The suspect isn't going to want to risk bringing your aunt out in the open. Don't go anywhere until you hear from me."

Without waiting for me to acknowledge his edict, Mike got out and started jogging in the direction of the Parthenon. He wasn't wearing a uniform or his gun, but the tension in his body and the way he studied the cars he passed screamed cop. I just hoped Kelly didn't see what to me appeared so obvious. If she did, Aunt Millie would be in even more trouble.

I watched the clock on my phone as the minutes crept by. Twenty minutes left. Nineteen. Eighteen. When my clock told me fifteen minutes remained, I opened the car door and got out. Thunder rumbled in the distance. The storm was getting closer.

I rubbed my arms with my hands and squinted at the Parthenon, trying to see whether Kelly was one of the people standing outside. It was hard to tell from here. I checked my phone. No messages from Mike, and there were fourteen minutes left. Yes, Mike had said to stay here, but the time crunch was making me nervous, especially being this far away from where in mere minutes I needed to be. Grabbing my purse from the passenger's seat, I hurried down the sidewalk.

Aha. I spotted a street vendor selling large canvas bags with the word "Nashville" on the side. Kelly expected me to arrive with LuAnn's purse. Since I didn't have that purse, I was going to do the next best thing. Bluff.

Armed with the bag, two Nashville travel mugs, gray sweatpants with a guitar decal ironed onto the ass, and a stuffed animal wearing a "Country Music Rocks" T-shirt, I put my now-lighter wallet back in my purse and shoved everything including my purse into the Nashville bag. Then I studied my work. Would Kelly believe I had LuAnn's enormous purple purse shoved inside? I sure hoped so, because it was the only idea I had.

Eight minutes remained until meeting time. A light rain began to fall from the sky. My phone dinged. I had a message. Hoping Mike was going to tell me that Millie had been found and the Nashville cops had Kelly in custody, I looked down at my phone.

Not Mike. The message was from Aldo. He and Killer were here at the park and were headed for the Parthenon, determined to help rescue Millie. Oh shit.

I didn't think. I just ran.

The raindrops were fatter and more numerous as I bolted down the sidewalk. The heels I had worn to my audition weren't conducive to footraces, but I didn't care. I needed to find Aldo before Kelly spotted him and decided to run or attack. Either option was bad.

I stepped on a crack in the sidewalk and turned my ankle, but I didn't stop running. The Parthenon was closer. And there—I spotted a woman with black hair. She was looking in the opposite direction so I couldn't get a clear view of her face, but I was pretty sure it was Kelly Jensen. Aldo and Killer weren't in view.

My cell phone buzzed. The message from Mike asked, "Where are you?"

He must be back at the car. Doing my best to shield the phone from the falling rain, I typed, "Went to meeting.

Aldo is here." Kelly's eyes settled on me as I was sliding my phone back into my pocket. She stood in the covered area between two massive columns. A folded umbrella was in her left hand, taunting me with the fact that she had the protection from the rain I currently was in need of. I quickly forgot about my wet state when I noticed her hand shoved into the bulging pocket of her stylish off-white trench. I had no idea what Kelly had in that pocket, but I was pretty sure I didn't want to find out.

Despite the fact I was still getting drenched, I slowed my pace. Kelly's eyes shifted from my face to the bag on my shoulder. At least a dozen people were standing in the Parthenon's columned entrance, looking at the falling rain, which made approaching Kelly slightly less scary. She wasn't going to attack me in front of witnesses. Was she?

"Stop right there," Kelly yelled when I was just steps away from the columns and the shelter they provided.

"It's pouring," I said, glancing behind me. Still no sign of Aldo. Maybe Killer had given Aldo trouble getting out of the car. Unless it was at the overpriced, incredibly pretentious dog salon Millie insisted on using, Killer hated getting wet. "Maybe you could step back? That would give me room to come inside," I suggested.

Kelly shook her head and shifted the hand in her pocket. "I want you to take the item I asked you to bring out of your bag and place it on the ground."

Now that I was closer, I could see the bump in her pocket better. Something was poking the fabric out and there was only one thing I could think of. A gun.

Swallowing down my panic, I said, "I want to see Aunt Millie. Where is she?"

"She's around."

"That's not good enough," I said. "How do I know you've seen her today? You might be taking advantage of her disappearance to get LuAnn's purse. You really should've grabbed it after you hit her with your car. Now that you've ransacked my hotel room and kidnapped my aunt, people are going to know you're behind everything."

Kelly frowned. "LuAnn was single-handedly destroying the legacy my husband left behind, not to mention putting the children we're here to protect at risk. All she cared about was money and feeling powerful."

"So what was the plan? You'd meet with LuAnn and convince her to turn over a new leaf?" Talk about optimistic.

"No, not exactly. I was going to offer her money if she'd admit to me all of the things she'd done and walk away from working with the competition. I was going to record the whole conversation. That way she couldn't bilk me out of my money. She'd have to go away and stay away. For good."

A couple unfurled an umbrella and walked past Kelly into the rain. They gave me a strange look, since it appeared I had chosen to stand in the rain instead of duck for cover.

Ignoring them, I said, "Clearly, that plan didn't work."

Kelly's eyes narrowed. "I knew it wouldn't. LuAnn always had to be difficult. Why should this time be any different? She came to the theater expecting Christine. When she learned I was the one who set up the meeting and that Christine had no intent to boot your team from the competition as she'd demanded, LuAnn got angry. She started screaming that I was a joke. How Christine and the competition only kept me around out of pity. That everyone knew I didn't have the flu when my husband died and that the other woman in the car was the mistress he was going to divorce me for."

Ouch.

The phone in my pocket vibrated, but I wasn't exactly in the position to answer as Kelly said, "I realized how stupid I was to think that LuAnn was only interested in money. She liked ruining people. So I climbed into my car. She yelled that she wasn't surprised I was running. That I was weak. That's why my husband was going to leave me and she was going to make sure people learned the truth. She was going to ruin my husband's memory and destroy the reputation I'd built just like she was going to ruin this contest. Fate had already taken my husband, daughter, and granddaughter. I couldn't let LuAnn take the only things I had left."

"So you ran her down."

"I'd originally planned on shooting her, but found I couldn't do it. I was lucky LuAnn goaded me into running her down."

"Lucky" wasn't the word I'd use.

"When I got home, I called the police to give them the tip that someone had killed LuAnn, only they were already on the scene. They said someone else had contacted them. For a while I was worried they'd be able to save her. I waited for the cops to come to my door. Instead, Christine called and told me that you'd found LuAnn dead. I was relieved until I remembered LuAnn's purse and the divorce papers she found that my husband filed right before he died."

"Why would it matter if that got out?" Call me crazy, but the man was dead.

"I spent my entire life dedicated to being the perfect wife and mother. It's the reason people ask me to sit on their boards and work on their charities. Without that I have nothing. Now give me the purse so all of this can end."

I saw the glint of metal as Kelly's hand shifted out of her pocket. The gun was small, but in this case I was pretty sure size didn't matter.

Mike and the Nashville police had to be nearby. I just needed a little more time so they could show up and save the day. Desperate, I latched onto the only other question I could think of. "Why did you call me and tell me to meet you at the theater?" If it hadn't have been for that, I'd have never found LuAnn or called the cops or ended up standing here taking a shower in front of the Parthenon.

Kelly shook her head as if disappointed that I wasn't smart enough to figure it out on my own. "The police needed someone to blame for LuAnn's murder. I chose you. Now give me the purse."

There was nothing wrong with Kelly's reflexes. One minute she was standing next to a fake Greek column; the next she was shoving me to the ground and grabbing the Nashville bag off my arm with her left hand. Her right hand still held the gun. I rolled to the right and sprang to my feet, ready to launch myself at Kelly, but a big growling puff of white got there first.

"Ow!" Kelly screamed as Killer's teeth clamped down on her wrist. Kelly kicked at the dog, but he didn't release his hold. Kelly had kidnapped Millie, and Killer was pissed.

People standing in the Parthenon shouted for help. And help came. As if by magic, a very wet-looking Mike and a number of cops appeared from every direction. Out of the corner of my eye, I saw Aldo huffing and puffing as he hurried in our direction.

"Nashville Police Department. Drop the weapon," someone yelled.

Maybe Kelly didn't hear. Or maybe she was just too angry to pay attention to the direction. She kicked at Killer and let out another scream as Killer chomped down on her arm and yanked it to the left.

That was when Kelly's gun fired. One of the cops fired back. A bright red spot appeared on the side of Kelly's white coat as she dropped her gun and fell to the ground.

Chapter 25

Cops hurried through the rain to restrain her. As if understanding his prey was down for the count, Killer let go and trotted to Aldo, who gave Kelly's downed body a satisfied nod. Then Aldo asked the important question, "Where is Millie?"

I had no idea.

"Kelly had her stashed at her home." Mike strolled over, holding an umbrella. "The police were verifying that Millie was there and safe before moving to apprehend. You'd have known that if you'd stayed where I told you to stay and waited to read the message I sent."

Oops.

Mike turned and put his hand on Aldo's shoulder. "EMTs are giving Millie the once-over now. If you want, I can have one of the cops drive you and Killer over to keep her company while she waits to answer some questions."

Aldo didn't have to be asked twice. He grabbed Killer's leash and made a beeline for the line of cop cars parked to the far side of the park. A few minutes later, Mike had worked out the details and Aldo and Killer were zipping off to be with the love of their lives.

The rain had stopped by the time Kelly was taken away. I had answered a bunch of questions, and Mike and I were finally given the all clear to leave. It was two hours until showtime. I was thankful the hotel wasn't far. We headed there for me to shower and change out of my still-wet clothes. As we drove, I expected Mike to express his displeasure at the way I'd disobeyed orders. Instead, he gave me a rundown on what I had missed while I was standing in the rain being threatened by a maniac. I guessed he was waiting to read me the riot act until I had stopped doing my impersonation of a drowned rat.

"The cops found your aunt tied to the living room armchair. Your aunt said Kelly picked that seat because she didn't want Millie to be unnecessarily uncomfortable. After all, she was Kelly's guest."

Kelly had gotten Millie to the house by acting scared of Killer, which prompted Millie to put him in the hall. Once Millie came back, Kelly brandished her gun. She then took Millie out to the back loading dock, where Kelly had parked her car. With a gun pointed at her head, Millie was forced to drive to Kelly's house, where she was then strapped to a chair. All in all, I'd say Kelly had an interesting take on hospitality.

"According to what I've heard from the detectives on scene, the inside of Kelly's house makes it look like the entire family is still alive and well. The dining room table is set with five place settings, the bedrooms all have clothes hanging in the closets and shoes lined up in front of the bed. In the middle of notes about what breakfast food to buy for her granddaughter were diagrams of the pulley system used to drop that light bar."

Creepy.

Mike pulled up to the hotel, and I waited for him to park before dashing to my room. The kids were already at the performing arts center, so I didn't have to worry about my appearance wigging them out. Which was good, because one look in the bathroom mirror had me freaking. Mascara ran down my cheeks, and the blue dress that had once made me look polished and professional was now covered with mud and grass stains that the most gifted dry cleaner would not be able to remove.

Twenty minutes later, I'd showered, dried my hair, and changed into the lavender dress I'd packed in hopes the kids would make it to tonight's final performance. The dress had floaty sleeves, a scooped back, and a drop waist. I thought it looked soft and romantic. The appreciative smile Mike gave me when I came out of the bathroom told me he agreed.

"Your aunt called." Mike stood and slid his phone into his back pocket. "She and Aldo are on their way to the theater to help the kids get ready. I told them we'd be there soon."

My aunt had been kidnapped and held hostage, and was still ready to work her makeup magic. The woman was a wonder.

Grabbing my purse, I studied Mike's expression. He looked calm and totally at ease. This was not the look of a man who was going to yell at me for going against his cop directives. I was both relieved and confused. "Why haven't you flipped?" I asked. "Normally you'd be screaming at me about how foolish I was to go to that meeting with Kelly."

Mike shrugged. "I decided to try a different tack. If nothing else, it'll set a precedent the next time something like this happens."

"You think there's going to be a next time?"

"Let's just say I wouldn't be surprised. You attract trouble." Mike smiled to soften the sting of his words. "The thing about today is that I don't blame you for doing what you did. It's not what I wanted, but you were worried about Aldo. And you were smart." He picked up the bag with the Nashville logo. "You found a way to make Kelly think you had LuAnn's purse, and you kept her talking long enough for the NPD to get into position. We were just about to take her down when she jumped you. I admit, seeing her point that gun gave me a bad moment. Killer is getting an extra-large box of dog biscuits from me."

"He prefers bacon."

"Bacon it is." He chuckled and reached for my hand. "Look, I can't promise that I won't yell in the future when I'm worried that you're doing something foolish or dangerous. There will be times I won't be able to help it. That's just how I react when someone I care about is in trouble. And when that someone is you . . ." His fingers traced a line along my jaw. "Let's just say those feelings go a whole lot deeper. I want to try and make this work. What do you think?"

Maybe it was because I had almost died (again), or maybe it was because Mike was being nice, but something inside me shifted. And I knew exactly what I thought. "I think it's going to be an interesting ride."

The kiss he gave me confirmed that. Wow.

Unfortunately, any more talk about the future would have to wait. Music in Motion was getting ready for their final performance, and I needed to be there. Mike held my hand as we drove. I gave him an overview of what would happen tonight. First up—the four finalists in the all-girls division would compete. Then our division would take the stage. Once all performances were over, the awards would be announced. I hoped, now that Kelly was in police custody, everything would go smoothly. Although, there were still one or two loose ends I needed to tie up.

Mike came with me to the staging room to check on Millie, who was brandishing a curling iron in one hand and a round styling brush in the other. Aldo and Killer were stationed nearby as if daring anyone to try to take her from them again. From the looks Millie was sending Aldo, I was pretty sure the two of them were going to be together for a long time.

A bunch of the kids greeted me with waves and cheers. I waited for them to launch into questions about Kelly's arrest. Instead they asked about my audition. How did it go? When would I hear if I got the gig? What did I sing? I tried to sound upbeat as I gave my answers and promised to give them more details after the concert was over. Until then, they needed to focus.

After Mike assured himself that Millie was not suffering any ill effects from her adventure, he went to buy a ticket for the concert. When he was gone, I huddled with Larry and Devlyn to find out what they'd told the team about today's events.

Nothing.

The kids had heard a rumor that someone had been

arrested for LuAnn's murder since that was the word buzzing around the theater, but the person's identity and the circumstances behind her arrest had yet to be leaked. In the interest of keeping the kids focused, Larry and Devlyn had made the call to keep Millie's kidnapping and my part in Kelly's arrest under wraps. I doubted they'd be able to keep it quiet for very long, but I was hopeful the media silence would last until our turn on the stage was over.

Once all the kids were in their costumes and Millie's hair and makeup emporium was finished working its magic, the team raced for the theater to watch the first round of the competition. I, however, turned in the opposite direction and headed for the Central Memphis High School staging room, where Nikki was giving her team a motivational speech. She praised the kids for the maturity with which they handled this week and the hard work they'd done. She then reminded them that they were first up in their division and that they should report back here after half of the teams in the first group had competed.

The kids were dismissed and headed out. Squeezing past two giggling girls, I walked into the almost-empty room and waited for Nikki to notice me. When she did, her eyes widened with panic.

"I stopped by to see how your team was dealing with the news that LuAnn's murderer was caught."

Nikki gave me a tense smile. "They're doing as well as can be expected. I appreciate you asking. Now, if you don't mind, I'd like to get a seat before the competition starts."

As Nikki hurried toward the door, I asked, "What did you do with LuAnn's purse?"

She froze. "I don't know what you mean."

"Yes, you do," I said, hoping my assumption was correct. The fear on her face spoke the truth louder than her words. I had hit a bull's-eye. "LuAnn drove her car here on the night she was killed. It was one of the three cars parked at the front of the building when I arrived. When I left, the car was gone. You came to the theater with LuAnn that night and drove her car back to the hotel after she died. You also ended up with her purse."

Nikki shook her head. "I don't know what you're talking about. I was at the hotel Wednesday night."

"You were also at the theater. I'm betting if the police search your hotel room, they'll find the purse that will prove it." I pulled out my cell phone, pulled up the Nashville Police Department's number, and waited to see whether Nikki was confident enough to call my bluff.

"Wait," Nikki said as I started to dial. "LuAnn's daughter left her keys behind after dinner. Before I gave them back, I decided to check and see if she had a key to her mother's car. I hoped to find something in the car that would help me keep LuAnn from getting the assistant coaching job. It was just bad luck that LuAnn came out of the hotel as I was in the backseat. There was a blanket on the floor, so I pulled it over my head and waited. I hoped she was coming to get something out of the glove box. Instead, she started the car. I had no idea she was going to the theater or that the building was even open. After ten minutes, I got tired of waiting and went inside to look for her. I heard voices outside the loading dock door and then a scream. By the time I was able to cross around right to the loading dock door, the car was peeling out of the parking lot and LuAnn was dead."

Technically, LuAnn had still been alive at that moment, but there was no point in splitting hairs.

"I panicked and ran back to LuAnn's car. It wasn't until I was at the hotel that I realized her purse was in the front seat."

"You looked through it?"

She nodded. "I was going to turn it over to the police. Then I realized what learning about that side of her mother would do to LuAnn's daughter. She'd already lost so much. I didn't want her to suffer more."

Neither did I.

"The lead detective on the case seems like a good guy. If you explain the situation, I'm sure he'll do his best to keep the information under wraps." Nikki looked even more panicked. I was counting on her fear of my spilling the beans to make her do the right thing. If not, well, Mike could make a call to his new cop friends.

"Wait," Nikki called as I headed for the door. "That's it?"

"No." I smiled. "Good luck tonight. I hope your team has a great show." After what they'd been through, they deserved it.

Nikki gave me a tentative smile back. "Good luck to you, too."

I watched from the back of the house as the first group of teams danced around the stage. When intermission started, I went to the staging room for one last powwow with my teens. The energy level was high. The kids were pumped. So was Larry, who could barely say two words without stuttering. But that was okay, because there wasn't much that needed to be said. The team was ready.

Standing in front of them for what would be the last

time at a competition, I looked from face to face. Megan. Chessie. Eric. Claire. Girls who had complained when I scheduled extra rehearsals. Guys who'd thought learning ballet technique was uncool. This year had changed them. It had changed me even more.

When it was time for our team to take the stage, I didn't see the flaws from yesterday as they twirled and spun. And when they hit their final pose, I couldn't have been prouder.

When all the performances were over, we all took our seats in the theater and waited for the awards to be handed out. Christine announced the all-girls division first. There were tears, shrieks of joy, and lots of applause as the kids ran up to get their awards. Then it was our division's turn. I felt my phone vibrate, and pulled it out of my purse as Christine McCann picked up the third-place award, which went to Scott Paris's team. As the kids raced up to get their trophies, I glanced at my cell phone screen. My already-nervous stomach took a tumble. Alan had sent a message. I clicked on it and felt my heart soar.

"Good news?" Mike whispered as Christine announced the second-place winner. A team from Minnesota. My team danced on the edges of their seats. They had either won it all or had placed in the bottom three.

After one last glance back down at the phone, I shoved it back into my purse, took Mike's hand in mine, and said, "We can talk about it tomorrow." The future could wait.

"And first place . . ." Christine paused for dramatic effect. "Goes to Music in Motion from Prospect Glen High School in Illinois."

The kids jumped up and down. Larry and Jim hugged. And Aldo got down on one knee. Between their happiness, the man standing beside me, and the news I'd just received, it was safe to say what a great future it was going to be.

THE WHITE HOUSE CHEF MYSTERIES FROM
NEW YORK TIMES BESTSELLING AUTHOR

JULIE HYZY

Introducing White House
executive chef Ollie Paras, who is rising—
and sleuthing—to the top…

"Hyzy may well be the Margaret Truman
of the culinary mystery."
—Nancy Fairbanks

"A must-read series to add to the
ranks of culinary mysteries."
—*The Mystery Reader*

STATE OF THE ONION

HAIL TO THE CHEF

EGGSECUTIVE ORDERS

BUFFALO WEST WING

AFFAIRS OF STEAK

FONDUING FATHERS

HOME OF THE BRAISED

M546AS0813